"What did you mean that you don't hit a guy with his family?"

"I know it sounds crazy, but there are unwritten rules about killing a cop, and one of them is you don't do it when he's with his family. You do it when he's on duty or alone somewhere."

"The protocol of cop killing." I was undressing sloppily, the last of my reserve energy petering out with the first light of day. Jack picked up my brown pants from the chair where I had dropped them and held them upside down to smooth them out and fold them. Seeing him do it, a small, caring kindness, I felt tears tumble down my cheeks.

He came over and held me, but all I could think of was Jean McVeigh at the St. Patrick's Day parade, standing on Fifth Avenue with her little boy on her shoulders, looking for Daddy.

By Lee Harris
Published by Fawcett Books:

THE CHRISTENING DAY MURDER

THE CHRISTMAS NIGHT MURDER

THE GOOD FRIDAY MURDER

THE PASSOVER MURDER*

THE ST. PATRICK'S DAY MURDER

THE THANKSGIVING DAY MURDER

THE YOM KIPPUR MURDER

*forthcoming from Fawcett Books.

THE ST. PATRICK'S DAY MURDER

Lee Harris

FAWCETT GOLD MEDAL • NEW YORK

A Fawcett Gold Medal Book
Published by Ballantine Books
Copyright © 1994 by Lee Harris

Library of Congress Catalog Card Number: 93-90724

ISBN 0-449-14872-6

Manufactured in the United States of America

First Edition: March 1994

10 9 8 7 6 5

The author wishes to thank
Ana M. Soler and James L. V. Wegman
for their patience, kindness, and invaluable information.

In memory of my friend in the pool.
It's not the same without you.

No more St. Patrick's Day we'll keep,
  his colour can't be seen,
For there's a cruel law agin the wearin'
  o' the Green!

        * * *

When law can stop the blades of grass
  from growin' as they grow,
And when the leaves in summer-time
  their colour dare not show,
Then I will change the colour, too,
  I wear in my caubeen,
But till that day, plase God, I'll stick
  to wearin' o' the Green.

> From The Wearin' o' the Green
> Anonymous, from an old Irish song

1

It was the first St. Patrick's Day in a long time that fell on a Sunday, so we had plans for the whole day and well into the evening. I had driven into the city on Friday and made myself comfortable in Jack's Brooklyn Heights apartment. Because he and his best friend, Ray Hansen, were in the Detective Division and worked regular five-day weeks, they were off duty on Sunday. The third member of the trio of friends, Scotty McVeigh, was still in uniform but had managed to get the necessary approval to avoid working his regular tour that day.

Although they were off duty, all three were marching in the parade and I watched like a kid seeing her favorite uncle dressing up to be Santa Claus as Jack put on his uniform for the first time since I had met him last summer.

"Stop looking starry-eyed," my guy said, buttoning the gold buttons on his blouse. "I think I have to lose a couple of pounds."

"You look good to me."

"You've lost your objectivity."

"I never had any."

He came over and kissed me. He smelled fresh and man-sweet, and his kisses made me tingle. We had gone to an early mass and come back to change for the parade, he to his uniform and I to a pair of brown wool slacks, a white cotton blouse with a small green silk scarf, and a brown suede vest that I had paid too much for and promised myself I would wear for the rest of my life. These were the first brown clothes I had bought since leaving the Franciscan convent where I had spent fifteen years. The Franciscan habit, which was obligatory, is brown, and I had surprised myself by re-

1

turning to the color less than a year after giving it up. Not
that you could compare what I was wearing today with what
I had left behind.

"Did I tell you you look gorgeous today?"

I rubbed my cheek against his. "So do you."

"Just fat."

I punched him lightly. "Tough," I said.

"We should go."

He got his service revolver from the closet and put it in
the holster on his belt, folding the Velcro flap over the top.
Usually, when he wore plainclothes, he used a shoulder holster. He helped me on with my coat, and we left.

Because of its historical preponderance of recruits with
Irish backgrounds, St. Patrick's Day is very much an NYPD
holiday. Almost everyone who isn't working marches, and
even people who haven't worn a uniform for years, don one
for the parade. Seeing all those men in blue go past me I decided the real reason they're encouraged to march in uniform
is to keep them aware of the fit. An awful lot of tight jackets
went by, those gold buttons straining to contain years of police experience and heaven only knew how many doughnuts
and Danish. I was pretty pleased to note that the women, as
a group, looked a lot trimmer than their male counterparts.
At least they looked as though they were breathing easier.

Jack had dropped me off west of Fifth Avenue, and I made
my way east to a corner of Fifth, just north of St. Patrick's
Cathedral. It was the last year before the Gay-Rights issue
threatened to halt the parade altogether, and there were nothing but good feelings among the spectators. Although the
idea of a parade thrilled me, the crowds proved a little too
much for my peace of mind, not to mention the noise and the
barely concealed beer drinking. It was a day recyclers could
have made an instant fortune. But the location was terrific.
Across the street we could just make out the cardinal on the
steps of the cathedral, where he stood to review the parade.

I was meeting Jean McVeigh, Scotty's wife; and Petra
Muller. We were one wife and two girlfriends that day, Ray
Hansen having separated from his wife some months earlier.
I knew both women, but not well. On one occasion all six of
us had been out together, and on two other occasions Jack

and I had gotten together with one couple and then the other. I liked Jean McVeigh enormously. She was a thin, redheaded, vibrant bundle of energy, the mother of two small children and a tireless volunteer for a number of causes.

I admired Petra. She was tall, dark-haired, and built like a model. When she walked, you half expected her to pivot to display the back of whatever she was wearing. She worked for a decorator whose name was apparently known to everyone in the world except me. I am still not entirely sure what a decorator does, but I know I can't pay for it.

Perhaps because I had met Ray's wife shortly before they split up, and liked her, I had been less than warm to Petra the first time we met. But the truth was she was a remarkable woman who seemed very good for Ray. She still spoke with the slightest German accent, having come over only a few years ago.

Petra shivered as the wind blew down the avenue. She wrapped her arms around herself, rubbing her coat sleeves with gloved hands. "I never get used to your winters here," she said.

Jean McVeigh, holding her son up, so he could see the marchers, laughed. "Better stay in the East then. People in Minnesota think this is summer."

"How can they stand it?" Petra said.

"Makes men out of them."

Petra smiled. "Then I stay away from Minnesota."

I laughed and jiggled Andrea McVeigh to relieve the weight on my arm. Her eyes were glued on the parade, searching for her father, who was marching with the Emerald Society, an organization of police officers who can trace their roots on one side or the other to the "auld sod." We were standing on the west side of Fifth Avenue, close enough so that we could see St. Patrick's Cathedral on the other side of the street, about a block south of us.

"There he is!" Jean called. "There's Daddy."

It took me a lot longer to spot him, but the children saw him in seconds and shrieked with delight. Scotty responded with a raised hand and a big smile. When Andrea announced, "That's my daddy," to the group assembled on the street around us, there were smiles and words from people who more normally probably moved through the city shunning both eye and voice contact. On St. Patrick's Day everyone is Irish and a member of the family.

Jack was marching with the Sergeant's Benevolent Association, and when I saw him, I called and jumped up and down like the kid I never was. I had known him eight or nine months at that point and I don't know why it took a parade to do it to me but as he gave me a quick grin, I said to myself: I love that man. I felt giggly and silly, but very happy.

The last of the three was Ray Hansen, who was marching with the Viking Society. For a city whose leaders talk a lot about the melting pot, the ethnic divisions in its police department sometimes confounded me. But there was Ray, finally, and Petra, like Jean and me before her, dropped her reserve and waved and called in a very undignified manner.

Jean had taken off with her children before the Viking Society came by, refusing my offer to accompany her. She was dropping the kids at her mother's and then returning for the afternoon festivities. Petra and I kept each other company for another half hour, then started our long walk west. The parade would go on for hours without us.

As it always does, the Emerald Society sponsored a huge celebration on a Hudson River pier in honor of the holiday. Literally thousands of people were expected, a bigger crowd than I find comfortable. Perhaps Petra was thinking the same thing, because she said breezily, "Maybe we should ditch the guys and find a nice quiet bar and talk about life."

"There isn't a quiet bar in New York on March seventeenth," I told her.

"Of course. Today is Christmas for bars. Well, OK. Then we go to the party and scream at each other."

"We'll talk about life another time, Petra. I expect you know a lot more about it than I do."

"Why? Because you were a nun? I bet you know wonderful secrets the rest of us don't know."

I gave her a smile that I hoped was suitably enigmatic but probably came off just looking like a schoolgirl grin.

It didn't matter much, because she turned toward the avenue we were approaching and cried, "Look, a taxi! Come on,

Chris. My treat!" and in thirty seconds we were settling back in a blessedly overheated cab on our way to the pier.

It was bedlam and mayhem in navy blue and green. Alcohol flowed in rivers, the fumes alone intoxicating me. It took over half an hour for us to find our men and quite a while longer till Jean McVeigh arrived sans children. Scotty had gone out several times to look for her, but we finally found her inside trying to ward off the tipsy advances of a rookie redhead suddenly enamored by one of his own.

Jean was in stitches after her rescue. "My first conquest as an older woman," she crowed. "I want to drink to that."

"I'll deck him if he tries it again," her husband said, less than thrilled.

"C'mon Scotty," Jack said. "I thought you like having a woman other guys admire. She came back to you, didn't she?"

"I don't know why," Petra said, with a sly smile. "He was pretty cute, don't you think so, Chris?" But she turned away from me to look at Ray, whose eyes were fixed on her with a look that could mean nothing but desire.

As I sensed the heat between them, I wondered whether other people were aware of a similar current that flashed between Jack and me on those occasions in public when I neglected to mask it.

Ray moved closer to Petra and put an arm over her shoulder. She was tall, and when she turned her head toward him, the kiss that resulted came very easily. I turned away, feeling Jack's hand take mine, and I saw Jean, her eyes fixed on the other couple, a look of contentment on her face, as though she were watching the results of her own matchmaking— which I knew was not the case.

"Let's say hello to some of the guys," Jack said, drawing me away from the group and into the sea of blue and green.

"Where's your green?" I asked as we made our way across the huge pier.

"I'll put it on when I change."

We ducked in and out of happy groups, some of them bursting unexpectedly into song, or, more expectedly, into laughter. Here we ran into an old friend from the Academy, there a guy who had worked in Jack's last precinct. Most had wives with them, some were alone or with girlfriends. Everyone seemed to have reached a state of euphoria before we ran into them.

We stayed a couple of hours and then found Ray, Scotty, and the women. They were ready to leave, as we were, and the six of us went outside to where the men had parked their cars. We were all going home to change and then meeting at Petra's apartment, where we had been invited for dinner. Walking through the huge, makeshift parking lot, we found Jack's car first.

"All right, everyone," Petra called. "Five o'clock. Don't be late."

We called our good-byes and got into the car. As Jack pulled out, I saw the other four walking ahead of us, inspecting the rows of cars as though they had forgotten where they had left theirs. Once we found our way out, it was a pretty quick trip to Jack's apartment.

The building Petra lived in was deeper into Brooklyn than Jack's. She had told me once that when she first came to New York, she couldn't afford an apartment in Manhattan and she didn't want to share. Brooklyn had been cheaper, and by the time she could afford something better or closer to where she worked, she had grown fond of the borough and the neighborhood and didn't want to move.

We left Brooklyn Heights about four-thirty and arrived at Petra's door practically on the stroke of five. Jack was now wearing a flannel shirt in a beautiful shade of forest green and Scotty was wearing one in the black watch plaid. Ray was in tan, without a hint of green. But the apartment was decorated with green carnations and party streamers.

"And everything you eat tonight is green," Petra announced. "After this meal, nobody eats green for another year." She set down a tray of grasshoppers and tinted potato chips, and we began the feast.

The men traded stories of past St. Patrick's Days until Jean insisted they stop. "Talk politics," she said. "Talk football. Anything but the job."

"Shit, if we can't talk the job, we'll all sit in silence," Ray said.

"No, you won't. There's a whole world out there that isn't NYPD."

"Where?" her husband asked, looking around for it.

"You're too much, Scotty," she said, laughing.

"Jean's right," Petra said. "I have an interesting job, Chris has an interesting job, and neither one of us has a gun. In fact, it's an accident we both know men who do."

"A lucky accident," Ray said lightly.

"Lucky for you," Petra tossed back just as lightly.

I got up and went to the bathroom. Although the apartment was in an old building, Petra's decorating had transformed it. The living room walls were done in fabric, the floors had been completely refinished to show off an intricate parquet, the windows were done in a way I couldn't even describe to myself, and all together the effect was both exotic and comfortable. What I liked best was her collection of baskets, carvings, and one-of-a-kind painted dishes that were remembrances of places she had visited around the world and that were placed strategically around the room so that each was visible and the total result was elegant, without a hint of clutter.

The bathroom was at the end of a short hall between the doors to the two bedrooms. The one on the left was slightly ajar, and through the crack I could see an unmade bed. On the right was Petra's study, the door propped open with a heavy-looking elephant carved out of stone. Even the bathroom had benefited from her magic touch. The building was old enough so that there was a small window of frosted glass on one wall, and several plants, standing and hanging, were positioned to take advantage of the light. The floor, which was made up of tiny hexagonal white tiles, and the fixtures testified to the age of the building, but a coat of flat white paint and a couple of white wicker pieces, each adorned with a single painted pink rose, made it look young, almost breathless. I decided to ask Petra's advice if I ever invited the two of them out to my house in Oakwood, where I had changed very little of Aunt Margaret's accidental decor of accumulated possessions since moving in last spring.

When I got back to the dinette, Ray was helping Petra clear the table and carry in the next course. I felt a wave of anger sweep through me. On the evening we had visited him and his wife, he had sat like a doorstop through the entire meal while his wife took care of everything. I had insisted that we not leave early because I wanted to help her with the dishes. Now, with a new woman in his life, Ray was the most helpful person in the room.

Even the dessert was green, a mint parfait with tinted cream whipped up in the kitchen seconds before Petra brought it out.

"You're amazing," Jean said, her eyes alight. "How could you do all this and still go to the parade?"

"Meet the superwoman," Ray said. "She's good at everything."

Why didn't I like him? Jack considered Ray his best friend. They bantered together with ease, making each other laugh. When I talked to Ray, he remained stony and laconic. His smiles were infrequent and often struck me as derisive. It couldn't be that he sensed my discomfort with his marital situation because he had acted just the same when he was living with his wife. Scotty and I got along fine. Was I trying too hard or not hard enough? Could it be that my background in the convent made him uneasy? I didn't know, and I had never talked to Jack about it. What I was sure of was that Ray Hansen made me uncomfortable and tonight was no exception.

"Want to go?" Jack said in my ear.

We had retired to the living room after dessert and coffee, and Jack was sitting next to me on the sofa.

"Yes."

He squeezed my hand and stood. "OK, guys. Party's breaking up. I just happen to work tomorrow."

"Me, too," Scotty said, getting out of his chair. "Let's go, sweets."

"Not so fast," Petra said. She darted into the kitchen and came out with green party bags, which she gave to each of us.

There were cookies inside and a four-leaf clover preserved in plastic.

"Petra, you're wonderful." Jean grinned at her. "I'm hiring you to do my next kid's birthday party."

"She's not for sale," Ray said. He was standing next to her, and he pushed her hair gently off her shoulder as he spoke. It was a gesture that was both proprietary and sexy. It struck me that every gesture he made toward her was sexy, and I wondered if there was a foundation of affection in the relationship or if it was all physical. Not that it was my business.

We said good night to both of them, and I thanked Petra for the wonderful meal and complimented her again on the apartment. Out in the hall, Jack rang for the elevator as the McVeighs said their good-byes. They arrived just as the elevator did.

"So where to?" Scotty said as we went down.

"Home," Jack said.

"Hey, it's early. I know a great place that you don't know and it's not fair to keep secrets from buddies. What do you say, buddy?"

"How far is this place?"

"Hop, skip, and a jump. It's on my beat, Gillen's Crossroads. Has a little lot you can park in off the street and you get the treat of your life driving there."

The elevator stopped, and we got off, walking through the empty lobby toward the front door.

"What kind of treat?"

"Heads up, buddy."

Jack turned to him and lifted his hand in a reflex action as something sailed through the air at him. "What's this for?"

"Keys to my dream car."

"C'mon, Scotty."

"It's a BMW, slightly used, better than new. Parked somewhere right near here. Gimme your keys and I'll lead the way."

"How much did you go into hock for this dream car?"

"It was a bargain."

Jack tossed his car keys over as Jean and I smiled at each other.

"Can't live a weekend without the beat," she said.

"This place makes Irish coffee like nothing you've ever tasted," Scotty told us.

"I think I'll have mine without the Irish," Jean said. "I hope the kids are OK."

"The kids are with Mama, right? When weren't they OK with Mama?"

"Let's go," Jack said.

2

I laughed as we went down the street.

"You're potted," Jack said, putting his arm around me.

"Just having a good time."

"That's Scotty." He stopped at a car, unlocked the door, and I slid inside. When he was behind the wheel, he looked at the dash for a moment before turning the key. "Scotty and cars," he said as he pulled out into the street. Down the block, Jack's car was already waiting, and as we approached, Scotty waved and took off.

It was a longer drive than we had expected, which, Jack assured me, was to be expected.

"Does it drive like a dream?" I asked.

"It's nice."

"You sound a little restrained."

"The guy's nuts. Nice nuts, but nuts."

"Give me the bottom line. Do you want one for your birthday or not?"

"About twenty birthdays from now. How's that?"

"I'll start saving. What's he doing?"

"Probably looking for the brake. C'mon, Scotty. Leave me with a car."

We followed Scotty blindly, sometimes waiting behind him at intersections while the two of them seemed to be deciding which way to turn.

"You don't like Ray much, do you?" Jack said suddenly.

The question, the fact that he knew, caught me completely off-guard. I had forgotten that reading people was part of his job, part of him. "I don't dislike him," I said.

"He's a little hard to get to know, but when you do, he's a friend for life."

11

"I know that."

"Will you try?"

"I do. I will."

"I know you will."

The promised parking lot was a few doors down from Gillen's Crossroads, on a block of low brick buildings housing small stores. We walked back, the men talking cars. Inside, we were greeted like visiting royalty, Scotty having obviously become an honorary member of the Gillen family. We were shown to a small table near the bar, thankfully away from a group of rowdy singers wearing jackets of various shades of green.

Everyone ordered the Irish coffee. I felt more relaxed than I had all day. With the McVeighs I felt included. With Ray, I felt judged.

"Jesus, I couldn't wait to get outa there," Scotty said. "I thought he was going to do her while we watched."

"Scotty!" Jean said. Then she added, "They're just newly in love."

"Fuck love. He can't keep his hands off her."

"It's more than that," I said, almost anxious to defend Ray for Jack's sake. "They have a relationship. They do things for each other."

"You ever see him lift a finger to help Betsy?" Scotty addressed everyone.

"Leave him alone, Scotty," Jack said. "He's having a hard time."

"So's Betsy." Jean looked serious. "A very hard time."

The coffees came, and the subject changed. We agreed the coffee was better than good and we all worked our way through the whipped cream to the good black stuff underneath.

As we sipped, Scotty began talking about his beat. "I really got lucky," he said. "Nicest people in the world here. Old Gillen's the salt of the earth. Lady who runs the Laundromat down the street's got six kids she's raising by herself and won't take a nickel she doesn't earn. Korean family has a grocery at the other end of the beat. I don't think they ever sleep. They set up in a building used to be a crack house. You wouldn't believe what it took to get it all together."

"You wouldn't believe how much of the work Scotty did," Jean said. "He took them by the hand and showed them how to get permits. He got inspectors to come. This beat is his real life. We're just a meal and a warm bed." But she said it with pride and she looked proud.

"Someone's gotta do it," Scotty said. "These are great people."

"Community cop of the year. Hey, we gotta go," I heard Jack say. "Chris has had it."

That brought me back from the edge of sleep. I pushed my arms into my coat sleeves and wrapped my coat around me.

"OK?" Jack said.

"Mm-hmm."

We got several warm goodnights as we walked past the green-jacketed group, whose vigor had abated with mine, and on to the door.

"It's freezing out there," Scotty said. "You girls stay here. We'll drive around."

I didn't argue. They went outside and turned toward the parking lot. I rubbed my temples, hoping to wake myself up.

"You look done in," Jean said.

"I guess I'm still a morning person."

"Scotty doesn't work till the four to twelve tomorrow."

"It's a great car, Jean."

"My husband," she said, with a smile. "Boys and their toys."

As she said "toys," there was an explosion somewhere, then another one. We looked at each other. At the same moment that she said, "Shots," I said, "Gunfire."

"Oh, God," Jean said, her voice breaking.

I pulled the door open, and we ran. All I could think of was Jack, Jack. Please don't let it be Jack. The windchill was awful. My eyes were tearing in the far corners. There was a third shot and tires squealed. A car with its lights out turned onto the street from the parking lot and took off away from us. As we reached the lot, Jean began calling, "Scotty! Scotty!" while I kept my scream inside.

I saw Jack first and called his name. He was holstering his gun and moving fast. "It's Scotty. He's been shot." He dropped to his knees between two cars as he spoke.

Jean lurched forward, screaming her husband's name.

"Get her *outa* here, Chris," Jack shouted. "Go back to the bar and call 911. Tell them 'shots fired' and an officer's down."

He had his jacket off. He folded it quickly and placed it under Scotty's head. I took my own coat off and dropped it over Scotty. "Keep him warm," I said, as though I knew something about first aid.

Jean was screaming now. "Scotty! Don't die, Scotty."

"Get her *outa* here, Chris," Jack roared, and I took Jean by the arm and dragged her away.

The bartender gave me a phone, and I made the call, hanging on to Jean to keep her with me. All the unwritten rules were operating now. An officer's wife is trouble on the scene if he's been hurt. You have to keep her away even if it looks as though her husband is dying. The corollary is that no policeman dies on the pavement or in a parking lot. Even if he seems to be dead, if there are no vital signs at all, he will be taken to a hospital where he will be worked over and worked over. Officially he will die in the hospital after everything possible has been tried.

I had few doubts and little hope for Scotty. My glimpse of him on the ground had left me chilled far beyond what the weather had done. Now I sat holding Jean. She had become very quiet, one hand clutching mine, her eyes far away. We had heard sirens almost from the moment I hung up and now they were arriving.

"They'll get him to the hospital," I said.

She didn't even nod. In the mirror behind the bar I could see the reflection of flashing lights.

We sat for several minutes without speaking. The evening host of Gillen's was keeping people away and trying to keep the patrons calm. Every time he glanced at us, his face looked grimmer. Finally the door opened and two young policemen came in.

"Mrs. McVeigh?" one said, looking our way.

We both stood as he came over. I had a strong feeling this was the first time he had been involved in anything like this and wished he were anywhere but here.

"Is he all right?" Jean asked in a half whisper.

"They've got him in the ambulance, ma'am. We'll take you to the hospital." A noncomittal answer. It wasn't his job to carry the news.

We went outside. A blue-and-white was at the curb. As I got in, a policeman in uniform came running, carrying my coat. I thanked him and put it on gratefully. The air was freezing.

As we passed the parking lot, I looked for Jack. He was standing almost where we had left him, near the row of cars, talking to someone who looked older and very serious. In a second we had passed by.

"Everybody loves Scotty," Jean said. "Everybody."

I held her hand tightly and felt tears on my face.

They took us to Kings County Hospital. That's one of the places Jack had told me police always take their own. In Manhattan, it's Bellevue. The emergency room staffers in both hospitals have a reputation for extraordinary measures to save police officers' lives, probably because they also see so much of the city's violence. Officers have been known to stuff a wounded comrade in a car and drive him to one of those hospitals rather than wait for an ambulance to take him somewhere else.

But no hospital could make a difference tonight. Jean found a phone while we waited and called her mother. Someone brought us hot coffee and nurses offered anything they could think of to make Jean comfortable. Eventually a doctor, accompanied by a police chaplain and a captain in uniform, came out and told Jean he was very sorry.

Jack showed up just as we were about to get driven home. He hugged Jean, and I turned away. There seemed to be a lot of people around all of a sudden, men and a couple of women, in and out of uniform. It occurred to me the news would have been broadcast by now and friends of Scotty's might have come, along with fellow officers who might want to donate blood.

"I have to call Ray," Jack said somewhere near me, and he went down the hall toward a coin telephone. While he was gone, a few of the men near the waiting room came in and talked to Jean. She looked as though she hardly heard them, but she said "Thank you" several times.

"Got him," Jack said, returning.

"I can take you home now, ma'am," one of the officers who had brought us to the hospital said.

"Thank you."

We all went in the same car, Jean sitting between Jack and me in the backseat.

"Tell me what happened," Jean said in a dull voice.

"Not now, Jean."

"You were there, Jack," she said firmly. "I want to know and I want you to tell me. Now."

He took a breath. "There was a car parked at the back of the lot, facing the street, right between the two rows of parked cars. I didn't see it till it was too late. He kept his lights out, and he must have started moving as I opened my car door."

"He was waiting for Scotty."

"He must have been. I had the key in my lock when I heard the first shot. I couldn't see anything because my car was parked on the left and Scotty was on the right and the shooter's car was between us."

"I heard three shots," Jean said.

"I got one off at the back of the car as it hit the street. First shot I ever fired."

I felt a chill down my back.

Jean put a hand over Jack's. "They take your weapon?"

"I gave it to the duty captain."

The police car stopped first at Jean's mother's house, which was only a few blocks from Petra's apartment. I went to the door with her and stayed a few minutes. I didn't envy her her morning when her children got up for breakfast. But her mother seemed in control and said I should leave.

The car then took us back to the parking lot where Jack's car was, where it had all begun. Ray Hansen was there, a solitary shadow standing near the crime scene tape and staring at the taped outline of his friend's body. The investigation team had left by then, and probably the TV crew along with them. A lone officer was posted to guard the crime scene until a daylight search of the parking lot could be made. Without the bright lights it was night again. The BMW was gone, along with most of the other cars that had been parked there. Jack's car was the only one on the left side of the lot.

"Show me," Ray said as we approached.

I watched them walk to the back of the lot where the shooter's car had been waiting and come back again. I heard Jack repeat substantially what he had told Jean and what I supposed he had told the investigators before he got to the hospital.

"He must've been facing the car door with his key," he said, "because he hadn't gotten the door open yet. The car was parked front end out."

"The door would've shielded him."

"Right. So the shooter must have started down when Scotty walked between the two cars. He shot once—probably hit him in the side—count two, then shot again."

"Hit him in the chest?"

"I think so." Jack turned to me. "Your coat bloody?"

"Just a little."

"Where's Jean?"

"With her mother," Jack said.

"It doesn't make sense. We talked a couple of days ago. He didn't tell me anything that could've brought this on. He said he was having the time of his life. Leave it to Scotty to get wrapped up in his beat. God, he loved the job."

"And you don't hit a guy with his family."

"Unless you're a very dumb son of a bitch," Ray said. "Or you just don't care."

"I gotta get Chris home."

"Talk to you tomorrow."

We got into Jack's car and drove to the curb. As we turned down the street, I looked back and saw the shadow of Ray Hansen standing and looking down at where the body of his friend no longer lay.

Inside the apartment, Jack removed the empty ankle holster and tossed it on the kitchen counter. It was the first time since I had met him that I didn't see him carefully put away his gun as he entered the apartment. For that matter, the last couple of hours were the first he had been unarmed out-of-doors since I had met him.

"Why did they take your gun?"

"To check it and because I wasn't suppose to shoot it."

I felt more than bewildered. I felt dizzy with fatigue, confused. I knew I could not have heard him right.

"The shooter was no longer a danger. He was a fleeing suspect. What I did was against the rules."

"He had just shot a police officer," I said, making a point he had surely not overlooked.

"But he had stopped shooting and was leaving the scene. He wasn't a danger to anyone at that point."

"Are you in trouble?"

"Not really." He managed a little smile.

Before hanging my coat in the closet, he looked at the stains on the lining. They weren't bad, but I didn't like to think of seeing them every time I put the coat on or took it off.

"What did you mean that you don't hit a guy with his family?"

"I know it sounds crazy, but there are unwritten rules about killing a cop and one of them is you don't do it when he's with his family. You do it when he's on duty or alone somewhere."

"The protocol of cop killing." I was undressing sloppily, the last of my reserve energy petering out with the first light of day. Jack picked up my brown pants from the chair where I had dropped them and held them upside down to smooth them out and fold them. Seeing him do it, a small, caring kindness, I felt tears tumble down my cheeks.

He came over and held me, but all I could think of was Jean McVeigh at the St. Patrick's Day parade, standing on Fifth Avenue with her little boy on her shoulders, looking for Daddy.

"Get some sleep, kid," Jack said. "Let's put this day behind us."

3

It made every news broadcast on radio and television, every newspaper. I stayed in Brooklyn on Monday, telephoning my sometimes employer, lawyer Arnold Gold, that I would not be in for a few days. In the morning, I went to Scotty's precinct and gave a statement. In the afternoon, I drove Jean and her children back home to Queens. A couple of neighbors and the wives of some fellow officers of Scotty's dropped in to help her out. They knew the ropes. One of them was a police widow herself. A few police officers and a PBA official came and went. Even in death there are police rules and duties that must be observed.

Before I left, Jack stopped over.

Seeing him, Jean perked up. "You didn't have to, Jack," she said. "It's way out of your way." But it was clear she was glad to see him.

We sat at the kitchen table, and I poured from a coffeepot that had been replenished all day.

"They found the shooter's car this afternoon," Jack said. "In Brooklyn, a couple of miles away." He didn't have to say away from what. "There's a bullet hole in the trunk and ballistics is checking out the bullet against my gun."

"They found the bullet?" Jean said.

"In the back of the backseat. It was a stolen car. The owner reported it about eight o'clock this morning."

"Any idea when it was stolen?" I asked.

"He parked it Friday night, in a spot that was good all weekend, and never used it. He went out to get it this morning and it wasn't there. Said he walked the neighborhood looking for it before he called in the report."

"Somebody really wanted Scotty dead," Jean said.

Jack nodded.

"Why, Jack?"

"I don't know. Nobody knows. There aren't any rumors, there's no dirt, nobody's speculating. There's nothing."

"Scotty's been walking that beat for over a year now," Jean said sadly. "He patted kids' heads and schmoozed with shopkeepers and went to PTA and precinct community council meetings. He really cared about those people, Jack. If there was a beef, he sure didn't know anything about it."

"We'll get the guy. They're scraping that car clean looking for leads. The whole city's working on this one."

"I know."

He looked worn and tired. He had barely tasted the coffee, then pushed it away. I had the feeling nothing tasted good to him today. "Look, Jean, you may have some benefits coming because Scotty was a vet. And the job has benefits for the family. You know where his department and discharge papers are?"

"There's a box of stuff upstairs. I'll look for it."

"Anything you need, you just tell me."

"I know."

He got up, took another gulp of coffee, and went to the sink to rinse the mug out.

"Go home, Chris," Jean said. "Everything's under control."

I stopped and said good-bye to the children, then to the women. When I had my coat on, Jean handed me a paper bag.

"Just a little supper," she said. "You don't need to cook tonight."

We hugged and she gave Jack a peck on the cheek. We left together.

"I got my interview and official dressing-down today," he said when we were outside. "Got called into the captain's office. He was very nice and very firm. 'I understand why you did it, but don't ever let it happen again.' That kind of thing."

"He would have done it himself."

"That's why it probably won't mean a complaint or a trip to Poplar Street to see Internal Affairs."

I hadn't thought of that as a possibility. To me the shot he fired was both justified and understandable. "I'm glad it's over."

"They took two slugs out of Scotty," he said. "They were forty-fours. The first one hit his shoulder. It was the second one that did it."

"And nobody knows why."

"Not a glimmer. Not a whisper. I'm not on the case, but I called everyone I've ever known who knew Scotty and I came up with nothing."

"Maybe the answer's on his beat. It was his life. Maybe it was his death, too."

"Chris, they've got guys out there talking to anything that moves. They're questioning the dogs and cats on the street."

It occurred to me it might not even have been something Scotty himself did. New York had become a conglomeration of sectors, each representing the old residents and the new, a variety of races and language backgrounds, and even among people speaking the same language, there were hostilities based on their national origin. In some neighborhoods the anger bridged generations, with sons carrying on their fathers' battles. The melting pot that my elders had spoken of with such pride had frozen into discrete chunks that rubbed against one another abrasively, more so when they shared the same turf. Maybe Scotty had smiled once too often at a member of one group and not enough at another. Maybe he had become the scapegoat of their internecine wars.

We kissed at my car and I drove home while he went off to his evening law class. The next time we would meet would be at Scotty's funeral.

The funeral was Thursday morning. I sat inside the church while Jack attended with his squad and members of the precinct, standing outside in the dreary cold. The burial was private and we drove to the cemetery in Jack's car, the rest of the police returning to Scotty's precinct. When we got back to Queens, we stopped at the McVeigh house. Ray and Petra had just arrived and were talking to Jean.

"Jean can't find Scotty's discharge papers," Ray said when we joined them.

"You have a safe-deposit box?" Jack asked.

"We should, but we never got one. We kept the kids' birth certificates and stuff like that in a metal box. I've been through it so many times I can tell you the order of the papers. I've even shaken things out, but there's no discharge there."

"I can call the VA," Jack said. "About when was he discharged? Six, seven years ago?"

"Oh, gosh, no. It must be about eleven years now."

"Eleven?" Ray's skepticism was bare and harsh. "Come on, Jean. He came on the job right after he got out of the army."

"You've got it all wrong. He went in when he was eighteen or nineteen. We got married when he was twenty-four and he'd been out awhile by then. Believe me, if he'd served while we were married, I'd know it."

"OK," Jack said. "It's just a little misunderstanding. I'll get in touch with the VA and see what they say. It might help if you had his birth certificate. You'll probably need that for Social Security anyhow."

"I'll go down tomorrow. He was born in Brooklyn. I've got his driver's license if they need it."

We changed the topic rather pointedly after that and spent half an hour listening more than talking. It was late afternoon when the four of us left.

But outside on the quiet residential street, we stood and talked for a few minutes. Ray was up in arms.

"I think she's lost it," he said. "Something is very screwed up in there."

"I know. I'll look into it in the morning."

"I mean, did I hear Scotty say a thousand times he went from the army to the job with only a couple of months between?"

"You heard it. I heard it."

"So what's she pulling?"

"She's confused," Petra said soothingly. "Something else happened when he was eighteen and she's mixed it up."

In Jack's car a few minutes later he came back to it. "It doesn't feel right."

"Maybe Scotty went in a little later than Jean thinks and

got out a little earlier than he told you. Maybe he was out of work for a year and didn't want to admit it."

"But there's no discharge. If you've got a box where you keep birth certificates, you keep your discharge papers there, too. You keep the important pieces of your life in one place."

I wondered if he was thinking the same thing I was. "Could it have been a dishonorable discharge?"

"I hope not." He looked grim and dropped the subject. When we got back to his apartment, I picked up my bag, kissed him good-bye, and drove home to Oakwood.

I live in a small town on Long Island Sound in the house my aunt lived in for as long as I can remember. When she died last year, she left me the house at 610 Pine Brook Road and her nest egg and a responsibility that was in no way a burden. Her only son, Gene, who is my age and whom I have known all my life, is retarded and lives in a group home that recently moved to Oakwood, about a mile from the house. Now that he's so close, I visit frequently and take him for overnights when he's in the mood. Although he misses his mother, he's made a great adjustment, and I feel, as I always have, that he adds to my life as I hope I add to his.

Happily, I have become part of the community. I go to council meetings and join in discussions. I voted in my first election on the school budget, pulling down all the Yes levers for what I consider are all the right reasons. And I have made friends in town, mostly the McGuires who live next door and the Grosses, who live down the block and across the street.

Some of these things happened slowly, some quickly. I was aware, during the years that I visited Aunt Meg regularly, that I was "that nun" who came to see Margaret Wirth. I like to think I'm now Chris Bennett, known for my personality, not the clothes I used to wear.

I had some work to do at home for Arnold Gold and I sat down to it at eight-thirty Friday morning, having walked and breakfasted. Part of it was proofreading, part typing. Arnold gave me an old word processor recently when he bought new ones for the office, and, never having used one before, I found it fast and easy to use while the women in his office thought it was so old and out-of-date they teased him until he broke down and replaced it. I was putting a brief on a disk when Jack called.

"Something's very crazy," he said.

"About Scotty's discharge?"

"He never served. There's no record of his serving in any of the armed services."

"Why would he lie?"

"You got me. But it gets worse."

"What do you mean?"

"Jean just called. There's no record of Scotty's birth certificate."

I felt a distinct chill. "Could she have the year wrong?" I asked, knowing Jean would have tried other years if they failed to find the certificate.

"She says she got someone to do a pretty thorough search. They know who she is. His name's been in all the papers. I don't like the feel of this."

I didn't, either. "What about his parents, Jack? I didn't hear Jean mention them, and they didn't seem to be at the funeral."

"They died years ago. At least that's what he said. Now I'm starting to rethink everything he ever said about himself."

"Maybe that's not a good idea. He was someone you knew and cared about. If he had some reason for lying about his age or his birthplace or his military service, it doesn't change the person you knew."

"I can accept that, but Jean can't. I haven't even told her about the service. She was pretty shook up when she called about the birth certificate. I'm going to talk to the captain about it this afternoon. He has access to Scotty's personnel records."

"You think he lied on his job application?"

"I don't know what to think. Listen, I'm way behind in my schoolwork. I'm going to pass on this weekend unless I get a lot done tonight and tomorrow. If I call Sunday, you think we could get together for a few hours?"

"Gosh," I said theatrically, "I'll probably be booked solid by then. My phone never stops ringing."

"Yeah, here, too. The hallway's lined with naked women waiting their turn."

I laughed. "Throw them a towel."

"I didn't say they were wet. I implied they were eager. I'll try for Sunday."

I finished my work and got it into the mail before the post office closed. On Saturday I put my house in order and did my shopping. Then I visited Gene and took him for lunch. Afterward, we went to a store that sold miniature cars, and I let him pick one out for his collection. I watched with pleasure and some awe as he made his decision, measuring the cars against one another by criteria I could not imagine. He started with seven and worked his way down to three, then finally two. He put them side by side, turned them over, ran them over the glass case and up his arm, his face intent the whole while. Sometimes when I watch him I wonder what kind of person he would have been if he had been born with normal intelligence. I'm almost positive he would have been smart, a thorough, careful worker, a kind and thoughtful human being.

Finally he said, "This one."

I smiled. "Good choice, Gene." I picked up the runner-up and handed both cars to the man behind the counter.

"No," Gene said. "Just this one."

"I think you deserve two today."

His smile was overwhelming. "Why?"

I gave him a kiss on the cheek. "Because you always play by the rules and you're the nicest person I know."

When we got back to Greenwillow, he had had enough of me. All he wanted was to play with his cars. I left him happy.

Jack called before noon on Sunday. "Feel like driving in?"

"Sure."

"We'll have a little food and a little fun."

"Sounds good. Jack, I haven't asked, but is there anything yet on Scotty's killer?"

"Nothing. It looks like a very professional job."

"That's what the papers say."

"If the guy left a print in that stolen car, no one's found it."

"Have they looked into old unsolved murders of cops?"

"It's the first thing they do. The Intelligence Division comes in right away on a case like this. Apparently they don't see any connections, but they'll be looking into copycats, crimes that are similar in some way."

"We'll talk when I get there."

We didn't talk when I got there. It was more than a week since we'd been together without the shadow of the murder over us. The shadow was still there, but we set it aside, our first kiss lighting fires.

"It's good to hold you," Jack said, holding me in a way that was both comforting and arousing.

I moved against his body and found his lips again.

"Mind if we have the fun first?"

"I'll mind if we don't."

"Yeah," he said, and we went into the bedroom.

Jack is a fantastic cook. He tells me I will be, too, after he develops my taste buds, which he thinks were warped by fifteen years of convent fare. He may be right. I have only recently begun to notice individual tastes, like lemon juice in the salad dressing and cinnamon in a meat dish he puts together that perfumes the apartment while it's cooking.

We ate about four o'clock to give me plenty of time to get home and him another evening to work. While we were eating he briefed me on what he knew about Scotty's murder. The crime scene unit had dug Jack's single bullet out of the backseat of the stolen car and he had gotten his weapon back. The car had otherwise been clean. Since the owner didn't have a certain recollection of how many miles had been on the odometer, it was impossible to determine how many miles the killer had driven. What *was* certain was that Scotty had been followed when he left Petra's apartment and the killer had lain in wait in the parking lot for him to come back.

"And since he had no idea Jean would stay behind with

you, you have to figure the guy was ready to kill Scotty with his wife sitting next to him in the car."

"And professionals don't do that."

"Right. But this guy is a pro. He broke into the car without leaving a scratch, hot-wired it, and left nothing behind."

"So he's a pro that wants you to think he's an amateur."

"Looks like it."

"You think he killed Scotty for something that has to do with the lies he told about the military or where he was born?"

"Who knows?"

"Are they looking into that?"

"Hard to say. Scotty never lied to the department. The captain had Scotty's original questionnaire package faxed over from Personnel. Scotty never said he'd been in the army."

"So it was a story he made up for his wife and his friends, kind of a macho thing."

"That's what it looks like."

"It's eerie," I said. "I feel for Jean. It's bad enough she had to lose her husband. Now she doesn't even know who she was married to."

"I've never lied to you," Jack said.

It took me by surprise. "I didn't think you had."

"Neither did Jean."

We finished eating and did the dishes together. As I was drying the silver, the phone rang. Jack turned off the water and picked up the phone.

"Yeah, hi," he said after he'd answered. "No, no one. I've been hitting the books. . . . They *what*?"

I stopped rattling the silverware and started to listen.

"Say it again. . . . Yeah, yeah . . . Shit, I don't believe this. . . . OK, thanks. . . . I'll call him. . . . Right. So long."

"What is it?"

He looked several shades paler than he had when he picked up the phone. "They've just arrested Ray. He's being charged with Scotty's murder."

4

Shock is hardly the word for it. Jack tried Ray's number, but there was no answer. Then he tried Petra several times until her line cleared. Yes, she had heard, and no, she didn't know why anyone would think Ray had done it. Jack said we were on our way over.

All I could think of was that it was preposterous; it just couldn't have happened. Ray had been with us, with Petra, and then at home. "Last Sunday," I said, trying to remember the sequence of events, "you called Ray from the hospital and told him Scotty had been shot. When we got back to the parking lot, he was there looking it over."

"I know." Although his eyes were following the traffic, he seemed to be somewhere else.

"What is it?"

"That was the second time I called."

So he had called earlier, but no one was home. I didn't want to pursue it. To me it was perfectly reasonable that he had left Petra's apartment and driven home at about the time of the shooting, but that didn't mean he had done it. A thousand other people had been in their cars in that part of New York at the same time. At worst, it was a small piece of circumstantial evidence that would need a great deal more to make a case.

Jack found a tight parking space right near Petra's apartment house, and we went upstairs. She looked disheveled in a way I had never expected to see her, her hair messy, her casual weekend clothes worn without her usual panache. But she was glad to see us.

"Come on in. I'm so glad you're here. I think I'm living in a bad dream."

28

We dropped our coats on a chair and sat. Petra went to the kitchen and came back with a tray of coffee mugs and some cookies.

"Tell me what to do, Jack," she said.

"Where's Ray now?"

"I don't know. He called from Central Booking. The PBA sent a lawyer. He said he'll come here after he talks to the lawyer."

"Petra, you and I know Ray didn't do this. We just have to hang in there and be there for him."

"But how could anyone even think he would do it? He was Scotty's friend—you know that. This is all crazy."

"You're right, it is crazy. But it's going to work out."

"I feel like I'm living in a dream." She looked around helplessly. "A bad dream. It didn't happen. He's innocent."

"We'll prove it, Petra. The truth will come out, I promise you. Just tell the truth when they question you and we'll find out what really happened."

"OK." She was about to say something when the phone rang. Instead she jumped up and ran to the kitchen.

"He couldn't have done it," I said. "Petra's right; it's crazy."

"Being innocent isn't good enough. Ray's situation stinks. He's got a wife and a girlfriend. The prosecutor doesn't have to be a genius to make him look bad. And he's not the kind of guy who bows and scrapes to anyone."

"There's no motive, Jack. You don't sit in a car and wait to gun someone down without a motive."

"They must have something. You don't make a collar in a case like this just to clear it. The department and the D.A. have to be convinced. Beats me what they've got."

Petra came back to the living room. "That was Ray. He just got home and he's knocked out. He's not coming to-night."

"OK. Let's go, Chris."

We left the building in silence. Whatever Jack was thinking, my own thoughts were a bundle of confusion. Could Ray Hansen really have left Petra, stolen a car, and driven to the bar to wait for Scotty—if he knew where we were going, which he didn't? I couldn't believe it any more than Petra did.

Jack unlocked the car door, and I got in. Before he walked around to the other door, he stood on the sidewalk and looked up and down the street. This was where it had started a week ago, four happy people leaving the building and driving to a disaster. Had someone been sitting in one of the many parked cars along the street, watching us? Had we been stalked all day by a killer just waiting for the right moment? Or had Ray followed us in a car he had stolen earlier in the day and parked on the street?

Jack got in and started the car. "I don't know how to say this."

I turned to look at him, feeling scared. He was going to tell me we couldn't see each other till this was over and my heart was going to break.

"I'm crazy about you, Chris. I love you. I want us to be together, not just a night here and a night there."

I put my hand on his. If this was a proposal of marriage, it was the craziest one I'd ever heard of. "Jack—"

"Let me finish. I'm going to ask you two things and I want you to know there's no connection between them. I want you to marry me. I want us to be married. Shit, I don't know the politically correct way to say it and I wasn't planning on saying it tonight."

I started to laugh even though I had tears in my eyes. We hugged awkwardly, the emergency brake between the two front seats keeping us apart.

"I really love you," he said softly.

"I do, too." It was the first time we had said it. I had dreamed of the moment we would say it, but I had not imagined it would be in a car on a cold night, with the shadow of a murder hanging over us.

"I wish you wouldn't cry."

"I'm not crying," I said, sniffing away my tears, laughing and crying at the same time.

He wiped my tears away with his hand. "We're gonna be a great family," he said.

"Yes. I think so." I felt warm and euphoric and sexy all together. I took a tissue out of my bag and dried my eyes, which had spurted again.

"It's a deal then," he said.

"Do you want to shake on it?"

He gave me the sweet smile that was half the reason I loved him. "Your word's enough for me. I have to ask you the other question now."

"The other question." I had forgotten he had said two. Somehow I knew the bad news was coming.

"If you turn me down on this, I want you to know it doesn't matter."

"Turn you down on what?"

"I want you to try to clear Ray. You've done it before, and you've done it when the police couldn't and the evidence was hard to come by. If anyone can clear him, I think you can."

"I see."

"I know you've had a hard time getting to know him, and I know how you feel about his leaving Betsy and hooking up with Petra. None of that makes him guilty. It doesn't even make him a suspect. I've known this guy for a lot of years, and I know he isn't a killer. Whatever they have on him, it's either a mistake or it's flawed. Something's wrong and no one's ever going to find out why because once they've got their man, the investigation is over. Ray didn't do it, Chris. Someone else did and he's got to be found."

As he spoke, he pulled out of the parking space and started to drive. I had just committed my life to this man and now he wanted me to clear his friend of a murder, a friend I didn't like, a man I didn't want to spend time with, someone I would feel very uncomfortable questioning.

Still, as Jack had just said, none of that made him guilty. I had known Arnold Gold long enough and had been involved in enough of his cases to know that people who are not very nice are not necessarily criminals. I knew, too, that Jack could not investigate this case, much as he obviously wanted to. He was hardly a disinterested party and, as he had just told me, the investigation was over. All they would be doing now was sewing up the case against Ray.

"I can't do what you asked me to do, Jack," I said. "I

won't try to clear Ray. I'll do what I've done before. I'll try
to find Scotty's killer. If I turn up evidence that's damaging
to Ray, I won't hide it."

"OK." The muscles in his face relaxed. "You're right. I
asked you something I shouldn't've. We need to find Scotty's
killer, whoever it is. I'll give you all the help I can. We can
bat it around between us if you want, and if you'd rather not,
I'll keep out of it."

"Of course I want to talk to you about it."

He reached over and patted my hand. I smiled and
squeezed his hand. I wanted to go back to his apartment in
Brooklyn Heights and consummate our engagement with the
release of the enormous passion I was feeling for him. Instead, he turned down a street I had never seen before and
slipped into a parking spot just as someone vacated it.

"Let's go talk to Ray," he said.

I had never been to Ray's apartment and didn't know
which way to turn. Jack took my arm and we started walking. It was a street of New York–style houses: brick, two stories, one family on each level. Usually the owner lived on
the main level, up several brick stairs to a front door. A trio
of young, laughing men came down the street toward us, and
I felt Jack tense till they passed harmlessly by. I wondered if
the reaction was rooted in his police background or whether
all New Yorkers reacted that way. Across the street I heard
someone running and glanced over. A woman with a long
cape or shawl covering her head was hurrying down the
street. Although the young men had seemed intent only on
getting somewhere, I automatically worried about the woman
should her path cross theirs. It was night in New York, not
a healthy time to be walking alone on the street.

"Let's cross," Jack said, and we went to the other side.
"He's in one of these houses, but they all look the same. I
think it's two-twenty-one."

"It's hard to see the numbers. They've all turned their
front lights off."

"It must be getting late." He dropped my arm and
bounded up a couple of steps. "Two down," he said.

Ray was in the basement apartment with the entrance on

the driveway. Jack pressed the buzzer, and Ray responded right away. "Yeah, I'm coming."

The door opened, and Jack said, "Can we talk?"

"Come on in."

It was one large room with a sofa that I assumed doubled as a bed. A refrigerator, stove, and sink lined one wall as though they were a natural part of a bed-living room. The place had a military fastidiousness about it. It could have passed white-glove inspection without a moment's warning.

"All right, let me hear it," Jack said. "All of it." His voice had changed from the one I knew to a harsh one that belonged to a police sergeant.

Ray shrugged. "You got me. The doorbell rang this morning and they put the cuffs on and read me my rights. I didn't know what they were talking about."

"What have they got?"

"I don't know yet."

"Tell me what you think."

Ray looked uneasily at me and then back at Jack. "Nothing that'll stand up in court."

"Give it to me straight, Ray." The sergeant talking again.

Ray got up and walked around. "How do you like my pad, Chris?" he said.

"It's nice. Compact." I watched him moving nervously. He was tall and lean, taller and leaner than Jack. Tonight he looked unshaven but not disheveled. He was wearing tan pants and a brown sweater over a tan shirt.

"It's illegal," he said. "They took a three-room and made two ones out of it. Put in a second bath with a Sears prefab shower. They make a little more in rent, but half of it's off the books. Nice little extra, three hundred a month tax free."

"What do they have, Ray?" Jack said again.

"I loaned Scotty some money."

"You should be in a psycho ward. What kind of a dumb thing is that to do? Money goes through Scotty's hands like water. You know that. You've known it for years. He used that money to buy a car he didn't need."

"He said he needed it. I had it. I gave it to him. It was before I split with Betsy. He said he'd get it back to me in a couple of months and he didn't. After we split, things got a little tight. I asked him for it back."

"How did you ask?" Jack said, and I got a sick feeling in my stomach.

"I wrote him a note."

"To where?"

"To the station house. I didn't want Jean to see it."

"He probably tossed it in his locker and they read it the day after Scotty was shot. How much was it?"

"Three thousand bucks."

"They should have you in a straitjacket. That's what he made in a month."

"Come on, Jack. You kill a guy who owes you money, you don't collect. Even loan sharks know that. There's something else."

Jack didn't say anything. He just looked at Ray as though he didn't want to face what was coming.

"I drove over to talk to Scotty a few days before St. Patrick's Day. I really needed the money back, or at least part of it."

"I don't think I want to hear this," Jack said. "How bad did it get?"

"We had some words."

"Tell me you didn't lay a hand on him."

"I pushed him around a little. It was nothing." But Ray looked nervous now.

"You pushed him around. *You pushed him around.* Where did this happen?"

"In the locker room."

"You invite the captain to watch it? How big was the crowd?"

"Ten or fifteen. I didn't hurt him, Jack. Hey, you saw us on St. Patrick's Day. Did it look like trouble?"

"Ten or fifteen witnesses to a fight that got physical."

"Come on, you see it every day."

"But this time the guy getting pushed around ended up dead. You say anything while you were slugging him that'll kill you in court?"

"I don't remember. Maybe."

Jack got up and walked to one of the windows. It was at

about eye level and probably offered an enchanting view of the driveway and the basement windows of the house on the other side of it. "All right, here's what we're going to do. Chris is going to look into Scotty's homicide and see if she can turn anything up. I'll give her whatever she needs."

"Forget it, buddy. This is no job for an amateur."

"Hansen, you are under arrest for Murder One, the killing of a police officer, a family man that you got in a fight with over money a couple of days before he got shot. You've got a dozen cops who'll take the stand and swear you threatened to kill him. Just who do you think is going to clear you?"

"They got no case, Jack. The whole thing's gonna fall apart."

"Listen to me. Chris and I have some ideas. We're all tired now so we'll come back in the morning to talk to you. Eight o'clock. We'll all be able to think a little better."

"Don't bother."

"Come on, Chris."

I got up and rebuttoned my coat, which I hadn't taken off.

"When did you leave Petra's apartment last Sunday night?"

"Never looked. We did the dishes, rolled around for a while. I got dressed and came home."

"Why'd you come home?"

"I always come home."

"You see her last night?"

"Yeah."

"Why'd you come back here?"

Ray gave us a small smile. "It may surprise you," he said, "but I like sleeping alone. OK?"

"OK with me, buddy."

Jack opened the door, we went up a few steps, opened the outside door, and stepped out onto the driveway.

My thoughts were such a jumble I couldn't sort them out. Whether Ray had been generous or stupid to lend the money to Scotty I could not pass judgment on. But to have talked to him about it in a locker room, to have, by his own admission, pushed Scotty around, filled me with disgust. And to have done it in front of other people, people in Scotty's precinct who could be counted on to side with Scotty and probably dislike Ray in the bargain, only made it worse.

We drove home without saying much, but when we were upstairs, Jack said, "Let's talk."

"Go on."

"I know what you heard upset you. I know how you feel about violence. What Ray described happens all the time. A couple of guys have a beef, they talk about it in the locker room or a car or the men's room, and it escalates. There's an undercurrent of violence in a cop's life and sometimes it just explodes. I'm sure Ray was sore as hell when he went over to ask for the money, but he wasn't planning to kill for it. You saw them on St. Patrick's Day. They were buddies."

"Did you ever lend Scotty money?"

"Nothing bigger than a five or a ten, and after the first time, I never expected to get it back. He paid me back sometimes. He probably thought he paid me back all the time. That's the way Scotty was."

It didn't make me feel any better about Ray.

5

I didn't sleep well. Little about last night's visit with Ray had made me feel better about launching this investigation. The little was that he was so casual about the charge, so certain that it wouldn't hold up in court. Did that mean he was confident of his innocence—or sure that no other evidence against him would turn up? And while I hadn't expected him to welcome my entry into the case with open arms, I had not been reassured by his response.

I slept till Jack's alarm woke me, although I usually wake up earlier on my own accord. Jack put breakfast together, using coffee his sister, the caterer, had given him to try. The smell got me going more than the alarm had, and by the time I sat at the little table, most of me was there.

"Feel OK?" Jack asked.

"A little tired."

"You didn't sleep well, did you?"

"I'm fine." I leaned over and kissed his freshly shaved cheek. "You smell good."

"So do you."

"Fiancé," I said.

"Yeah." He kissed my lips. "I didn't give you anything to seal it."

"Yes, you did."

"That doesn't count."

"We should talk about this morning, about seeing Ray." I was inordinately nervous about it. Everything he had told us was very likely already known by the District Attorney. If Ray had written to Scotty at the precinct house to ask for the money back, and Scotty had left the letter in his locker, it was now part of the case against Ray. The witnesses to the

37

locker room fight had probably all made statements by now. If there were any other little secrets, it was unlikely Ray would disclose them to me or in my presence. I felt I would have to work around him, rather than with him.

"Let me tell you a couple of things about Ray," Jack said. "He and Betsy haven't had the smoothest ride together. This isn't the first time they've lived apart and it may not be the last. Whatever goes on between them, he keeps quiet about it, and I respect him for that. I think he was nuts to lend Scotty money—anyone would be nuts to lend him money— but whatever you think of Ray, he's got a heart."

"That's a lot of money to have lying around," I said.

"He's a careful guy. Betsy does some part-time work. I think her folks may have given them the down payment on the house, or at least some of it. I have money put away," he said, looking at me. "OK?"

"You're single."

"And I don't drive an expensive car. Ray doesn't, either."

"You think Scotty really used that money to buy the BMW?"

"I'm afraid to ask."

Boys and their toys, Jean had said on St. Patrick's Day. How could Scotty have thought he could return the money in two months if he'd sunk it into a car?

"There are three things we have to look into," I said, drawing together the fruits of my several sleepless hours. "Scotty's beat. Jean said that was his life and I still think the answer to all this is likely to be there. The second is unsolved murders of cops. I know there are some, and I know they've been investigated to death, but there could be a connection. And the third is these crazy things about Scotty himself, the lies he told his friends and his wife about his military service, and where he was born, and who knows what else."

Jack had taken a sheet of plain white paper from under the saltshaker and folded it in half once, then once again, in his familiar pattern of note-taking. As I spoke, he wrote 1, 2, and 3 along a folded edge and made brief notes.

"Because the homicide occurred on his beat, it's been canvassed, I can tell you that. And since it's about ten blocks long, with a lot of stores and apartment houses, it's much too big for you to go over by yourself. I'll get hold of the D.D.5s from the interviews and the unusuals and anything else that's been put in the file and either we'll go over them together or I'll pull out what I think should be looked into again."

"Fine."

He glanced at his note sheet. "I'll get the files on the unsolved cop killings. There aren't many. The guys break their backs on those cases and even if they can't bag the killer, they often have a good idea who he is and they're waiting to find him or waiting for him to make a false step so he can be picked up. The third thing, I don't know what to say. I don't know how it fits in or what it means. We'll just have to keep digging." He looked at his watch. "We should get going."

We took care of the dishes quickly and left the apartment. We were a little later than we'd planned. Jack works the ten-to-six shift and then goes off to law school four nights a week. We took two cars, so we could go our separate ways. I followed till we turned into Ray's street. After we parked, we met at Ray's driveway and walked to his apartment together.

Ray took my coat, but Jack kept his on. Ray was dressed in a a tweed jacket, white shirt, and tie. "They've got my two .38s and they took my ID so I can't run out and buy another one, and they put me on modified assignment," he said in answer to Jack's question. "They'll find some papers for me to shove around or have me sign in at the borough office for appearances."

"At least you'll draw a paycheck." Jack outlined our three avenues of investigation, and Ray listened and nodded.

"I don't know what to make of Scotty's military service and the birth certificate," Ray said. "I talked to a lot of guys last week and they were as surprised as I was. It doesn't make sense."

"How did he plan to pay you back?"

"He just said he'd have the money."

"He give you any paper on the loan?"

"I didn't ask, he didn't offer."

"Jean know about it?"

He wavered before answering. "Yeah, she probably knows."

The phone rang, and he went to answer it. "Yeah," he said. Then he listened, his face changing. He glanced over at us. Then he said, "Hey, hold on a minute." But the caller had apparently hung up. He looked at the phone before replacing it. "This is crazy. Some guy, I don't know who, said the troops were on their way over with a warrant. No name, no nothing."

"You have something to hide?" Jack asked.

"No, I don't have anything to hide," Ray said irritably, but he looked worried. "And I think you should get your butt outa here before they come. You, too," he said to me.

"I'll see you later," Jack said.

I watched him go. When the door closed, I said, "Maybe we can talk, Ray."

"There's nothing to talk about. You know as much about this as I do." His whole face was screwed up with tension.

"Is it a mistake that they've charged you or is it a set-up?"

"I didn't think about much else last night. I don't know. I don't know why anyone on God's earth would want Scotty dead, and I don't know why anyone would want to frame me for his murder."

I didn't like the way he was looking nervously around. Something was bothering him, and it wasn't my presence. There were voices outside and I looked toward the door.

"Sounds like they're here," I said. When I turned back, Ray was closing the closet door.

The doorbell rang and he went over and opened the door.

Three men walked into the apartment. The oldest of them introduced himself as Captain Browning and handed Ray a search warrant.

"What are you looking for?" he asked.

"The weapon used in the murder of Scott McVeigh."

"I don't have it. Go ahead and look."

The captain turned to me. "Who are you, miss?"

"Christine Bennett."

"Your address?"

I gave him my address in Oakwood, and he wrote it in a notebook.

"Mind telling me what you're doing here?"

"Don't answer that, Chris," Ray said. "It's none of their business."

"I'm a friend of the family," I said.

They got to work. I was sure they wouldn't find a gun, but the warrant gave them the right to look almost anywhere a gun might be, so they could well turn up something else quite legally. I kept my bag on my shoulder. I was glad I had hung up my coat. Heat was hissing out of the radiators and the temperature must have been near eighty.

The men worked quickly, looking in all the obvious places a gun might be hidden. Ray didn't look at them, but I did. I thought it wouldn't be a bad idea to have someone on hand who wasn't the accused and wasn't part of the search party.

The man going methodically through the dresser drawers opened one and tapped his fingernail on something metallic. Then he pulled out a gray metal box, put it on top of the dresser, and opened it.

"Want to tell me what some of these things are?" he said, turning to Ray.

"That's an extra car key," Ray said, walking over to the dresser.

"Extra key for your cuffs?"

"Yeah."

"This one?"

"Locker key."

"What's this?" He held up something that looked like a metal stick from where I was standing.

"That's an aluminum cleaning rod. I like to keep my weapons clean. There should be a silicon rag in there, too."

"There is." The man laid it on top of the dresser. "Two dump pouches." He put two small black leather pouches on the dresser. They looked like Jack's. Each one could hold six extra rounds. Jack had told me that only young cops or guys who thought they were immortal walked around without them.

The man opened each pouch and poured the contents into his hand. Then he put the bullets back in the pouches. The last thing he took out of the metal box was a cardboard box. I was too far away to see it clearly, but I assumed it was a

box of bullets to replace any that were used. The man whis-
tled as he opened it.

"Two copper-jacketed .44s," he said. "You own a
.44-caliber weapon, Sergeant?"

Ray's face had gotten very pale. "No, I don't, and I've
never seen those before."

The captain had walked over to see the bullets. "We'll
have to take these with us. Better take the whole box."

The box went into a plastic bag, the searcher made a couple of notes on the outside of it, and the men continued their
search. They took the bed apart, went through the stove and
refrigerator, including the ice cube trays, and spent some
time in the bathroom. The furniture was disassembled,
squeezed and poked, then put back together. There wasn't
much. It was a bachelor apartment with only four walls and
a bathroom. Even the closet yielded little. Ray owned a few
pairs of shoes and an assortment of pants and jackets hanging
neatly.

As the man going through the closet came to my coat, Ray
said, "That's Miss Bennett's." He walked over to the closet,
took it out, and held it over his arm.

It seemed as good a time to leave as any, so I took it from
him, put it on, and said good-bye. To my surprise, Ray said,
"Why don't you stay awhile?"

But I didn't want to, and the search was practically over.
I said good-bye again and left.

6

If someone had broken into Ray's apartment, it almost had to be yesterday. Had the bullets been planted earlier, there was a strong chance Ray would have found them. Assuming they were a plant and that they were planted yesterday, perhaps someone had seen the perpetrator. After everyone had left Ray's place, I rang the doorbell of the apartment on the main level.

A young woman carrying a two-year-old opened the door. "Yes?"

"I'm a friend of one of your tenants and I—"

"Which one?"

"Ray Hansen."

"Tell me he isn't the one I've been seeing on the news."

"He probably is."

"Oh, my God, in our house. He's gonna have to go, that's all there is to it. I have children. I can't have a killer running around downstairs."

I sympathized with her fears, but I felt Ray deserved that presumption of innocence we're always told the law grants us. "There hasn't been a trial yet and he's working at his job, just the way he did last week."

"They take his gun away?"

"Yes."

She gave me a quick smile. "So what can I do for you?"

"I wonder if you noticed anyone around his apartment yesterday."

"Why? Did somebody break in? In this house?"

"I'm not sure. Did you see anyone?"

"My God. My husband'll have a fit. I don't think I saw anyone, no. Is something missing?"

43

"Not exactly. Did you hear anyone down there during the day?"

"We never hear anything. The construction in this house is really good. And he's quiet and he isn't home much."

"If you saw or heard anything when he wasn't home—"

"I really couldn't tell you. Not that I noticed. I have to go. The baby needs changing. Who did you say you were?"

"Chris Bennett."

"OK. Thanks."

I tried a few more houses with no more luck. Most of Ray's neighbors had never seen him, didn't know how long he had lived there, and had been surprised to find out he had been arrested. One old woman had seen a police car before noon but had left her window soon after. Several people had spent the afternoon visiting. For all most of the block knew, Ray had never lived there. New York can be like that.

I had only tried six houses, three on each side of the street, and several doorbells had not been answered. It was a few minutes after eleven, and I went back and rescued my car from the mechanical broom that was lumbering down the street.

A few blocks away I found a pay phone and called Jean McVeigh. She was home and said she'd be happy to have company. Since I don't know my way around New York very well, especially Brooklyn and Queens, she gave me directions, which turned out to be very good. When I got to her house, she had coffee ready and some sandwiches for lunch. The children were playing upstairs and the police wives had left. It was her first day on her own since Scotty's death, a tough day to get through.

"Jack called when he got to the station house," she said. "He told me you're looking into . . . what happened."

"I'm giving it a try. You know the principals a lot better than I do. Do you think Ray could have done it?"

Jean smiled and shook her red head. "It's all wrong. The guys were friends, I mean real friends. They loved each other. There was no reason, no motive. He didn't do it, Chris. There was nothing bad between Scotty and Ray. They had different jobs, they didn't compete with each other. I don't know what's going on, but I don't believe Ray ever even had a bad thought about Scotty."

"Did you know Ray lent Scotty some money?"

"I knew." She looked down at the table. "I didn't know till after Scotty got it or I wouldn't't've let him take it. Anyway, that's not a motive. Scotty was going to pay it back."

"Do you know why he borrowed it?"

"Oh, gee." She sighed. "I suppose it was for the car. He was a real sucker when it came to cars. Someone was selling the BMW real cheap and he just had to have it. But for all I know, it was for something else. Scotty was a man of surprises."

"I really hate to ask this," I said, feeling very uncomfortable, "but how did he plan to pay it back?"

"We had some money coming in, a bond that was coming due. He would have had it." She seemed so down talking about it, her eyes misty, her voice low and occasionally choking up.

I really didn't want to go on. Every question would be painful, and she had suffered enough. "You make a good sandwich," I said.

Jean began to laugh and cry at the same time. She pulled a tissue out of a pocket and used it on her eyes, but she was smiling. "Oh, Chris, I know how hard this is for you. And wouldn't I rather talk about tunafish sandwiches myself. It's OK. Ask whatever you have to. I don't think Ray killed Scotty and my God, I want to know who did. If you don't do it, I don't know who will."

"Tell me about those papers of Scotty's, the birth certificate and the military one. Have you found out anything?"

"Only that Scotty never served and that he wasn't born in Brooklyn under the name Scott McVeigh."

"Did you know his parents?"

"He told me they were dead."

"My parents died when I was young. Maybe he got moved around and lost track of where he was born."

"Maybe that's it." But she didn't sound as though she believed it any more than I did.

"Do you know his parents' names?"

"Edward and Mary Margaret."

"My father's name was Edward," I said. "When I was a Franciscan nun, I was Sister Edward Frances, after both my parents."

"I see you and Jack together and I can't believe you were ever a nun. You must have repressed a lot of feelings for a long time."

"It wasn't like that. I loved what I was doing. I got a fine education and I taught wonderful students. It was a very fulfilling life. I still feel close to the people at the convent."

Jean smiled, the tears gone. She got up and brought the coffeepot to the table. There was a burst of giggly laughter from upstairs, and she walked to the stairs and stood and listened for a minute before returning to the table.

"Ray is a tough person to get to know," I said, admitting my own limitation. "There seems to be a shell around him, a barrier that I just can't negotiate."

"He's been under a lot of stress. Petra's really very good for him. Betsy's a nice woman, but she wasn't a partner. She lived in his shadow. Ray's tough and he needs a little—I don't know—someone who can stand up to him. Petra does that. She's pretty tough herself. Listen to me." She laughed. "I've got everyone in the world figured out except myself and Scotty. If anyone lived in her husband's shadow, it was me, and he's gone. Maybe that's why I've been so cold this last week. There's nothing to wrap around me anymore. I feel so exposed, so out in the open."

"We'll help, Jean," I said.

"I know you will, Chris." She had tears on her face again. "And I thank you for it."

I didn't know what else to do before I heard from Jack on the unsolved homicides of police officers and the interviews with people along Scotty's beat. I didn't want to call him from Jean's house, or from a pay phone, because I might have to take notes. So after another cup of coffee and some more conversation, I drove home.

Unless Ray had murdered Scotty, I wasn't any closer to finding out who did. None of the neighbors had seen anyone try to enter Ray's apartment yesterday, and those two copper-clad, .44-caliber bullets were going to be powerful evidence against him. Even if they never found the murder weapon, the bullets looked very bad.

But for me the bullets came close to tipping my feelings in favor of Ray's innocence. He was such a neat, fastidious person. If he had gone to all the trouble of stealing a car, acquiring a murder weapon, lying in wait, and executing his friend, how could he have been so lax as to leave two damning bullets in his drawer? He'd been a detective—a detective sergeant—long enough to know that a search warrant would turn them up. On the other hand, if they'd been planted, I was absolutely certain it had happened yesterday. If they'd been there earlier in the week, Ray would have seen them when he went to clean his guns, which I was sure he did regularly, probably on the weekend. I turned into my driveway and stopped in front of the closed garage. The garage was detached and set way back, a style of building no longer used. Aunt Margaret had liked it that way, and except that I had somewhat more snow to shovel in the winter, I didn't mind it much myself. When the car was put away, I went to the mailbox at the curb and took out a pile of catalogs and a few bills.

In the house I took my coat off, seeing the bloodstain on the lining once again. I had seen it this morning when I'd given my coat to Ray and again when I put it on. I really wanted to get rid of it, but this was the only winter coat I owned, and it was still too cold to do without it. Maybe, I thought, my friend and neighbor, Melanie Gross, would have something to lend me for the few days it would take to have the coat cleaned.

7

"Got a lot of stuff for you," Jack said in my ear. "Got a pencil handy?"

"Yes, I'm listening."

"Nothing in any of the interviews really stands out. A lot of people said they loved him. A lot said he was very honest. A couple told nice stories about him. One place wouldn't talk."

"Oh?"

"Remember he told us about a Korean grocery? They all claimed not to know a word of English when they were interviewed. The canvassing detective was persistent and went back with a translator, but the Koreans said they didn't know Scotty well and didn't know anything about him. A little fishy after what he told us."

"They probably don't want to get involved. Police can be very threatening."

"My guess, too. The interviewer is a hundred percent sure one guy speaks perfect English, but he just couldn't get through."

"I'll give it a try. I need to do some grocery shopping anyway."

He gave me the address and the name of the owner of the store, Mr. Ma. "Now about the other thing," he said. "There are three open homicides of police officers. None of them were shot with a .44, which doesn't rule out a connection. But there's almost nothing that could tie them to Scotty, even using a lot of imagination."

"Tell me about them anyway."

"One was a black cop walking home at night in Harlem about two years ago when he got off duty. His name was

Roscoe Boyd, he was twenty-seven years old, wearing street clothes, and the theory is it was a mugging that went bad. The perps probably didn't know he was a cop till they'd shot him. They took his wallet and gun and haven't been seen since. There are several possible suspects, but not enough evidence to bring them in."

"Was the gun they stole a .38?"

"Yup. Smith and Wesson. They shot him with a .22."

"OK."

"I've gone through what I could of his record and Scotty's and there's nothing to tie them together. They were a couple of years apart at the Academy and their careers never overlapped."

"What's the next one?"

"The next one is someone Scotty may have known. His name was Gavin Moore and he was part of a buy-and-bust drug team in Queens. About two and a half years ago, he was on his way to a buy and ended up dead. He wasn't where he should have been, and the guy he'd gone to meet has the perfect alibi. He'd been picked up for some traffic violation about the time of the homicide. There have been a lot of leads in this case—you wouldn't believe the size of the file—but nothing has panned out."

"You said he might have known Scotty."

"It looks as if they were at the same precinct for about a year a couple of years before Moore was killed."

"What was the murder weapon?" I asked.

"Nine millimeter."

"Ouch."

"Right. And here's the third. This one is really different. Harry Donner, an older guy, about fifty-five, probably putting in his last years before retirement. Described in different ways by different people. Some said he was a sweet old guy who never ruffled any feathers, donated a lot of time to good causes. Other people said he was a tough, savvy detective, ice water in his veins, that you couldn't put anything over on him."

"Sounds like an interesting guy," I said. "How did he die?"

"You'll like this. It was in a parking lot."

I felt a chill. "Go on."

"Not a bar. He was widowed and lived alone. He'd gone to a shopping center on Long Island one night about three years ago and got hit coming back to his car."

"So he may have been stalked the way Scotty was."

"Could be. Unless it was random. A lot of people have been shot or mugged in parking lots. There's something else. I knew him."

"You," I said. "How?"

"He was at the Six-Five when I first got there." The Sixty-fifth is Jack's precinct in Brooklyn.

"Which description do you think fits?"

"Probably both. I didn't know much about his charitable activities, but he was one hell of a detective. And a nice guy. He'd talk to you, show you, a natural teacher for new gold shields. But he didn't tolerate stupidity."

"How about a connection to Scotty?" I asked. "Besides the parking lot."

"I can't find anything. Donner had a long career in Brooklyn and Queens, but it doesn't look like he overlapped with Scotty anywhere along the way. And he was shot with a .38. So all three—all four—are different."

"But if you think about it," I said, "there are some similarities between all of them and Scotty. The first one, Boyd, was a uniformed cop."

"Doesn't mean much. You gotta be something, and most cops wear uniforms."

"You said the second one, Moore, was in Scotty's precinct for a while. And this last one got shot in a parking lot. Jack, I think two and three are possibilities."

"So do I. But remember, Intelligence has checked this out."

"I know. Is it OK if I talk to their families?"

"Sure. Gavin Moore had a wife and a couple of kids." He dictated an address in Brooklyn, and I took it down. "Donner's a problem. He was widowed, no children."

"Give me his last address."

It was in Queens, but not close enough to the McVeighs to be any kind of connection. I was already thinking through what could have happened to Donner's estate. If his house was sold, the money had to go somewhere. Maybe one of Arnold Gold's paralegals could research Donner's will for me.

"Got it?" Jack asked.

"Yes. This is really good stuff. I've got a lot to do now."

"Tell me about this morning. I haven't been able to find Ray anywhere."

I told him about the two copper-clad .44-caliber bullets in Ray's metal box. He hissed an obscenity as he heard it.

"It looked like a thorough search," I went on. "Ray was pretty nervous when it started, but he seemed cool as they went along, except when they found the bullets."

"I can believe it. This really stinks."

"I'll talk to you tomorrow, after I've made a start. I'll only have the afternoon so I won't get much done. Maybe I'll just buy some produce at the Korean grocery."

"See if they have Uglifruits. My sister says they're terrific."

"I'll give them a try."

8

Tuesday is my teaching day. I teach a course in Poetry and the Contemporary American Woman, and by March, I was on my second semester, an all new class. Over the Christmas break I had revised my lesson plan somewhat, as a result of my first-semester experience. For a while it was touch and go whether I'd teach this course or another, but I persuaded the department to let me keep this one. I always feel I do a better job the second time, and it seemed a shame to have to drop something just as I was about to improve it. Happily, the administration agreed to keep the course.

The college is a small one in Westchester, and I teach the whole week's worth in one morning, leaving me free the rest of the week to do other things. It's a very comfortable arrangement, if not lucrative. But I don't need a lot of money. For one thing, I've spent half my life living on practically nothing. When I was at St. Stephen's I often left the convent with no more than the price of two phone calls in my pocket, a situation that required some conscious alteration when I took up residence in Oakwood.

I had a quick lunch in the college cafeteria after my class and then drove to Brooklyn. In my bag was a list of fruits and vegetables that would provide my reason for visiting the Happy Times Grocery.

I got out of my car and took a leisurely walk along Scotty's beat. It was like visiting a place you've read about and never thought you would see. I kept thinking of Scotty in his uniform, stopping to talk to this one and that one. The Laundromat he had spoken of was there, and inside I could see the woman who owned it taking someone's clothes out of a washer and dumping them into a large plastic basket, heading for the dryer. I wondered if she knew how much Scotty had admired her.

Farther along, the parking lot where Scotty had been gunned down looked benignly different in daylight. It was simply the space left by a razed building between two other buildings. The crime scene tape was gone now and a couple of cars were parked near the back end. I crossed the street and went back on the other side.

It looked like any shopping area you might find in the middle of Brooklyn. There was a bank, a stationery store, a coffee shop, a store with about a hundred T-shirts in the window. Just around the corner of the street I was walking on was a small used-car lot and a body shop next to it. I passed a Chinese takeout, a used-clothing store, and found myself in front of Happy Times.

Like other Korean groceries, Happy Times had good-looking produce arranged very attractively, oranges and grapefruits in pyramids, several kinds of apples, also in careful rows, lettuces, cabbages, everything clean and carefully set out. I spied Uglifruits when I came in but kept away from them. They would give me the chance to ask a question and find out if anyone spoke English.

There was an attractive, youngish woman at the cash register, an older tiny woman walking around, rearranging fruit and keeping a sharp eye on the customers, and two men doing other kinds of work. One of them, a fellow probably only in his twenties, was sweeping the floor with a large broom. The other, a stern-faced man who may only have been in his thirties, was at a table in the back, writing.

I decided that the older woman wasn't likely to know much English, so she would be a good one to ask. With luck, she wouldn't understand me at all and would lead me to the expert who would. Before asking her, however, I filled several small bags, so she would see I was a serious customer.

When I went to ask her, I made my face pleasant but unsmiling. My observations about Koreans in New York indicated that smiling was a form of intimacy they did not indulge in with strangers, something that has probably led to a great number of misunderstandings. "Excuse me," I said politely, "I wonder if you have any Uglifruits today." I used enough words so that the important one could easily get lost in the string of sounds.

She shook her head and said something that may have been English and may have been Korean. Then she walked to the back of the shop to the man sitting at the table.

They exchanged a few words. Then he said, "What are you looking for?" in flawless English.

"Uglifruits," I said. "I think they're in season now."

"Yes, we have some." He got up and walked to where they were stacked.

"Thank you," I said, and took two. "Do you have sweet onions, too?"

"Bermudas. Over there."

"Yes. I see them now. This is my first time here. My friend, Officer McVeigh, told me to shop here just before he died."

"You are police," the man said, his dark eyes fixed on me.

"Oh, no," I said, trying to sound shocked. "I'm a teacher. I know his family. He said he came by here every day."

"He did. He was a good man. He was good to my mother." He turned toward the little woman, who was watching us.

"I don't know why anyone would kill him." I took a couple of Bermuda onions and put them in a bag.

"It was a mistake. Somebody who thought he was rich. Officer McVeigh was a good man. Ask anybody. You know his wife?"

"Yes. I know the family."

"You tell his wife, she comes here, I give her a big bag of fruit. Free. You understand?"

"Yes." I felt myself smile slightly, but he kept his mouth stern. "Thank you."

"No. We thank him."

I nodded and carried my bags to the cash register. It cost me almost twenty dollars, but I felt it was worth it.

I put the bag on the front seat next to mine and got into the car. I was about to drive away when I thought of something. I took a quick look up and down the street, didn't see any lurking police, and made a U-turn. At the corner, I turned right and pulled into the used-car lot.

It didn't look like a busy day. If there were customers, they weren't outside. I went to the building, opened a door painted a bright red, and stepped inside.

"Help you with something?" a paunchy, graying man behind a dilapidated desk asked as he saw me.

"I'm a friend of Officer McVeigh's," I began.

"Ah, Scotty. My God, what a shame, what a shame. You his sister?"

"A friend. I drove in his new car before he died."

"The BMW. I sold it to him. Nice piece of machinery, huh? Purrs like a cat. You looking for something like that yourself?"

"Not just yet. I wanted to ask you something about Scotty's car. His wife's going through his papers and they're kind of a mess. She needs to know what he paid for it."

"Nothin'."

"What?"

"It was a trade-in. He gave me his old car, I gave him the BMW."

"But his old car wasn't worth anything like what that car's worth." I had no idea what his last car had been, but it certainly hadn't been a luxury car.

"For Scotty McVeigh it was even-steven. I couldn't take money from him. The man made my life livable. You know what it is to have a small business in this city? It's like hell. You spend twelve hours a day filling out forms. Then they send it all back and say do it over again. He worked it out for me. He pulled a couple of strings, made a few calls, smoothed the road, you know? It was worth one used BMW. On a trade-in."

"Could I see the paperwork on the car?" I asked.

"Hey, lady, what is this? You the IRS or something?"

"I'm Jean McVeigh's friend. She was under the impression Scotty paid a couple of thousand dollars for the car."

"So let her think it."

"She'd like to know the truth."

"The truth I told you the first time around. From now on it's fairy tales. What do you want I should say? Two thousand? Fine. Officer McVeigh paid two grand for the car. Plus the trade-in."

"What did he trade?" I asked, giving up on the cash.

"A little Buick, good condition. I sold it already. It's not on the lot."

"Thank you," I said. I opened the door. "How much did you say he paid you?"

He gave me a big smile. "Two thousand dollars cash. You wanna try for three?"

I didn't.

My map of Brooklyn was in the car, and when I sat down I looked up the street where Gavin Moore had lived. It was some distance away, but since I was already in Brooklyn and it was still early, I drove over. The house was a one-family, on a street that had an old apartment house in the middle and one- and two-family houses on either side. In New York, the older, prewar buildings are often distinguished by their lack of style and anything approaching beauty. The front of an apartment house is contiguous with the sidewalk, every square inch of property used for the building. There is no shrubbery along the front, often no setback for the entrance. On many streets, buildings line up like a fortress, the side of one touching the side of another. While it was certainly an economical use of space, I have often wondered whether the designers and builders cared about anything else like the value of greenery, of space not covered with concrete.

The Moore house was several down from the large, red six-story building. It had a big *M* on the door and a small station wagon in the narrow driveway. I pulled in behind the car and went to the front door.

The door was opened by a nice-looking woman who was not much older than I. She was on the tall side and was wearing a running suit in a pretty shade of rose. I introduced myself and told her I was a friend of Scotty's. She invited me in.

"Everybody's looking for a connection," she said when we'd sat down in the living room. "This is the fourth un-solved killing in less than four years."

"What do you think?" I asked.

"I think there's nothing there. They knew each other, you know."

"I know."

"Not well, but they were in the same precinct for about a year. Then Gavin got transferred into this team and they probably never saw each other again. The work they did, it was completely different. You don't think this Hansen guy killed McVeigh?"

"No."

"They've been pretty quiet about a motive," Mrs. Moore said. "Something about borrowed money."

"They were friends. Jean McVeigh doesn't think Ray did it. I didn't really think I'd talk to you and come up with something the police missed, it just seemed to be something I ought to do."

"I know what you mean. In Gavin's case—"

The front door opened as she was speaking, and a man called, "Sharon?"

"Hi, honey. I'm in here."

A strapping, good-looking man came into the living room. He was in jeans and a sweatshirt, but the gun on his belt told me he was a police officer.

"This is Joe Farina," Sharon Moore said. "This is Chris . . ."

"Bennett," I said, shaking his hand.

"Chris is a friend of Scotty McVeigh's. She wanted to know if there was a connection with Gavin."

"Nice to meet you," Farina said. "You're not the only one looking for a connection. Wish I could help you." He turned to Sharon. "I need a nap." He leaned over and kissed her. "Good luck," he said to me, and went upstairs.

"We're friends," Sharon said. "We live together. It's been almost three years since Gavin died."

"He seems very nice," I said.

"He is." She shook off her embarrassment. "What I was saying about Gavin. I think he got careless. They had a plan every time they went out. There was a back-up team, they knew where they were going, they had a timetable. You want to know what I think happened? I think he had to take a leak. He got shot in a little park that was sort of on the way to where he was going. He probably stopped because he had to pee. I never knew anyone who had to go as much as

Gavin did. They think it was a bunch of kids who killed him. They don't have enough to charge anyone, and everybody's keeping quiet. One of these days one of those guys'll make a mistake and he'll give them a name and plead down his case. I really miss Gavin. He was a funny, sweet guy. You do that kind of work, you have to have a sense of humor or you go crazy. We had a lot of fun together. If he'd had a better set of kidneys, he'd probably be alive today."

I caught Jack before he left for law school and told him about my interviews. He seemed cheered that the grocery had offered something to Jean and assured me you couldn't believe anything a used-car dealer told you. He also thought that the story about Gavin Moore rang true, and he agreed with Sharon Moore's assessment of how the killer would eventually be found. The name Joe Farina rang a bell when I mentioned it. They had known each other at some point, but Jack wasn't sure where.

"I've gotta run," he said finally, "but I picked up some scuttlebutt today. Someone I know knows someone in IAD and the word is, there's a lot more to the D.A.'s case than the loan and the fight."

"Is that it?"

"That's all I heard. I'll keep trying."

I had half of my first Uglifruit at dinner and it was truly a treat. Greenish-yellow and misshapen on the outside, the inside was glorious, juicy and a pale orange color. Without much difficulty I could become a gourmet. If I could afford it.

9

On Wednesday morning I drove to Queens to see what I could find out about Harry Donner. His house was not far from the Nassau County border, the start of Long Island, so it wasn't surprising that he did his shopping there. Long Island has shopping centers with convenient parking and a lower sales tax than the city. His house was small and unassuming, with the usual tidy lawn, nice shrubs, and a still-dormant dogwood tree spreading its branches delicately. It didn't seem likely that the people who had bought the house from Donner's estate would have known anything about him, so I tried the house next door on the right. No one was home. Two doors down I found a young mother who had moved in two years ago and knew nothing about Donner. I walked back to the house to the left of his and tried again.

A plump older woman opened the door and asked what I wanted.

I told her my name and gave her a little summary of why I was there.

"Harry Donner?" she said. "Sure I knew Harry. We were friends with him and Dottie for years. It was a shame how he died. I don't think they ever found out who did it."

"They didn't. I'm trying to find people who knew him, relatives."

She hesitated, then invited me in. "There weren't any relatives that I knew of. Dottie died a long time ago, a couple of years before Harry did. Cancer. She was a lovely person. He spent every free minute with her when she was sick. They were really devoted. They never had children."

"Brothers? Sisters?"

She shrugged. "They never talked about them. She could

59

have had a sister, now you mention it. I don't know what her name would be. Or if she's alive."

"Where did they spend their holidays?" I asked.

"Well, sometimes with us. Or they'd get in their car and go somewhere. They'd visit his aunt sometimes."

"He had an aunt?"

"Well, yes, now that I think about it. He used to talk about her. She had a funny name. Like a man's name. What was it?" she asked herself.

I sat waiting and hoping. "Aunt Jo?" I suggested.

"No, nothing like that."

I tried to think of other names. Lou seemed too much like Jo to suggest. Danny for Danielle? Gabe for Gabrielle? I watched the furrowed face, the set lips. She was trying hard.

"Who's that comedian who died a long time ago?" she said.

"I don't know," I said helplessly. If it was a long time ago, how could I know?

"He was on radio. You know."

"Fred Allen?" I ventured. Aunt Margaret used to talk about Fred Allen sometimes.

"The other one. Jack Benny!" she said triumphantly. "Aunt Benny. That was her name. Harry always used to talk about his aunt Benny. I don't think she could be alive anymore, do you? Harry would be about sixty now, I think. How many people have aunts when they're sixty?"

It was a long shot and I didn't know how to find someone whose last name I didn't know. "Did she live around here?"

"No. They always took the car to see her. And Harry would bring her things, you know? She was probably old and poor and needed Harry to take care of her."

Then he would have left her at least part of his money. I thanked the woman and went back to my car. It was time to get Arnold Gold to help.

"I remember that shooting," Arnold said over the phone. He had called me back at the pay phone I had found and he was taking notes. "The case is still open."

"I'm looking for a link between that one and the McVeigh

shooting. Jack doesn't think Ray Hansen did it and I agree there's a good chance he didn't."

"I think I'll nominate you for the saint of lost causes," Arnold said.

"I learned from you. And anyway, the post is filled, Arnold. St. Jude has it."

"The Catholic church thinks of everything."

"Someone has to."

Arnold promised to have one of his paralegals track down the Donner will. I hoped it wouldn't be too much work. Arnold never lets me pay for work that his office does for me, although I've offered to pay by putting in hours. He told me the Thirteenth Amendment prohibits indentured servants, but to me it just sounded like a simple case of bartering.

Since I was in Queens, I decided to drop in on Jean McVeigh. I didn't really want to drop in on her unannounced, but I was out of change and it's hard to come by in New York. So I drove over and rang the bell.

"Oh, Chris, I'm glad you're here," Jean said when she saw me. She looked bedraggled and her eyes were red. "Come on in. I'm doing something I don't want to do and you're a good excuse to stop."

"I know I should have called first, but—"

"It doesn't matter. Just make yourself comfortable. Want some coffee?"

"Only if you do."

"I should really cut down." She dropped into a chair in the living room. "I've been going through Scotty's clothes." She pulled a tissue out of her pocket and blew her nose.

"Maybe it's too soon, Jean."

"Sure it's too soon. It was too soon for him to die, too soon for me to be alone. My mother picked up the kids this morning and it just seemed like the right time to get started. Tell me how things are going."

"I've got a great idea," I said. I told her about the Happy Times Grocery and the offer they had made. "Put your coat on and let's drive over there now. I'll sit in the car and you can go in and get a bag of apples for the kids."

"That sounds good. Let me wash my face and we'll go."

I put my coat back on and took my keys out of my bag. Jean returned looking a lot fresher, a little color in her cheeks and on her lips. She opened the closet and took out a huge black shawl and wrapped it around her. "Nice?" she said. "We found it in a shop that sells Scottish woolens. I just love it. When it's cold out, I wrap it around my head like this." She flipped it up, so it covered the red hair, and my heart took a tumble. She was the woman I had seen Sunday night hurrying down the street away from Ray Hansen's apartment as Jack and I were arriving to talk to him after his arrest. We had been at Petra's when he called to say he was going home and would not see her that night.

"What's wrong?" Jean said. "You look like you've seen a ghost."

"You were at Ray's apartment Sunday night."

"No. What makes you say that?" Jean gave a nervous little smile.

"I saw you leaving. You were wearing that shawl around your head."

We looked at each other. She knew she'd been caught, and I didn't want to say anything to gloss over it. There was no question in my mind what had happened. Ray had called her, either from the police station or when he got home, and she had said she would come over. But he had also told Petra he would come to her place, and he had had to cancel one of the two meetings. If Jack and I had arrived five minutes earlier, we would have walked into a very big surprise.

"I just wanted to tell him I believed in his innocence, Chris. He needed to know that. He was arrested out of the blue. I didn't want him to think—" She stopped, but I didn't fill the silence. "I wanted him to know I believed in him."

"Come on. Let's get you some fruit."

As we drove, I told her about my brief look into the lives of Gavin Moore and Harry Donner. She was familiar with their cases but was sure she knew nothing else about them. We tried to fit Scotty into some kind of pattern that would include either of the other two but couldn't.

"Scotty was never out of uniform," she said. "He was never in a precinct where Donner was. I can't imagine they ever saw each other even by accident."

"And Moore?"

"Scotty never did undercover work. If he was once in the same precinct as another guy on the job, well, that's probably true of hundreds of them. Brushing shoulders isn't a connection, Chris. I don't know why this happened, but I'm sure it has nothing to do with Ray."

"Besides the three thousand," I said, "was there anything else?" I made the question broad enough to include anything she might want to confide in me.

"Not that I know of." Jean looked straight out the windshield.

I parked at a hydrant across the street and a little bit down the block from the Happy Times Grocery. Jean went in, and she disappeared from my view. I looked around at the shops I had passed on my walk yesterday. If someone in one of them had had a grudge . . .

But it had to be more than that. Just because you have a grudge, you don't necessarily know how to steal a car so cleanly you don't leave a trace of your identity. Having a grudge doesn't automatically mean you own a handgun. Scotty had been followed, and that took planning and time and a certain expertise. I looked at a paunchy man smoking a cigar in front of his video store. What were the chances he could have pulled off such a clean killing?

Jean emerged from the grocery. She was smiling broadly. As I watched, she bent over to hug the little woman, then the young woman who had left her place at the cash register, then the young man I had seen with a broom. I felt my eyes tear. They had told her good things about Scotty, shedding their own fears and inhibitions. The last one out was Mr. Ma. He was carrying two shopping bags that were bulging with produce. Jean pointed to my car, and he started across the street. She threw kisses to the others and followed him.

I got out of the car and opened the back door for the bags of fruit.

"Thank you for bringing Mrs. McVeigh," Mr. Ma said. "Very nice lady. My mother happy to meet her."

Jean joined us before I could say anything. Her face was tearstained. "Thank you, Mr. Ma. Thank you so much." She wrapped her arms around him and was rewarded with a smile. "You're very kind."

She got into the car, and I pulled away as she daubed at her face with a tissue. "What nice, warm people," she said. "I can't believe anyone would think they're cold. They said such wonderful things about Scotty. He was such a good person, Chris. . . . Hey, let's find a place to have lunch, my treat. Take a left up ahead. I'll show you where to go."

I drove feeling the situation was muddier than before. The Koreans had smiled, and Jean had gone to Ray's apartment after his arrest, and Jack had heard rumors about Ray. Nothing was making any sense, and although I had no idea about it then, it was all about to get much worse.

10

Jack called a little while after I got home. "Where've you been? I've been trying to get you."

"In Queens, trying to find out something about Harry Donner. What's up?"

"What's up is that I did a little digging and turned up something that somebody missed. You know that Korean grocery you went to? Happy Times?"

"Yes. Jean and I went there again this morning. They were wonderful to her, said all kinds of nice things about Scotty."

"There may be more there than meets the eye. The guys working on the case checked along Scotty's beat to see if any storeowners had a registered handgun. This guy Ma, who's listed as the owner, doesn't have one. But there's another guy who works there, someone named Joo. Guy in his late twenties."

"I saw him."

"He's probably a cousin or something. He has a .44-caliber automatic registered in his name. I called the team and turned it over to them."

I didn't know what to say. The police had probably shown up on the heels of our departure, making it look as though I had betrayed them.

"You having a crisis of conscience?" my guy asked.

"Yes."

"Chris, honey, somebody did it. If it turns out to be this guy, it's not your fault. You know that."

"I know. I just don't believe it. They're such hardworking people. They were so nice to Jean. It wasn't a put-on. They were genuinely happy to meet her because they genuinely liked Scotty."

"If you're right, the gun'll check out. All this guy Joo has to do is turn it over and Ballistics'll make a determination."

He was right, and I assured him I knew it. But it didn't make me feel any better. At least, I thought, looking for the bright side, the police had one small piece of information they could follow up on in a case they wanted to close.

I made a salad for dinner, and sat down at the table with the *Times*. The metropolitan section seemed to be a mirror of the international news, full of ethnic violence and hatred. There were articles about trouble between Dominicans and Colombians, between some blacks and Koreans, between a group of Jews and a group of blacks, between two high school basketball teams, one Catholic and the other largely Protestant. It was enough to make poor old Thomas Jefferson turn over in his grave.

Last summer a group of Oakwood citizens had fought tooth and nail to prevent my cousin Gene's residential home from moving to town. The reason had been pure fear of the unknown, fear of a group of retarded men and women who had never hurt anyone in their lives but who, our good citizens said, might. That "might" almost kept Greenwillow out of Oakwood. Happily, it didn't. They have been here since January, and not only have there been no incidents, but the residents are contributing to the community in a way they were never able to in their old home. Several of them have been hired to perform useful tasks in the town, and last year's grumbling has all but disappeared. Somehow, I felt, it ought to be possible to work something out on a larger scale.

I had switched from metropolitan ethnic strife to the pleasures of food and drink in the next section when the phone rang. It was Jean and it was clear she hadn't called to rehash the day's events.

"I just got a crazy call," she said. "From a man. Did you have the feeling we were being followed today?"

Icicles down my back. "No, I didn't. What's going on?"

"He just called. No name, no kind of identification. He said he wanted to talk to you."

"He knew my name?"

"No. He called you my friend who's working on Scotty's murder."

It certainly sounded as though I'd been followed. How else could anyone know I was more than just a friend of Jean's or of the family? Unless ... "Is that what he said, 'Scotty's murder'?" I asked.

"I think so. No, he said 'your husband's murder,' or maybe 'the murder of your husband.' I grabbed a piece of paper when I realized what was going on, but I was only able to jot down a word here and there."

"Why does he want to talk to me?"

"He said he has something to tell you, something about Scotty and Ray."

"Did you tell him to go to the police?"

"Yes, I did. I said he should do it right away. He said he couldn't. He asked me for your name and I practically told him to go to hell. He said how about the phone number? I said nothing doing. He said he had to talk to you—and if he couldn't call, you'd have to meet him somewhere. He gave me a place and time."

I picked up the envelope that the bill from the water company had come in and turned it over. "I'm listening."

"Friday night at midnight in Damrosch Park. Do you know where that is?"

"Frankly, no."

"He said it's on Sixty-second Street, near Lincoln Center, near the ramp to the underground garage. There's a sign on the wall with the name of the park. And in case you haven't been watching TV lately, he said to come alone, that you'd be perfectly safe. I guess he doesn't watch the news."

The appointed day was Good Friday. "Jean, it's crazy," I said. "If he calls back, tell him it has to be daylight. Is that it? Do you remember anything else? Background noises or anything like that?"

"It was quiet. He kind of talked as though he was keeping his voice down so no one would hear. But that's all I can remember."

"Anything more on Scotty's birth certificate?" I asked.

There was a silence. Then she said, "Nothing."

I thanked her and got off the phone. On Monday morning

I had left Ray's apartment near the end of the official search. I had sat in my car till the search was over, then asked his landlady and some neighbors if they had seen anyone around Ray's place the day before. If someone had been watching me, he would have seen that not only was I connected to Ray, but I was doing a little investigating on my own.

I took my notebook out of my bag and flipped back a couple of pages. I had had lunch with Jean that day, establishing a connection there if someone was following me. But it certainly looked as though he hadn't followed me home or he'd know how to reach me in Oakwood. Unless . . .

There it was again. I had given my name to Sharon Moore and Joe Farina. Although Scotty's connection to Gavin Moore was very tenuous, maybe there was something there after all—and maybe Joe Farina didn't want me to find out about it. A police officer would have no trouble tracking down a license plate, and my car had been parked in the driveway when he came home.

So why hadn't he called me himself or driven up to Oakwood? I got up and drew the curtains in the living room. The thought of being followed was very frightening. My car, my license, my address. And then it hit me. It was still less than a year since I had last registered my car. The address on record was St. Stephen's Convent, a healthy drive up the Hudson River. As I was still living in New York State, I didn't have to reregister when I moved here last spring, and Motor Vehicles did not as yet know my change of address because I had neglected to inform them, probably some kind of misdemeanor I was not going to worry about at this point. Much as I didn't want to admit it, the best way to find out if Joe Farina was the caller would be to show up at Damrosch Park on Friday night and see if he was there.

But suppose it wasn't Farina? Suppose it was some elusive person who was following me? He could have tailed me easily enough on Monday from Ray's apartment, but I couldn't see how he could have picked me up on Tuesday. I'd started from the college and driven to Brooklyn to the Happy Times Grocery, and then to Sharon Moore's. And today I'd started in Queens, in Harry Donner's old neighborhood, and then gone to Jean's. Maybe it was Jean he was watching. But then why wouldn't he talk to her?

As for meeting someone in a park on the West Side of Manhattan at midnight, forget it. I wanted all the information I could get on Scotty's killing, but I wasn't about to risk my life to get it. I decided that although Jack would want to hear about this new development, it could wait for morning. Nothing was likely to change overnight.

11

I talked to Jack sooner than I had expected. He called shortly after eight Thursday morning, while I was sipping the last of my coffee.

"I didn't want to get you up last night," he began. "There's been an interesting development in the case of Mr. Joo's gun."

"You're not going to tell me it was the murder weapon."

"No, I'm not. I'm going to tell you it's missing."

"Stolen?"

"So he claims. Says his apartment was broken into on March eighteenth, conveniently one day after St. Patrick's Day. He says he doesn't carry it every day—and that Monday was a school day so he left it home. When he got back, it was gone, along with a couple of other things."

"Did he report it missing?"

"Nope."

"I assume they searched his apartment."

"You bet. When he said he didn't have it, they got a warrant."

"None of this makes him guilty," I said uneasily.

"You're right. None of it does. But it is a violation of the rules under which he holds his gun permit. The theft should have been reported ASAP."

"Is any of this taking the heat off Ray?"

"Probably not, but it's raised some questions. I expect Ray's lawyer can use it to his advantage."

"How much trouble is Joo in?" I asked.

"Enough. They'll be scrutinizing him and the grocery."

I knew what I had to do, but it was too early. "Let me tell

70

you what happened last night." I sketched my conversation with Jean.

"I tell you what," Jack said when I finished. "I think you ought to get off the case. I shouldn't've asked you in the first place, and it's getting too hairy. This guy probably picked you up outside of Ray's place. I don't like someone following you, and I think the whole thing has gotten out of hand."

"I have an idea," I said, without agreeing or disagreeing. I told him that I thought it could be Joe Farina who made the call. "If he doesn't agree to a daylight meeting, suppose we just go to Damrosch Park and see if he shows up."

"Suppose I just keep my eye on Farina on Friday. See if he goes home, see if he stays there."

"Suppose we do both."

He made an *Mmm* sound. "I'll get back to you. Meanwhile, stay home."

I gave Arnold Gold plenty of time to get to his office, although he's usually the first one in, and then called him. When he got on the line, I could hear his usual classical music playing softly in the background. Arnold is devoted to WQXR and turns it off only when he has to. I told him about Joo and the missing .44-caliber handgun. "Arnold, I know I cost you a lot of money, but I think this fellow needs a lawyer."

"Does he speak English?"

"I'm not sure. One person there, Mr. Ma, does. But if Joo is going to school, he must know some English."

"I can get an interpreter. I'll look into it."

"Thanks, Arnold."

"And don't apologize for costing me money. As long as I can afford it, that's what I'm here for. I've got some answers for you on Harry Donner's will. Terry tracked it down yesterday. The late Mr. Donner bequeathed his entire estate to the Catholic church."

"God bless him," I said. "Sounds like that's a dead end. What did he do, leave it to his parish church?"

"He gave them a lump sum, yes. But the bulk of it, including his house, went to a hospital. Maybe that's where his wife died."

"That's possible." I picked up a pencil. "Can you tell me the name of the church and the hospital?"

"Hold on." He rustled some papers and muttered some incoherent syllables. "St. John the Baptist." He read off an address in Queens that sounded fairly close to the Donner house. "And Our Lady of Mercy Hospital, but that doesn't seem to be in the city." The address was somewhere upstate. "I don't know why his wife would go to an out-of-town hospital when there's a hospital on every street corner in New York."

"Maybe she didn't," I said slowly, something finally clicking into place. "You're a doll, Arnold. Thanks a million."

What had occurred to me during our conversation was very simple. A Catholic hospital is likely to have an affiliation with a convent. A convent has nuns. If Harry Donner gave his estate to a Catholic hospital, it was a good bet that Aunt Benny was one of the sisters.

I decided to use my connection to St. Stephen's to avoid being given a runaround. I called my friend and former spiritual director, Sister Joseph, the General Superior at the convent.

"Chris, how nice to hear your voice," she greeted me. "Are you traveling this way soon?"

"Possibly. I'm looking into the murder of a police officer."

"The one that happened on St. Patrick's Day?"

"Yes. He was Jack's friend." I had told her about Jack not long ago.

"I thought I saw in the paper that they arrested the killer."

"They may have the wrong man. Right now, I'm looking into connections between this killing and other unsolved police murders. And I think I need to talk to a nun." I explained more fully, giving her some details.

"Yes, I know the hospital. It's run by Dominican nuns and it's about twenty miles from here. I'll give them a call and get back to you."

I have to admit that my heart sank when she said Dominicans. The only nuns I was ever afraid of as a child were the Dominican sisters at a church that used to compete with mine in athletics. They wore the traditional white habit with only a bit of black on the belt and veil, and one of those sisters always looked ten feet tall to me and absolutely terrifying. Remembering those childhood fears, I assured myself that anyone who would let herself be called Aunt Benny couldn't be very intimidating.

While waiting for Joseph to call back, I put my house in order. Now that Oakwood does a lot of recycling, I find I have bags and containers that need to be put at the curb according to a schedule much more complicated than my own. Having missed the paper day this week, my newspapers and magazines more than filled a grocery bag. And the container with bottles and jars was nearly full. I had just gotten everything neatly arranged when the phone rang.

"I think you may be on the right track," Joseph said. "I talked to the superior, who says they have a thriving community, including a villa." The villa is where older nuns live when they've retired from an active life. "One nun who's over eighty is named Benedicta."

"Yes," I said eagerly. "May I visit?"

"I can't see why not."

"Thanks so much, Joseph."

"Just don't forget to visit us."

"I'll do that soon."

I didn't want to show up empty-handed. Harry Donner's neighbor had said he visited her and took care of her. I got to the bank early and withdrew some money. Living without a credit card, I have to think in advance what I'm going to spend. My next stop was a bath shop in a nearby town where everything is always discounted; they happened to be running a sale. I bought two thick white bath towels and washcloths and a box of three large cakes of soap. I looked around the store to see if there was anything else. The owner kept referring to things as "decorative," and I merely smiled and shook my head.

"I have a lovely little hand mirror that's marked down to four ninety-five," she suggested.

"I'm afraid that wouldn't be appropriate." Sister Benedicta had probably not seen her reflection for sixty years. Finally I picked up a little bag to hold personal laundry.

There was no way to wrap things, but it didn't matter. A

shopping bag was good enough and could be used over again. I paid my bill and left.

The drive took about an hour and a half, then another quarter of an hour to find Our Lady of Mercy Hospital. The convent was beside it. The Mother House was a big old red brick building that might once have housed a wealthy family. A young nun opened the door for me and welcomed me in.

"The villa is just behind us," she said. "You can go out the back way and save some steps."

I could hear the sound of pots and pans banging around in the kitchen. Lunch would be over by now. I had had a sandwich in the car a little while earlier.

The backyard had old snow covering the grass and high shrubbery around the perimeter for privacy, but the privacy was an illusion. The hospital was several stories high; patients looking out windows would have a clear view of the nuns sitting in the summer sun.

"Right over there," the sister said, pointing.

"Thanks." I went through a break in the hedge and came to a smaller building, also old red brick.

An old Dominican nun wearing very thick glasses and the fearsome white habit of my childhood opened the door. But when she smiled, she looked quite friendly.

"I'm looking for Sister Benedicta," I said.

"Come with me. I think she's just back from the hospital."

"Is she ill?"

"Oh, no. She reads to patients. I can't do that anymore. My eyesight's nearly gone."

More was gone than her eyesight. She leaned heavily on a cane and walked slowly.

"There she is." We were at the door to the common room. "She's probably asleep in her chair."

"Your distance vision is pretty sharp," I said.

"It's not bad. It's just small print I can't read anymore, newspapers and books. I wish they made more in a size that first graders read."

"I'll send you a book if you tell me your name."

"Oh, you don't have to do that." She laughed. "I'm Sister Domenica."

"I'm Christine Bennett," I said, and went over to the big chair with the sleeping nun.

I didn't want to wake her. I sat on a sofa a few feet from her and set the shopping bag down carefully. I took my coat off and folded it so that the dark stain of Scotty's blood didn't show. As I laid it down, a voice said, "Can I help you?"

Sister Benedicta was wide awake and watching me.

"My name is Christine Bennett," I said. "Sister Benedicta?"

"Yes." She said it with a slight questioning sound, or a note of apprehension.

"Harry Donner was your nephew."

"Harry was my nephew. He's dead. Been dead almost three years."

"Sister, another policeman has been killed. He was a friend of mine. I'm trying to find out if the two murders could be connected."

"How would I know that?" She was sitting very straight now, and I could see she was a tall woman. If she stood, she might be taller than I, although that was unlikely in a woman of her age. Why was it my luck to have my childhood fears revisited?

"You're Harry's only living relative, the only one I could find. I know he visited you. Did he talk about his work?"

Her face was long and inflexible. "He was all I had," she said. "My sister's boy. I never thought I'd outlive my only nephew."

I realized I had moved too fast. She wanted to dwell on her loss. Here she was in retirement and still giving to the patients in the hospital, and her only relative, her only comfort, had been taken from her.

"I've heard he was a very nice person, a man with a good heart."

"He had a good heart."

"He called you Aunt Benny, didn't he?"

"How did you know that?" she asked sharply.

"I spoke to the woman who lived next door to him. He talked about you. She didn't know you were a nun."

"That would be Mrs. Keppel. The Keppels were good friends of Harry's."

I could imagine Harry Donner's visits with his aunt. She would talk about her work and the nuns, and he would talk about his friends so that she would almost know them. And maybe he would talk about his work.

"I understand you read to patients."

"It's about all they'll let me do," she said, a trifle irritably. "I used to do bookkeeping, but they've got computers now. I'm sure I could have learned how to use a computer, but you get to be a certain age and they think you can't do much."

I was afraid to sound patronizing. She seemed as sharp and aware as the younger people I ran into in the bank, and probably a lot smarter. "I can see why Harry enjoyed visiting you," I said.

"He did enjoy it. We always had a lot to talk about." She looked at me as though sizing me up for something. "Stand up," she ordered.

I stood.

"Turn around."

I turned a slow circle. I was wearing a black skirt and white blouse with low-heeled black shoes. My face had only a faint touch of pink on the cheeks and one of those lipsticks that scarcely adds any color. When I completed my turn, I stood facing her, half expecting her to pin up my skirt.

"You were a sister at St. Stephen's Convent, weren't you?"

"Yes, I was."

"The superior called here this morning. I wouldn't have guessed it otherwise. Your hair's still short, but it's grown in. When did you leave? Last year?"

"At the end of the spring semester." I felt like a child called before the principal for having done something bad. I knew, of course, what the something bad was. I had defected. I had given up the life this woman cherished.

"I left my order once. Almost forty years ago. The war was over and the fifties had begun. Something happened, a situation I found intolerable, so I took a leave of absence. I thought I would never come back. I moved in with Harry's family. He was just a youngster then, in his early twenties. He hadn't joined the police force yet."

I sat down on the sofa. Her story had shocked me. Nuns of her vintage didn't leave their orders, except perhaps if they were young and fell into a hopeless passion. She had been in her forties and gone to live with her family.

"That must have been very unusual," I said.

"It was. It was indeed." A trace of a smile touched her lips. "They say it takes nine months to make a baby. It took ten to make me a nun again. It was Harry more than anyone else who influenced me to go back. He honored my work. And through him, I came to honor it, too."

"I think what you do now is honorable," I said. "It's better than that."

"Twenty years later it was Harry who wanted to leave his job. My sister was gone by then, and my brother-in-law. His wife had never been happy that he was a police officer. But I was. Harry was a brave man and an honest one. Those are the people who should protect us."

"I agree with you."

"We talked and talked, and he stayed with the job. Do you think he was killed because of his work?"

"I don't know."

"I don't know, either. I have tried very hard to forgive the man who killed him."

"I know," I said. Forgiving is never easy, and her nephew's death must have weighed heavily on this old woman, especially since she had convinced him to remain on the job. Perhaps it was herself she was having trouble forgiving.

"I don't know how I can help you," she said.

"Did he talk to you about his work?"

"All the time. But one story ran into another."

"Did he ever mention the name Scott McVeigh to you?"

"I don't remember."

I swallowed and took a shot in the dark. "Jack Brooks?"

She looked into the distance. "I'm not sure."

12

During the drive home I was unable to get warm. The heater functioned perfectly, but I kept shivering. If I was looking for connections, there was certainly one here, and it had nothing to do with Scotty. Sister Benedicta thought Jack's name rang a bell. Jack had known—and liked—Harry Donner. On St. Patrick's Day, Scotty and Jack had switched cars on the way to the bar and in the dark it was possible the shooter had identified not the man but the car he drove. There was a chance that a case Jack was working on now connected with Donner, and the person who had killed Donner had now killed Scotty in error.

I drove faster than usual, bordering on recklessness. I wanted to reach Jack before he left the station house for his evening law classes. Suddenly I had changed my mind about meeting the anonymous caller in Damrosch Park. It wasn't Scotty's murderer I was looking for anymore, but someone who was out to get Jack. Everything else was error or coincidence. Ray was an accidental victim, picked because he had been stupidly generous first and stupidly aggressive afterward.

I pulled into my driveway and left the car there, too much in a hurry to open and close the garage door. I grabbed my mail without bothering to look at it. When I called the Sixty-fifth Precinct, they had to look for Jack, but while I held, they found him.

"What's up?" he said in the casual tone I was used to.

"I've been to see Harry Donner's aunt."

"I thought you were dropping the case."

"Listen to me, Jack. I don't have time to argue. She's a Dominican nun in an order that runs a hospital up the Hud-

78

son. Donner talked to her about his work all the time. When I asked her if she knew the name Scott McVeigh, she said she didn't remember. When I asked her if she knew your name, she said she wasn't sure. She looked as if it rang a bell."

"I've got a common name. Half the guys on the job are named John or Jack."

"Listen to me!" I insisted. "You and Scotty switched cars when we went to the bar. The killer was watching the car, not the driver."

"Chris, this is so farfetched—"

"It isn't farfetched. Something may have passed between you and Donner, or maybe there's a case you're working on now that he once had something to do with."

There was silence. "It's possible," he said. "I don't know, honey. We didn't work on any cases together, but I have a couple of old ones that haven't been closed."

"Will you check on them?"

"I'll look into it, OK?"

"You have to check every possible connection you could have to Donner. I thought about the cars a little after it happened, but now I'm sure."

"You know, Scotty and I look so different. You couldn't see the two of us walking together and mistake one for the other."

"That's true. But the parking lot wasn't lighted. The killer is sitting in a car at the back, waiting for you. He sees the two of you turn into the lot and he ducks down. He doesn't even see which of you goes to which car because he doesn't want you to know someone is sitting at the wheel of his car. He looks up and you've both more or less disappeared next to your cars. All he knows is that he's after the guy who drove the BMW that night. He drives down to the car, shoots the person opening the door, and gets away. He doesn't even know till the next morning that he's killed the wrong man." I had worked it all out on the drive home, and I had convinced myself that the events of that awful night were exactly as I now saw them.

"OK, it's possible," Jack said.

"It means he's still after you, Jack. Whatever the reason,

he's still after you. I think I have to go to Damrosch Park tomorrow night and find out what this informant knows."

"Forget it."

"Well, someone has to go."

"It's not going to be you."

"Please watch yourself," I said, my voice not as steady as I wanted it to sound. "He's still out there—and he's going to wait for the right time to get you."

"I promise I'll be careful," he said.

"Damrosch Park," I reminded him.

"I'll talk to you when I get back from my class."

Arnold called after I'd picked at my dinner and decided I wasn't very hungry. He had seen Joo and would represent him, but he said the chances were Joo would never again get a license for a handgun. Failure to report its loss was taken very seriously by the police department.

A little while later Jean called. "I just talked to him," she said.

"Will he make it during the day?"

"He says daylight is out because he can't take a chance of being recognized. And he works nights, so midnight is the earliest he can get there. He's calling me back later."

"Tell him I'll be there."

"You're crazy," Jean said.

"I'm not saying I'm going. I just want to make sure he'll be there."

"Have you found out anything?"

"Not very much. I talked to an old aunt of one of the cops killed a few years ago. Scotty's name didn't ring a bell."

"Don't go tomorrow, Chris," Jean said. "This will work itself out somehow. It's not worth your getting hurt to find out what happened."

"I'll see what Jack says," I told her.

Jack called when he got home. He said he still thought my scenario was wild, but he had worked something out for tomorrow night. A friend who owed him a favor had agreed to watch Joe Farina from the time he left work until midnight. If Farina went anywhere near the West Side of Manhattan, we would know, whether we saw him at the park or not. The friend had a cellular phone in his car; we could check with him during the evening to see what Farina was doing.

"What about the meeting?" I asked.

"Come down to Brooklyn tomorrow when you get out of church. We'll have dinner and we'll drive over to the park early and look around. I haven't been there for a while, but there may be some construction in the area where I can get a look at where you're supposed to make the meet."

"What about me?"

"You can sit in the car ... out of the way."

"We'll talk about it."

"Chris, why don't you leave this alone?"

"Because you're involved. And that makes me involved."

"You know, you're starting to sound more and more like those tough old nuns of my childhood and less and less like that sweet girl I met last summer."

"Are you taking back your offer?"

"My mother won't let me."

"I'll see you tomorrow."

Sister Benedicta had said very little more to me after I had asked her if she recognized Jack's name. I was very curious about the reason she had taken a leave of absence in the fifties, although it had nothing to do with either Harry Donner's death or Scotty's, but I felt she would have volunteered the information if she had been so inclined. I was equally interested in the reason why Harry Donner had wanted to leave the job, although that had been some time ago and surely had nothing to do with his subsequent murder.

What I wanted to do now, or rather what I thought I should do, was talk to Ray Hansen. I caught him at home Friday morning before he left for work.

"It's Chris, Ray," I said.

"Oh, Chris, yeah, hi."

"I'd like to talk to you. Can you meet me for lunch?"

There was enough of a pause so that I knew he was thinking of how to say no. "I don't usually eat lunch, Chris."

This man really brought out the worst in me. "Make an exception today. Give me a time and place I can meet you."

"Yeah, OK. There's a little Italian place. How's twelve-thirty?"

"Fine."

He told me where it was and how to get there. When we finished, I would go to church. Today was Good Friday.

Before leaving I called Melanie Gross and told her I had a strange favor to ask.

"You want to borrow a child for a day or two?" she asked hopefully.

I laughed. "If you have an old coat, I'd like to have it till I can get mine cleaned." I didn't want to explain about the bloodstain, but it had begun to bother me.

"Take your pick. They'll all be a size too big, but you can have your choice. Come on over."

"I'll be there in fifteen minutes."

I took my winter coat out of the closet and emptied the pockets. I would need the gloves, but the rest of the stuff could go into the garbage, except maybe for a safety pin, which I put in a drawer. There was a dirty Kleenex, a couple of supermarket receipts, and a folded-up envelope that I didn't remember putting there. Smoothing it out I hoped it wasn't an overdue utility bill.

It wasn't. It was an envelope with no return address—and it was addressed, in ink, to Ray Hansen at his precinct. That was crazy. How could a letter addressed to Ray find its way into my coat pocket?

I had no right to read it, but I had a right to know how it had gotten there. The last time I had seen Ray was Monday morning during the search. I had taken my coat off, and Ray had hung it in the closet. The police had come and . . . And what? When they had gone to the closet, he had made a point of saying this was my coat. Then he had given it to me. I pushed my memory back a little further. When the doorbell rang, he was at the closet.

I sat down. *Ray had put the letter in my pocket so that the search team couldn't touch it.* If I had stayed till they left, he would have taken it back before I put my coat on.

But I hadn't and he hadn't. I had told Jack I would not try to clear Ray; I would simply try to find Scotty's killer. In my hand was a potential piece of evidence. I pulled the single folded sheet out and opened it.

It was very brief. It read:

Dear Ray, It was terrific. Let's do it again. Love, Jean.

Ray was coming down the street from the opposite direction when I got to the restaurant. He looked the way he usually did, no sign of strain and no sign of anything else. At least when Jack was happy or irritable or angry, there was a visible sign.

We said our hellos and went inside. Ray steered me to a table for two in the back, and we gave our orders to a waitress who was obviously no stranger to him.

"So how's it going?" he said.

"I've been looking into the unsolved police murders: Roscoe Boyd, Gavin Moore, and Harry Donner."

"I remember them."

"Did you know any of them?"

He pursed his lips into a negative. "Don't think so. Boyd was the one up in Harlem. Moore, they found him in a park in Brooklyn when he should have been somewhere else. Maybe he was visiting a girlfriend."

A rather different explanation from Moore's wife's. "You think a girlfriend did it?"

"Probably some neighborhood punks. They'll get 'em."

"You remember Donner?"

"He was an older guy. Jack said he used to know him."

"I met his aunt yesterday. She's a Dominican nun in her eighties."

A very faint smile. "So you had something in common with her."

"A little," I said. "Very little."

"You find out anything about where Scotty was born?" Ray asked, changing the subject abruptly.

"Jean didn't know anything last time I asked."

"That's the key to this thing. Scotty obviously led a double life. Someone crossed the line from the other one into this one and wasted him."

"Why?"

"I figure he did something once, hurt someone. Someone kept a grudge, looked for him, found him, shot him."

"It would have had to be a long time ago. He was married in his mid-twenties, and he's been on the job almost that long."

"Some pain doesn't go away." He said it as though he were talking about himself.

"What could have happened when he was in his teens or early twenties?" I asked. It wasn't really a question; it was something I would have to think about.

"The way I see it, something happened that kept Scotty out of the army. Whatever it was, he couldn't deal with it. He made up the whole story about being in the army to cover up the truth and seem like a regular guy. Everybody else had an army record, so he had one, too. You listen to enough stories, you can make up your own pretty easy."

It was a lot of words from a man who rarely acknowledged my existence. I wanted to keep them flowing because it was clear he had done a lot of thinking about Scotty, more than I had. "Let's push it a couple of steps further. Those .44-caliber bullets they found in your apartment, they weren't yours, were they?"

"Hell, no. They were planted. I was gone all day Sunday. Anyone could have gotten in and put them there."

"That's what I think. I asked some of your neighbors if they saw anyone Sunday."

His eyebrows went up. "And?"

"No one saw anything. Most of them weren't home that day."

"Figures."

"Ray, if someone killed Scotty because of something he did a long time ago, why would they set you up as the killer?"

"There's a lot of pressure to close a case like this fast."

"But a fellow police officer?"

"Let me explain something to you. In case you haven't noticed, I'm not a nice Irish cop. I'm not a member of the Emerald Society. My behavior isn't as upstanding as some people think it should be. I'm not living with my wife and

I have a girlfriend. It boils down to I'm an easy guy to sacrifice. 'Brother officer' only goes so far."

It gave me the shivers. "What do you think they have on you?"

"If someone's been tailing Scotty, he knows we're friends."

"But does he know you lent Scotty money?"

"If he's a cop, he does. The story of our little fight has made the rounds by now, and Scotty probably left my letter in his locker. So it's evidence."

"But it can't be a cop if it's someone from Scotty's long-ago past," I said. "It doesn't fit together."

"Maybe it isn't a setup. Maybe the morning after the shooting they empty out Scotty's locker and find my letter telling Scotty I needed my three grand back. And then someone remembers the fight and blows it up into something it wasn't. The team working on the homicide picks it up and runs with it. Then some overzealous guy on the team drops the bullets in my drawer when I'm out. Once they think they've found their man, they stop looking and just work on closing the case. Nice and neat."

"Besides the loan, what else would make them think you could have done it?"

"They think I had opportunity. After St. Patrick's Day, they interviewed me—and Petra—and contrived a time frame that shows I could have been waiting in that parking lot. According to my calculations I couldn't, but that's what they'd expect me to say."

"Talk to me about motive," I said.

"You can always find a motive if you work at it. I found out they interviewed Betsy before I was arrested. I don't have to tell you Betsy isn't happy we split. I didn't tell her about Petra because I didn't want to hurt her. But the guys interviewing her did, just dropped it in her lap and watched her react. Who knows what she said?"

About what? I wanted to ask, but I didn't. Ray was artfully skirting the substance of my questions while seeming to answer them fully. Sure, Betsy could have said mean, nasty things about her husband when she heard he was practically living with someone else. And although she hadn't struck me as a vindictive person, no one could foresee how she would respond. It came down to whether she had told the truth, not whether she was vindictive. But Ray had made up his mind that he would not talk about substance.

"Have you spoken to Betsy since your arrest?" I asked.

"Once."

Nothing doing there. "What have they got you doing on the job?"

"Make-work. All you need to know is the alphabet. Counting is one step up."

"It's better than sitting in your apartment."

"Yeah, I guess it's better."

"Any other ideas?" I asked. We had pretty much eaten our lunch by that time.

He gave me a faint smile. "I thought you were the idea person."

What I thought had to be obvious. He had eyed my coat when I took it off. The letter from Jean hung between us like bait on an invisible hook, enticing each of us to bite, but Ray would not. He knew what it said, but he couldn't be sure if I did, if I even knew of its existence.

"I found the letter this morning," I said. "After I called you."

"Where is it?" he asked quickly.

"At home." I took a deep breath. "I read it, Ray."

His face showed nothing. "It's not your business," he said evenly. "It isn't anyone's business."

"I'm investigating a murder. I want an explanation."

"Look at the postmark. It was written a long time ago. It was nothing. Something that happened between two consenting adults."

"Who else knows about it?"

"No one. We kept the shades down."

The man really riled me. "Ray, we're talking about a motive for homicide. If one other person knows—"

"You're the other person, Chris. That letter isn't your property. It got into your coat by accident and you should destroy it."

It was pointless to pursue it. I had gotten more from him

than I expected. "I think there's a lot missing," I said. "I don't suppose you know who did it."

"I haven't the faintest. I don't know anyone who'd kill Scotty." He laughed. "Except maybe me. And I didn't do it."

13

I went to a nearby church and got there in time for the Good Friday service. When it was over, I went to Jack's apartment, showered, and changed.

As always when I waited for Jack after not seeing him for several days, I felt the accumulating desire of sex. Whoever first used the word "hunger" to describe that feeling had done so with great accuracy. Not only was the word right on the mark, but the two activities, sex and food, making love and eating, were so bound up together in our lives that it was sometimes hard to separate them.

I almost always saw Jack at a mealtime—and we almost always delayed the food in favor of the other, satisfying one hunger and increasing the other. I rather liked the commingling. The smell of food or the taste of something good often gave me a sexual jolt.

"You're nuts, Kix," I said aloud, and laughed.

Jack came home, and we made the usual decision to satisfy the usual hunger first. Although we had passed the spring equinox a week earlier, it was dusky in the bedroom, where we left the lights out. The sheets were fresh and crisp. I had changed them, as Saturday was Jack's day for the Laundromat and cleaner. The room was almost too warm, the heat hissing from the radiator, blanketing the sounds of our love, the whispers and murmurs, the small yelps and bigger cries, the words I had heard only a few days ago for the first time and which I would never tire of hearing. Our bodies knew each other well now and worked with a beautiful rhythm. I could not have been happier.

* * *

We sat at the table eating one of Jack's creations, fish with a marvelous tomato sauce with olives and other goodies topped with feta cheese. It even looked professional on the serving platter, and it smelled wonderful.

I leaned over and held his wrist before he dug in. "I want to say something."

"Talk."

"I love you."

He swallowed. "Before fish?"

"Away from the heat of passion. Calmly and coolly." I had not said it before, and I had thought a lot about a time and place. I hadn't exactly selected "before fish," but it was as good a time as any.

He touched my face, my hair. He took my hand and kissed it. "Accepted," he said. He kissed my hand again. "And returned."

"Bon appétit."

"It isn't dinnertime conversation," Jack said after we'd dipped into the fish, "but I'm going to tell you what I heard today. It's about that IAD rumor I told you about."

"It's bad, isn't it?" Since my lunch with Ray I had a pretty good idea what was coming.

"Very bad. It started out as 'unsubstantiated information on an overheard.' That's what it's called when someone picks up some scuttlebutt on a cop and reports it. Eventually it finds its way into a D.D.5." A D.D.5 is a form used in the Detective Division to report interviews, information, almost anything that's relevant to a case.

"Overheard information? That's outrageous."

"It may be outrageous, but Internal Affairs collects this stuff. Someone said Ray jumped Scotty's old lady."

I didn't need a translation. "It's true, Jack." I told him about the letter, which I had left home, so Ray wouldn't be able to talk me out of it. "You think Ray bragged?"

"Knowing him I'd say no."

"And I'm sure Jean didn't. How does information like that find its way to Internal Affairs?"

"I don't know yet."

"Jack, why would Ray keep that letter? All it could do is cause him trouble."

Jack put his fork down. He looked troubled. "Let me tell you something about cops. If you looked in a cop's locker tonight, a nice guy with a wife and kids, you'd find some things that would surprise you. There might be what you'd call girlie magazines, even bordering on pornography. You'd find letters from women, civilians he met while doing his job, flattering, admiring letters. There might be snapshots of women, sometimes with the cop in them. A guy who goes to church with his family every Sunday, who speaks out loud and clear about adultery, a guy who never wears anything but jeans and a T-shirt and a pair of sneakers when he comes to work, has a designer suit, a clean white shirt, a silk tie, and a pair of hundred-dollar black shoes in his locker for a night when he tells his wife he's working overnight."

I sat still, my eyes on his face as he spoke, the inevitable questions forming in my mind.

"And when that cop dies, like Scotty, someone in the station house goes into his locker—they don't need a warrant to do that, by the way; it's Police Department property—and they sanitize the contents before sending it home to his widow." He stopped and met my eyes. "So when you ask your question, why did Ray hang on to a letter like that, it's what cops do, Chris. He was just a little smarter than most of them; he took it home, where it was safer. Because he never expected to have his apartment searched because he would never do anything that would warrant a search."

I said, "I see," although I didn't see it all; I didn't see most of it.

"You don't know cops, Chris, and there's a lot cops don't tell their women. You know me, you know Ray a little, and you knew Scotty a little. I'm not saying we're different. It's pretty obvious that we're not. You're part of a group with a lot of strong macho bonds."

"It's OK, Jack."

"I know you're wondering. I'd wonder, too, if I were in your shoes."

I put my hand on his to stop him, but he went on.

"A week after I met you, I cleaned out my locker. And the week before I started law school, I cleaned it out again."

I kissed his cheek, feeling honored.

When we finished dinner, Jack made a phone call. I knew immediately it was to the man watching Joe Farina.

"Sal, it's Jack. What's up?" He listened for a brief time. "OK. I'll keep in touch." He hung up. "Farina went home after his tour."

"Home to Sharon Moore?"

"I think that's the only home he has now. Anyway, he's still there. Lights are on. No one's come in or gone out."

I felt a little uneasy. It was eight o'clock, four hours till midnight. We had not yet discussed what was going to happen. "Maybe he's not the guy."

"Maybe he's waiting for eleven o'clock to leave for Manhattan."

"What are we going to do, Jack?" I had cleared the table and Jack was starting to do the dishes. I stood next to him, the dishtowel in my hand.

"We'll drive over there. There's plenty of time. Whoever he is, I don't think he's going to be a couple of hours early. It's too cold, and if he picked the site, you can bet he knows it."

We finished the dishes without talking about it, but it was the only thing I could think about. Crazy things went through my mind. Did this man know something or was this meeting an elaborate way to get me alone for purposes having nothing to do with Scotty's death? Was he someone who knew the killer—or knew about the killer—and if so, how could he? Jack was certain there had been only one person in the car he shot at. Or could it be the killer himself? Had I accidentally stumbled on something that I had not yet recognized as a lead—and did he want to erase the possibility that I would put everything together and discover the evidence that pointed to him?

Jack turned off the water and said, "Leave the rest."

The silverware was dried and put away, but I hadn't finished the dishes. I hung the towel to dry. Jack took my hand, and we sat on the sofa.

"Here's what we'll do. We'll leave about ten. It won't take more than half an hour to get there from here. I'll park a block or so away and walk back. I want to find a place that'll give me some cover. I have to be able to see that meeting point."

"What about me?"

"I'll make that decision when I see if I can find a place for myself. In any case, I want to be there to see if this guy comes."

"We'd better take my car," I said. "He's probably seen it. I don't want him to know your plate number."

"OK. Nervous?"

"Scared to death. I wonder if he's going to tell me it's you they were after."

"Don't even think about what he's going to tell you. He may not show. He may have nothing to do with the homicide. He may just be some wacko that gets his kicks from meeting women in parks at midnight."

I didn't want to think about all the possibilities. Midnight would come soon enough and I would deal with the single reality at that time. Instead, I told Jack about the rest of my lunch with Ray.

"He says the answer to everything is in Scotty's mysterious past. How am I going to find out where he was born and who he really was?"

"Jean should know that by now. Scotty had to submit a birth certificate before he entered the Academy. I think she's asked the department for a copy."

"She's never said anything."

"This is very rough on her."

But I had to know. If Scotty had been the intended target, Ray might be right about where to look for a motive. "I'll talk to her," I said. "This is a tough case, Jack. It's full of pain. Almost everyone I talk to has suffered a terrible loss— Jean, Sharon Moore, Sister Benedicta. It's not like questioning neighbors whose strongest feeling is curiosity. These people are all *involved*." Jack was watching me. "You know all this, don't you?"

"Yeah."

"I guess you'd have to." But for me it was new. I had investigated three homicides since leaving St. Stephen's and in all of my questioning had spoken to few deeply bereaved relatives. The pressure of these women's pain had begun to weigh on me. Even finding Scotty's killer would not diminish it. I had to keep telling myself my job was to expose the truth, uncover the facts, provide a reason for the madness of killing. I was not in the business of alleviating pain.

"Tell me about the nun," Jack said.

"She's a Dominican and I've been scared of Dominicans since I was a kid." I smiled at him.

"Come on."

"It's true. And she was the incarnation of the nun that used to terrify me."

"But you talked to her. You got something from her."

"She's very honest," I said. "She doesn't hide her feelings under her habit. You sense a real person, someone who's had great difficulty coming to terms with loss. She said she'd tried to forgive the man who killed Harry, and I felt what she was saying was that she hadn't succeeded. But she held a lot of things back."

"Like what?"

I told him about Sister Benedicta's leave of absence.

"Back in those days that must have been scandalous."

"But she did it. She's tough and she has strong opinions. But she never said why she left, and she didn't say what Harry's problems were when he wanted to leave the department."

"Donner wanted to leave?"

"A long time ago. Twenty years, maybe more. He's the one who talked her into going back to her order, and she convinced him to stay on the job. But no details. I'll have to try again."

He kissed me and said, "Let's get ready."

Jack changed into black corduroy pants and a black turtleneck. I was wearing jeans and a sweater and wasn't going to dress up to meet an informant. But Jack took something out of his closet and tossed it on the bed.

"Put this on under your sweater."

Shivers ran through me. "What's that?" I said, although I knew.

"A bulletproof vest. Your sweater's big enough to cover it."

"What about you?"

"I'm the guy who's hiding in the construction, remember? You'll be out in the open—if we decide you're going through with it. Put it on."

It wasn't made for a woman's body, but it more or less fit and covered a lot more of me than it probably did of Jack. The sweater was a bulky cotton knit and it just made me look as though I'd tacked on ten pounds between my waist and shoulders.

"Not bad," Jack said. He changed his shoes, putting on heavy low boots with thick soles that looked as though they could grip any surface.

It was almost ten when we were ready. I put on the camelhair coat Melanie had lent me and took my bag. I had half emptied it, removing cash and ID. The cash I left in the apartment; the driver's license and car registration I put in my coat pocket. If he didn't already know who I was, my possessions wouldn't tell him anything.

We were at the door when the phone rang. Jack went back and answered. I heard him say, "Stay with it, Sal," and he hung up.

When he came back he said, "Farina's on the move. Looks like he's heading for Manhattan."

14

Damrosch Park is at the southern end of Lincoln Center, which is a collection of buildings devoted to the performing arts built around a central plaza with a fountain and lights. On opera nights the limousines drive up and deliver their wealthy occupants, who then take their places in reserved boxes in the Metropolitan Opera. Besides the Met, there are theaters, concert and recital halls, restaurants and shops. The West Side subway rumbles underneath as it makes its way up and down Broadway.

Quite naturally, the Juilliard School of Music relocated at the north end of Lincoln Center and Fordham University has built to the south. It was there that Jack thought some lingering construction might afford him cover.

When we arrived at ten-thirty, one of the theaters was emptying. There were plenty of people in the area, on the streets and in restaurants. By midnight, most of them would be gone and the place would be deserted. Jack drove along Sixty-second Street, from Amsterdam to Columbus Avenue, to show me where the meeting point would be.

There was no construction for a square block. But across Sixty-second from the park was a small security booth with a uniformed guard. That seemed to please Jack.

After our swing around the area, he drove to a bank of phones and got out to call Sal. He was back quickly.

"They're crossing the bridge into Manhattan. I'll try to call him again before midnight. Let me have a chat with the guard on Sixty-second."

He parked on Amsterdam Avenue, near Fordham. A fence separated the sidewalk from the construction on the other side. The windows I could see were dark and the street was fairly empty. The Lincoln Center crowd kept to Columbus Avenue and Broadway, one and two blocks east, where the night spots were. The only action here was the occasional dog walker.

"I'll see you soon," he said cheerfully. "Lock the doors."

"You look like a second-story man." He had a flashlight poking out of one pocket and an absolute lack of color anywhere.

I reached over and pressed the button to lock the door as he left, watching him until he turned the far corner. The wait was longer than I expected, or at least it felt that way. I probably have the last analog clock in an automobile; its advantage is that you can read it even when the motor is off, something you can't do with the newer digitals, but it was too dark to see and I didn't want to turn the dome light on because I didn't want to draw attention to the car. Joe Farina was on his way to Manhattan and I didn't want him to drive by and see me alone in a car in the passenger seat. So I sat in the dark and waited.

A couple went by, talking. They were having a good time, joking around, moving and turning as they walked. Across the street a small dog used a car tire instead of the traditional fire hydrant and then moved along with its master. From behind me, a man in a too-long overcoat came slowly even with my window. He wasn't looking at me, and, as I watched him, I realized he was one of the many homeless you can see almost anywhere in the city these days. He sat next to the fence and drew blankets over himself, but he didn't lie down. He took a bottle out from under his coat and drank from it, wiping his mouth with a gloved hand. After a minute or two, he put the bottle away, got up with difficulty, and continued slowly up the block toward Lincoln Center. It was too cold a night to be sleeping outside, but he looked as though he was used to the rigors of street life.

I could feel tension building. How long should it take to get the security guard to let him stay in the booth? Maybe he had changed his mind and found some other place or had fallen and was hurt in some out-of-the-way cranny I could not find.

Someone suddenly turned the far corner. I kept my eyes

on the figure as it passed under a streetlight. It wasn't Jack. I refocused on the corner, telling myself he was capable and careful, knew what he was doing, and would show up when he was ready. A woman walking a good-sized dog went by. It must take up half her kitchen, I thought, trying to imagine it lying down in an apartment-size kitchen. Come on, Jack, where are you?

A single figure crossed the street, coming toward me. It shuffled rather than walked, moving with apparent difficulty. As it passed under a light, I recognized the homeless man who had stopped for a drink several minutes earlier. This time he was coming straight at me and I didn't want to be seen. I ducked in the seat, giving him time to pass the car. When I tentatively raised my head, he was gone. In the side mirror I could make out what looked like his back several car-lengths behind me.

"How're things?" The door opened, and Jack slipped inside.

"I'm glad to see you. I was starting to hallucinate."

"Nothing to worry about. All I did was flash my shield and it was, 'Yes, Sergeant' 'You got it, Sergeant' 'Anything you want, Sergeant.' "

"Jack, I've been thinking."

"Uh-oh, bad sign."

"Whoever this person is, we assume he followed me on Monday when I left Ray's apartment."

"Right. That's how he knows you know Jean."

"What if he saw both of us that morning, maybe when we got to Ray's apartment? That puts you and me together. So he gets me here tonight, but what he's really looking for is you because you're the one who was supposed to get shot on St. Patrick's Day."

"You're making a lot of assumptions."

"But if I'm right, he isn't coming to talk to me, he's coming to get you."

"He isn't going to see me, and if you don't show, he won't see you."

"He may not show himself until I do. He could also be sitting in a car somewhere around here, waiting. Or maybe he's already seen the car and knows I'm here and all he has to do is wait for you to get back to Sixty-second Street."

"Anyone take a look at you while I was gone?"

"Just some dog walkers." I thought. "A young couple." I liked this whole thing less and less. "Jack, a homeless man." I told him rapidly.

"Stay here." He got out of the car and started down the street.

I locked his door and got out and followed him, staying enough behind so that I wouldn't be in the way. He moved fast, jogging along, and I ran to keep up. We passed Sixtieth Street, where one of the buildings of John Jay College of Criminal Justice was; Jack had pointed it out earlier as we surveyed the area. As I stepped up on the curb, I stopped short. Jack was almost at Fifty-ninth Street and he was talking to someone. I walked slowly toward them.

I heard Jack say, "OK, take care," and then he turned and caught up with me, putting his arm around my shoulder. "He's clean. Which means he's filthy, and he stinks of alcohol. If he's someone pretending to be homeless, he's gone too far. That's not our guy."

"OK."

"Let's stop in for a cup of coffee and a little warmth."

We went into a coffee shop, and I ordered hot chocolate. I needed the heat, both outside and inside. My watch showed after eleven.

Jack went to call Sal for the last time. He came back and dropped into his chair, looking troubled. "I can't raise him."

"He's not in the car?"

"Either that or he's turned off the phone to keep the sound down. I don't like it."

I didn't, either. He had promised to stay with Joe Farina till midnight.

"I'd be a lot happier if you'd stay in the car, right where it's parked."

"And if I don't?"

"If you don't, here's what I would do. At a couple of minutes to twelve, I'd drive up to Sixty-second, turn the corner, and leave the car. Double-park if you have to. Then get out, cross the street, and stand near the sign. Don't look in my direction. I'll have a clear view of you. If he shows, talk to him, then get into the car and drive around the corner to Columbus, down to Sixtieth. Take a right and stop. I'll meet you there."

"OK."

"Don't go anywhere with him, don't get into any car except your own. You get nervous, you put your hand up to your face." He touched his own right cheek. "It's a decoy cop's signal to his backup to move in, a nice, natural move. Got it?"

"Got it. Don't worry."

"Feel warmer?"

"A little."

"There's no rush. When we go back to the car, I'll walk on the other side of the street. I'll watch you every step of the way."

"You're sure about that homeless man?"

"Absolutely positive."

I left the coffee shop first and walked north, keeping my pace at a kind of New York night normal speed, adhering to all the rules: Don't make eye contact; hold your purse close to your body; don't dawdle. I had the car key in my coat pocket, so I wouldn't have to open my bag and look for it. Without glancing around, I knew Jack was there and I knew he was watching me, giving me a feeling of security that lasted until I sat behind the wheel. I fixed my eyes on the street corner a block ahead, hoping to see him turn into Sixty-second Street, but I never did. In the pit of my stomach I felt sick. Had I merely missed him in the dark or had something happened? "Maybe this isn't the life for you, Kix," I said out loud. Where was he? Had he gone a block farther north to circle around to Columbus? Or turned around after I was in the car and cut across Sixtieth? I checked the rearview mirror and the side mirror. I looked across the street and back to the corner ahead of me. There was no Jack.

I put the key in the ignition and turned it enough clicks for the radio to go on. CBS was pretty good about telling you the time, but I had to wait several minutes to find out that it was 11:36. I turned off the radio and sat back and waited.

The usuals walked by. Two dogs barked at each other as they passed. A siren sounded several blocks away and faded without getting any closer. A truck lumbered by noisily. Two women walking alone passed my car. I never think of women being out that late by themselves in New York, but I guess if you work at night, you've got to get home somehow.

The homeless man came back.

This time I was scared. He walked right up to the place where he had sat the last time and maneuvered himself down on the sidewalk. He pulled the bottle out from under his coat and took a gulp. He was sitting north of the front of my car and several feet away, across the sidewalk, so it was impossible in the dark to tell whether he was looking my way or not. But after he drank the whiskey, I saw him reshape himself as he lay down and drew blankets over himself.

I turned the key again and put on the radio. I guessed that five or ten minutes had gone by, but to my surprise the announcer said it was 11:55 and time for the business news.

It was time for me to get ready.

I counted to sixty. Jack had said a few minutes before twelve. Somehow, I knew I would rather be late than early. The homeless man had stopped moving. Now he was merely a large bundle of rags along the fence. I sat for some long seconds and turned the radio on again. CBS was going into its pre-top-of-the-hour news headlines. I turned on the motor and pulled out.

I drove to Sixty-second and made my right turn, the midnight news coming on just as I stopped the car. I turned off the radio, double-parking as Jack had suggested, and looked around. The street was empty. I put the car key in my coat pocket, took my bag, and got out of the car. I was almost relieved that the hour had come, that finally something would happen. Without moving my head, I could see the security booth down the block, its light dimmed. There was a dark figure inside, but with my cursory glance, I couldn't tell if there were two.

I crossed the street and walked down the block toward Columbus Avenue, stopping when I made out the bronze sign on the white marble wall at the edge of the park. DAMROSCH PARK. A nice way to be memorialized, I thought, a park at the edge of a music complex. I looked back the way I had come, but no one was there. I scanned the area, from my right slowly around to my left, my eyes lingering only slightly on the security booth. A couple walked down the other side of the street silently, but there was no one else.

It was very cold. I moved my scarf to protect more of my neck, feeling the weight and discomfort of the bulletproof vest. I could see why officers were reluctant to wear them. They must be killers in summer, I thought.

Come on, I said in my head, addressing my absent anonymous informant. You set this up. At least be on time. In my mind, the man was Joe Farina. I could see the tall, handsome cop who had taken up residence with Gavin Moore's widow. Even in the shadows I would know him by his height, and I was pretty sure I would recognize his voice, even though I had only heard a few sentences.

But he didn't come. I walked into the pool of light cast by a nearby streetlight and looked at my watch. Ten after twelve. I went back to stay in Jack's line of sight. I looked inside the park, in case Jean had gotten the instructions wrong, but no one was there. I rubbed my gloved hands together and moved my arms around, feeling a mixture of relief and disappointment. It had all been for nothing, the planning, the uncertainty, the anxiety. A car came down the street and turned right at Amsterdam. A quarter after. I felt angry now. Come on, Joe. Don't do this to me. You had something to tell me. Do it. I could be in a warm bed with a warm man instead of freezing on the street.

A couple walked by me. As they passed I heard the woman say something about me. I almost laughed out loud, wondering if she thought I might be a hooker in Mel's proper winter coat, my blue jeans, the colorful cotton knit sweater, and the bulletproof vest.

I started pacing to keep warm. Jack had said give him twenty minutes and then go back to the car. It was twenty minutes now, and although I had given up entirely, I waited. Maybe he'd had a flat. Maybe Sal had seen him stop and gone to help him, feigning coincidence. Maybe it wasn't Farina. Maybe it was someone who had taken the subway, and the train had stopped in a tunnel for fifteen minutes for no reason anyone could imagine, the way they always seemed to do. Give him till twelve-thirty. If he calls Jean tomorrow and tries to set something else up, tell him to forget it. I've had it.

There was a sound like a gunshot; I drew in my breath and turned toward Columbus Avenue. A dark figure was suddenly running across the street toward me.

"It's OK," Jack's voice said calmly. He put his arm around me.

I was shaking now, more with fear than with cold.

"A car backfired, that's all it was. It's OK. He didn't come. Let's go home, baby. It's all over." .

I was ashamed of my fear, angry that I hadn't stayed cool. Jack held me as we walked to the car.

"The homeless man," I said. "He came back. He sat down in the same place." I was shaking like a leaf.

"We'll check it out."

We got into the car, and Jack circled around and drove back to where I had been parked. A car with signs in the windows in English and Spanish, proclaiming the absence of a radio, had taken my space. There was a suspicious lump along the fence. We both got out, although Jack had told me to stay put.

The lump was covered with blankets. Jack flashed his light along it. There was no movement. Then he switched the beam to the sidewalk. Next to the sleeping man was an empty pint bottle.

"Let's go," Jack said.

We drove home.

I had never thought of fear as an aphrodisiac, and maybe it isn't. Maybe it was the removal of fear, the relief, the sense of peace in being warm and out of danger, but that night something turned us on as nothing before had. Instead of fatigue, I felt awake, alert, alive, full of incipient passion. The bulletproof vest fell to the floor with the rest of my clothes, with his, with ours, here, there, this room, that one, a trail to the bed, to the quick inevitable. It was over almost as it began, leaving me weak, panting, happy, clinging, grasping.

He was the same. He kissed me and held me, keeping me close. "Maybe I was wrong," he said finally. "What I said on the phone. About you being like the nuns of my childhood."

"What if I am?" I said. "What if we're all the same?"

"Oh, my misspent youth," he said.

15

The call came after I had fallen asleep. Jack got it on the second ring.

"Sal. Where the—? I know. I tried you about eleven-thirty. . . . He *what*? Yeah. Yeah . . . I don't believe this. . . . Yeah, I'm listening." He listened for some time, then thanked Sal and got off the phone. "I hate coincidences," he said.

"What happened?"

"Farina drove into Manhattan and went straight to the Midtown North Precinct. Sal followed him inside. There was a crowd; he asked what was going on. It seems two guys were just arrested for a misdemeanor and they found one of them carrying a police .38. The suspect admitted to being part of the group that killed Gavin Moore. Says he wasn't the shooter and wants to deal the information."

"Any chance he killed Scotty?"

"Sal says it doesn't look that way."

"Why was Farina there?"

"Someone at the precinct called Mrs. Moore to tell her they had a suspect. Farina came down to see what was going on. He's not our man, Chris, and there's no connection between Moore's death and Scotty's. Go to sleep."

"That nun has to know something," I said.

"She probably knows a lot, but I think it's a long shot she can help us."

The only times Jack can study are weekends and early mornings. We fit our time together in small blocks before and after work and study, his and mine. Sometimes I hang around reading the paper or a book while he studies in the other room, but I know I'm a distraction. He feels if I'm there we should be doing something together, I've had a hard time getting him to believe that I'm happy doing in his apartment what I would otherwise be doing alone in my own house.

Best of all I liked him to visit me in Oakwood, although that was difficult during the semester. By now I had gotten over my ambivalence at having an overnight guest, although I'd been told one of my neighbors didn't like it when his car was there in the morning. I wasn't angry at the neighbor and I didn't talk to her about it; I was just sorry that something I would not change in my life caused pain in hers.

On the Saturday morning after the Damrosch Park no-show, we breakfasted together before Jack went out to do his weekend chores. Then I called Jean to give her the news.

She answered quickly. "Chris? I tried you at home. What happened?"

I told her and listened to the disappointment in her voice.

"Have you heard from him?"

"Not since he called Thursday night to make sure you were coming."

"Have you heard the news about Gavin Moore?"

"A friend of Scotty's called a little while ago. He said there probably isn't any connection."

"That's what Jack heard." I was stalling, trying to decide how to ask her what she would prefer not to talk about. "Jean, have you gotten Scotty's birth certificate yet?"

She hesitated. "I don't want to talk about it."

"Maybe if we sit together . . . ?"

Suddenly she was in tears. "I don't know."

"May I come over?"

"Sure," she said, her voice tight. "Why don't you meet me at my mother's? She's here with the kids. We'll have some peace and quiet."

Jack said to come back later and we'd go out to dinner. I had time before meeting Jean, so I got in my car and drove to Scotty's beat.

I went down the whole ten blocks, stopping for lights, looking at the people crowding the streets on this last Saturday in March. At this point, I no longer knew whether Scotty had been the gunman's target or had been killed in error, but there were questions that needed answers and maybe the answers were on his beat.

I went back to the used-car lot and pulled the car onto the blacktop. The man I had spoken to earlier in the week came out of his office as I got out of the car. Today he was wearing a plastic badge that said CAPPY.

"It's you," he said, recognizing me.

"Good morning."

"You decide you want a car?"

I patted mine fondly. "Not yet. I want the truth about how much Scotty McVeigh paid for the BMW."

"What is it with you?" he blustered. "You ask me questions even the cops don't ask."

Maybe they should, I thought. "Tell me."

"I told you already. I gave him a trade-in and he gave me a thousand dollars."

I looked at him.

"Two thousand," he corrected himself as he avoided my eyes. "That what I said last time? Two thousand?"

"But that isn't the truth," I said.

"It's what you want to hear, lady. And that's all I'm telling you."

He turned his back on me, and I got into the car. He would never give me the truth now. I was angry at myself, not him. I had been too direct, too confident he would tell me the truth. I took a right at the corner, thinking that I would stop in and see how Mr. Joo was doing, but there was no place to park. I went several blocks before someone gave up a space. Then I started walking back, looking in shop windows. I knew the street had been canvassed, but I stopped into a pharmacy and asked about Scotty. He was a wonderful man, the pharmacist told me, honest and helpful. Made you feel safe having him around. The dry cleaner next door said pretty much the same thing, as did the woman behind the counter at the variety store.

The next shop was a jewelry store. I stopped and looked at the display. Several small gold items lay on black cushions and draped white satin. The name on the window was *Bedrosian*. I went inside.

There were two men and a woman, all obviously members

of the same family. I introduced myself and told them I was a friend of Officer McVeigh's. They all started talking at once.

The woman—the sister?—shushed her brothers. "You know the family?" she asked.

"I'm a friend."

"Tell us what to do. Officer McVeigh ordered a birthday present for his wife a few days before he died. It isn't finished yet. Should we send it or give her the money back?"

"He paid for it?"

"Every penny. It was almost a thousand dollars. Wait, I'll show you."

She went into the back and returned with a wooden tray containing several intricate links of gold. She arranged them, so I could see what the whole would look like when it was finished.

"It's magnificent," I said.

"Eighteen karat. Every piece we make by hand."

"I think she would love to have it," I said, hoping I wasn't making a terrible mistake. She might need the money, but she would never have anything so beautiful again.

They seemed happy with my decision and asked for Jean's address. Scotty had been going to pick it up himself and take it home. I gave them the address, and we all shook hands. When I got to the car the meter had expired and it was time to go to see Jean. Joo would wait for another day.

Her mother's house was quiet and empty, no children, no cake in the oven, no hovering mother, maybe just some nice old memories. Jean tossed her coat on a chair and dropped on the sofa. I could see her as a teenager doing the same thing. But she looked a lot older than seventeen today, her face worn and prematurely aged.

"Those fruits are really something," she said, and I had to think a minute before I remembered our visit to the Korean grocery. "They really loved him."

"Tell me about Scotty," I said.

"His name wasn't even McVeigh." She opened her bag and took a paper out and handed it to me.

It was a birth certificate for a seven-pound baby boy

named Scott Allan. The mother's name was Carol Hanrahan. The father was listed as Unknown. The place of birth was a hospital in Brooklyn. He had told the truth about that.

"Maybe she had to give him up," I said.

"I don't really care what happened. I don't care if his mother was a lioness. Why didn't he tell me?" Her voice shook and her eyes were wet.

"Because he couldn't," I said. "Because he didn't know how. Because he was afraid of what you would say. Because he had suffered and he didn't want to inflict his suffering on you." I threw the reasons out knowing they didn't answer the question, that no answer would be adequate.

"I was his *wife*." She said the word with such vehemence that its meaning was crystal clear. She had not been a woman he was sleeping with or living with or who had borne him children and baked him bread. She had occupied the supreme position in his life. And he had failed to tell her who he was.

"Jean, I didn't know him well, but I feel—"

"I don't know who I am now. Am I still Jean McVeigh? Should my name be Hanrahan? Or maybe it should be 'Unknown,' for that man who got his mother pregnant. What do I tell my children about their father?" She had gotten up and was walking around erratically, her red hair moving this way and that as her anger flashed.

"You're you, Jean. You're Jean McVeigh. It's the name Scotty picked for himself or was adopted into. You're his wife and you're the mother of the children you both created. And you're your own self, the person who grew up in this house, who made a certain kind of life."

"I didn't make *this* life. I'm not ready for it. I'm not ready to be a widow or a single mother. I appreciate the help everyone's been giving me, but I hate the pity. I just want Scotty back. I think I'll want him back the rest of my life, but it'll never happen. And you know what else I want?" She was crying now, but she started to laugh. "I want to kick him for doing this to me, for not telling me, for thinking I wouldn't understand. I would have understood anything."

"I'm sure he knew that," I said. "It was the burden he was sparing you."

"He really spared me a burden." She wiped her face with

her hand. "I want that bastard who killed him. I will never forgive him. I won't even try. Forgiving is for the last scene in a TV movie, when the good guy has the killer in his sights and he drops his gun and lets him be arrested. I'm not one of those good guys. I'd pull the trigger myself if I had the chance."

I thought of Sister Benedicta, who had been trying for three years to forgive. "Jean, do you think there's any chance Ray could have done it?" There were those two bullets in his drawer and no one had seen anything the day Ray was arrested. If they'd been planted, it had been done by an expert. But there was a chance Ray had left them there himself, confident that no one would find them because no one would consider him a suspect.

"Chris, that's just ridiculous. Ray's been good to us. What reason would he have to kill Scotty?"

Dear Ray, It was terrific. . . .

I couldn't think of anything I was ready to say out loud. "You said Scotty was expecting some money. Would you tell me where it was coming from?"

"From a bond my dad bought us when we got married. My dad had crazy ideas about money. He said we both had good jobs and we didn't need anything, but seven years later we would. So he got us a treasury bond. It paid us interest twice a year and after seven years it would come due. It just did. Ray'll get his money back just like Scotty promised."

The birth certificate was still on my lap. I handed it to her; she looked at it sadly before putting it back in her bag. "I started calling Hanrahans out of the phone book yesterday. I even found a Carol, but she was seventeen years old. She'd have to be at least fifty now, right?"

I agreed. I wondered how I could ever find out anything about her. Besides her name, the birth certificate had shown only the hospital where she had given birth.

"Let's get out of here," Jean said. "We can have lunch somewhere. There's a place a couple of blocks from here we can walk to."

I got up and put my coat on.

"I hate this house," Jean said.

Her comment startled me. "It looks like a pretty nice

place," I said mildly. In fact, it reminded me a little of my own house, inherited from my aunt.

"It's awful. My mother never changes anything. The stove in the kitchen is older than I am. The bathroom looks like it was built by the cavemen. She could afford to make it pretty and comfortable but she won't. I don't think she's painted for twenty years. There are stains on the wall in my old room that go back to when my brother threw things at me."

"Maybe she's just happy with it, Jean. Maybe she just doesn't want to go through the trouble of moving furniture and patching plaster."

"Let's get out of here. This place gives me the willies."

I spent a lot of time with her that afternoon. She was struggling with anger and heartbreak and felt she was losing on both counts. For my part, there was little I could say to ease any of her pain or problems, but it didn't matter; she wasn't listening, except to the sound of her own voice.

But although it was repetitious and eventually somewhat boring, I forced myself to listen carefully to everything she said, hoping for a slip or a voluntary admission, something that would help to explain the letter she had written to Ray Hansen. It never came, and finally, after a slow lunch and too much coffee, she wore herself out and there was silence.

She sat looking far away, a pretty redheaded mother of two young children now totally devoid of energy. "He took my youth," she said.

"He didn't do anything of the sort, Jean. You're young and you're gorgeous and you're going to live and work and raise those kids."

"Thanks, Chris." She gave me a wan smile. "You're the first person who's let me say it all without interrupting. Everybody else cuts me off, changes the subject, pats me on the head. You listened. I had to say it out loud. I didn't want to be like the tree in the forest that doesn't make a sound when it's falling because there's nobody there to hear it. I finally got heard."

"How do you feel?"

"Empty, exhausted." She laughed suddenly. "Wasn't I awful?"

"No."

"Let's take a walk. It's a lot warmer out today and I really don't feel like going home—unless you have somewhere to go."

"Not till later."

We had paid our bill an hour earlier, so we put our coats on and left. Jean asked me about Jack, about Jack and me. I didn't want to say we were engaged because it seemed an inappropriate time to express my own happiness, but from the way she talked, she assumed we would marry. She had known Jack for a long time and had met several of the women he had dated, none of whom she liked as much as me and none of whom she considered worthy of him. I rather enjoyed listening. It was a very different monologue from the one in the coffee shop.

"He'll make a great lawyer, too," she said. "He's very thoughtful and careful. Ray jumps to conclusions and Scotty turned to mush whenever he heard a hard-luck story." It was interesting the way she always talked about them in threes, always compared them. "Here's Petra's building."

"Really?" It all looked so different in daylight. "She's close to your mother's house."

"Sure. That's why we all came back here after the parade." She was suddenly silent again, the parade and its aftermath having intruded on our walk. We had stopped at the entrance to the building.

"I'd ring her bell, but they're probably in bed together. It's Saturday afternoon, right?"

"Right." I didn't want to talk about it. "I'm completely lost. How do we get back to your mother's?"

"The way we came."

We turned around toward the corner we'd just come from. In five minutes we were back at my car.

16

"So she let it all hang out," Jack said when we were sitting at a table in a restaurant.

"I guess that's what you'd call it. She felt better afterward, but I don't feel I learned anything helpful. I have the name of Scotty's birth mother, but I don't know what good that'll do."

Jack gave me an impish look. "Maybe she became a nun."

"You're a tease."

"But I take *you* seriously. When do you want to get married?"

"I don't know. I haven't thought about a time or a place or anything else."

"Think."

"I'd like to be married at St. Stephen's."

"My mother's gonna love this," he said, his tone of voice indicating his mother had assumed that a woman without a family would be happy to be married in her fiancé's church.

"You asked."

"Right."

"It's a beautiful place."

"We'll talk about it tomorrow."

We didn't talk about it the next day because I went home after dinner. I had promised to take my cousin Gene to Easter mass before I became engaged, and I never break a promise to Gene.

I picked him up, admired his suit and new tie, and we went to church together. Afterward, I took him for lunch and then dropped him off at Greenwillow.

It was the last day of March, and like the old saying, the month was going out like a lamb. That mysterious something that signals spring was in the air, and I was so delighted to breathe it, I had to work to keep from hyperventilating. When I turned into Pine Brook Road, I spotted Melanie Gross working around the shrubs in front of her house, I pulled into her driveway to say hello.

"Stranger!" she called, clapping her cotton-gloved hands together to brush off the earth. "It's good to see you. Whooping it up in New York?"

"Oh, Mel, that's not an easy yes-no question."

"Nothing I ask you is. Listen, I've got a pot roast in the oven. Can you come to dinner?"

"I'd love to. I think I'll do some gardening first and work up an appetite."

I did exactly that. A neighbor had rototilled a rectangle behind the house, and I had packages of seeds ready to be planted. In twenty minutes I was dressed for work and had the wheelbarrow out with Aunt Meg's old rake and trowel and spade and a new bag of five-ten-five fertilizer. It was time to sow the cold-weather vegetables—peas, lettuce, and broccoli—and I spent a refreshing afternoon doing just that. When I finished, I went inside and planted my indoor seeds—tomatoes, eggplants, and green peppers. I had been told to do that on March fifteenth, and it was now two weeks late, but I promised myself I would talk to my seedlings and urge them along. Maybe that would be worth a fourteen-day push.

My house is equipped with the proverbial sunny window, in fact quite a number of them, and I had bought a starter kit that was like a miniature greenhouse. Using some good potting soil that I lightened with a little vermiculite and sphagnum moss, I planted seeds in small square plastic containers, using a sharpened pencil to dig the hole in the center of each. When I was finished, I had such a sense of satisfaction you would have thought I'd harvested a ton of vegetables rather than planting a few ounces of seed. Before I went to bed that night, I must have checked the containers half a dozen times, although I can't say I really expected to see any sprouts. But it was another first for me. Like the homesteaders of the last century, I was laying claim to my land by enriching it, by making it produce. By the end of the summer I might have a new husband and a first crop. That, I decided, is what happiness was made of.

Hal Gross took the kids out for an early fast-food treat, leaving dinner in the dining room for the grownups. The smells in the house were enough to make me run out and buy a shelf of cookbooks and devote myself to a life in the kitchen. Although she was about my age, Mel had somehow managed to learn culinary secrets that I usually attribute to women twice her age, probably some faulty reasoning on my part. A square tin of brownies emitted an aroma from the kitchen table that threatened to make a child of me. The fast-food dinner had not caused even temporary amnesia in her own children. Two of the sixteen cut squares were conspicuously absent, and it appeared to me that the kids had somehow divined which two pieces were a microounce larger than all the others.

We ate and talked and eventually the Grosses asked what I was working on, and I told them.

"Sounds like you've got a lot of things going," Hal said. "A murder the police think they've solved, an anonymous informant who doesn't show up for a midnight meeting, a missing handgun, and a nun who won't come clean."

I laughed at his brief summary. "If you can believe it, there's even more. Scotty McVeigh wasn't born Scotty McVeigh, he lied about serving in the military, and his wife never knew a thing about it till he died."

"How terrible for her," Mel said.

"I'm sure she wants to know about his birth family. When she finally got his birth certificate, she started calling people in the phone book with his mother's last name."

"Where was he born?" Hal asked.

"Brooklyn. Kings County Hospital." It was a sad irony that he had died, at least officially, in the same place.

"I've got a paralegal going over to Brooklyn to the Records Center tomorrow to research something for me. It'll only take an extra few minutes for her to look up the woman's address."

"Hal, that would be a great help. I didn't even know there was a place that had that information."

"Oh, definitely. It's a very ugly building over on the Flatbush Avenue Extension in Brooklyn. New York has been keeping records for a long time, and if you're investigating something, they're helpful. I can have the information tomorrow evening."

I gave him the name and Scotty's birthday. With an address, I could ask neighbors if they remembered the Hanrahans, even if the Hanrahans no longer lived there. New York apartment dwellers tend to live in the same place for a long time, especially if their rents are controlled or stabilized. A girl becoming pregnant in the early sixties was something people might remember more easily than if it happened today.

At nine, I got up to go. Like the gardener I believed I had already become, I promised Mel all the tomatoes she could eat next summer. It gave me such a feeling of munificence to make the offer that I immediately recognized more than a flicker of the sin of pride. But beyond that, and sinlessly, I felt again the happiness of using the land. The house on Pine Brook Road had been the home of my aunt, uncle, and cousin since I was a child. I never doubted their right to own it and never questioned my own ownership when I inherited it last spring. But ownership is a legality. What gave ownership a meaning to the people along my road was the shrubs and trees and grass that they planted. I walked along the dark street, inhaling the scent of spring, of peat moss, even a little manure, which made me wrinkle my nose, and I felt part of them, these homeowners who were my neighbors.

Inside my comfortable little house, I took a last look at the brown earthy squares where my seeds were spending their first night on the road to germination and went up to bed.

I knew when I awoke on Monday morning that I wanted to see my friend, Sister Joseph. Besides being my dearest friend in the world, she is smart, clever, levelheaded, logical, and imaginative, a combination of traits that make her a remarkable leader. We have known each other since the night I entered St. Stephen's as a frightened fifteen-year-old, and our relationship has necessarily changed over those years. Before taking the series of steps that led to my leaving the convent, it was Joseph that I consulted with most, and most frankly.

I had visited the convent several times since leaving, but I had never invited her, or any of the nuns, to visit me. It isn't that I hadn't thought about it. I had, but something always stopped me. Now I decided to rectify that.

An early morning call brought her to the phone. "I've been waiting to hear from you," she said, with spirit. "Have you been to the Dominican convent?"

"Yes, and I left with more questions than I came with. But that's not what I'm calling about. I want you to visit me."

"That sounds like a wonderful idea. Did you have some date in mind?"

"I want you to choose the date. There's nothing except my Tuesday morning class that can't be changed."

"Well, that is certainly an offer I can't turn down. By chance, I'm going to New York tomorrow. I had thought I'd go by train, but if I drive, I could stop off in Oakwood."

"You could stay overnight, Joseph. I'd really like you to."

"Mm. That is a lovely idea. It might keep me from falling asleep at the wheel."

"Let me tell you how to get here," I said.

I was as excited as a child. The first thing I did was call Melanie and ask her to suggest something I could cook for dinner. A true friend, she offered to do the cooking for me, sneak it into my house, and let me pass it off as my own.

My laughter cut her off before the entire plot unfolded. "This is a friend," I assured her, "not a future mother-in-law."

"Well, there may be one of those soon, and my offer stands."

"It's also a person that I have an open, honest relationship with."

"Chris, you're so adorably old-fashioned. So all you want is a recipe?"

"For something that won't take all day to cook. I'm teaching in the morning."

"All right, let's see." She went through a monologue of murmurs and mutters punctuated with a lot of, "No, that's no good" and "That takes too long." Finally she said, "I think a stir-fry is your best bet. You can get most of the real work done in advance and put it all together at the last minute. It'll look good and it's fail-safe. We'll throw in snow peas and a red pepper and the colors alone will enchant her."

"Mel, you're wonderful. Fail-safe sounds like what I need. I've got my pencil. Dictate."

We worked it all out, including a dessert of apple cobbler that she assured me would be a smashing success and *no work at all*. It sounded wonderful. I could shop today, prepare almost everything after my class, and go into production while Joseph and I carried on a conversation. Too good to be true, perhaps, but worth a try.

When she had finished dictating, Melanie said, "I'd love to meet her some time, Chris. You've met my mother and mother-in-law, but I've never even laid eyes on anyone from your deep, dark past. Except for Margaret Wirth, of course."

"I'll give you a call when she comes."

"Oh, how super. I'll blow away the dust."

"Just don't say anything about Jack. I haven't told her yet."

"Trust me."

List in hand I went to the very upscale supermarket that serves this area and bought my ingredients: a flank steak; a red pepper; snow peas; mushrooms; scallions; a piece of ginger root that looked like a contemporary sculpture; and a can of water chestnuts. It looked like enough food for twice the number of people, but I'm used to leftovers and the convenience of reheating.

At home, I reviewed Mel's instructions. They included washing, cleaning, slicing, and plastic-bagging before Joseph arrived, all of which I could do in the hour or so after I returned from teaching. Confident that my culinary career was about to be launched, I called Jack to let him know.

"What a day," he said when he came to the phone. "Jerry McMahon didn't show up this morning and the you-know-what hit the fan a little while ago because someone tried to cover for him."

"What happened?"

"Who knows? Last year about this time he called on a

Monday morning and said, 'I'll be a little late. I'm in Bermuda and the plane's been delayed.' "

"Bermuda! That must have been some weekend."

"It was. Turned out he picked up a girl on Friday night and they hopped a plane on Saturday morning. It rained the whole weekend, but I don't think Jerry knew what the weather was till he left for the airport."

I felt a tingle of admiration for a soul more adventurous than my own. "Where did he call from today?"

"Nowhere. He hasn't called. He's probably sleeping one off somewhere and there'll be hell to pay when he gets back. How're you?"

"My friend Joseph is coming to visit tomorrow."

"Sister Joseph?" he said after a moment's delay, indicating a rather satisfying note of jealousy.

"Yes. She's staying overnight and I'm cooking dinner for her."

"Well, that'll be an experience. How long has this friendship lasted?"

"A long time, and it has a long time to run. Melanie Gross designed a dinner for me to cook easily."

"Three hundred sixty-five ways to cook chicken?"

"I'm doing beef."

"See? I told you you were pretty daring. I didn't do anything but chicken for years."

I thanked him for the compliment. "Jack, may I tell her about us?"

"Sure you can. It's a done deal. Isn't it?"

"Yes."

"Tell anyone you want. I love you, babe."

"That feels good."

Hal Gross called while I was eating leftovers and reviewing Melanie's instructions and gave me the address Carol Hanrahan had listed when she had given birth to Scotty. It could wait till Wednesday.

17

I retrieved my coat from the cleaner's on my way home. Joseph was a little late, which gave me time to do everything just as I wanted. Franciscans wear an obligatory habit, and I wasn't surprised to see a couple of small children across the street staring at my guest as she stood on my threshold. We hugged as she came in, something we didn't do often at St. Stephen's.

"It's a wonderful house," she said, with such enthusiasm that she surprised me. "You have grass and trees and shrubs and inside you have all these rooms. You must love it."

"I do."

"I've brought you a housewarming gift." She opened her very large black handbag and pulled out a gift-wrapped package.

"Joseph, that was absolutely—"

"Unnecessary," she finished. "Yes, it was. If it hadn't been, I probably would have made some excuse for not getting it."

"Thank you." I opened it carefully. The box was several inches long and a couple wide and deep. Inside, in a flannel bag, was a tea strainer with a cup to set it in. I could tell without looking that it was silver. "Joseph," I said, my eyes tearing, "it's simply beautiful."

"You deserve it. Use it happily. You used to make such a good cup of tea with that ratty old strainer, I didn't want you to switch to tea bags."

"I will use it," I promised. I felt very humble, almost guilty. Here I was a homeowner, a landowner, a free spirit learning to fly, not to mention make love, and Joseph was spending her savings on something beautiful and unnecessary.

"No tears," she said firmly, and I nodded and busied myself putting my gift in its bag and finding a place for it in a drawer.

We sat in the living room and talked for a little while before I asked her if she'd like to visit Melanie Gross.

"I'd love to. It'll give me a chance to see your little town."

"Not much of it," I said, going to the phone. "She lives just down the street."

Melanie said she was ready and would put the coffee on. Joseph and I, after taking a minute to walk around the outside of the house, went down the road to the Grosses'.

Mel, who usually wore a running suit or pants, had put on a denim skirt and an elegant white blouse for the occasion. "This is a first for me," she said when we were inside and our coats hung in the hall closet. "I used to see Chris sometimes when she visited her aunt, but I've never had a nun in my house before."

"I think I may never have been in the home of a Jewish woman before," Joseph said. She was looking at Mel's menorah, which I had seen her light at Hanukkah when I came over for potato pancakes and some festivities.

"How amazing," Mel said.

"Most of the homes I visit belong to relatives." She turned to me. "And friends. Most of my close friends are Catholic."

"This is a pretty diverse town," Mel said, pouring coffee into exquisite cups that I had never seen before. "We couldn't live here if it weren't. But there's certainly a clannishness below the surface. But Hal and I have friends that are almost everything you can think of. We invite and we get invited, here and in the city."

Joseph turned to me. "And you do, too, Chris."

"Yes," I said, thinking of an investigation I had done into the murder of an old man on Yom Kippur about six months earlier. "I like it. I've even picked up a surrogate father, Arnold Gold, the lawyer."

"Yes, you told me about him." Joseph looked pleased. "Your aunt picked a place to live that suited her and it ended up being the right place for you, too."

"A stroke of luck," I said. "So much in my life has been luck. I met Mel because we both take an early morning walk. I might never have run into her otherwise."

"Chris walks," Mel explained. "I run. We've managed to adapt."

"I suppose that's what friendship is all about. Maybe even life. Chris has a lot of experience adapting. Melanie, this is wonderful cake. You baked it, didn't you?"

"I do that one a lot. It's a sour cream cake, my grandmother's recipe. It puts pounds on here, here, and here." She touched three somewhat ample parts of her body.

Joseph laughed. "Well, I hope it does it in equal proportions. I'd like another piece."

Melanie glowed.

We walked it off by circling the block, a pretty long distance.

"I see why you're happy," Joseph said. "You have lots to do and friends who love you."

"There's another reason." I knew as I started to say it that I was terrified of Joseph's reaction. "I'm going to be married."

"Chris!" She turned to me with a big smile. "Chris, that's wonderful."

The sincerity of her words and voice washed over me in a huge wave of relief. "It was something that just happened. I wasn't looking for a relationship, and at the beginning I tried—"

"Stop excusing yourself," Joseph said. "It happened and it's wonderful. You're a person who's tried very hard to plan your life carefully, with a time for this and a time for that, and nothing has ever happened on schedule or the way you thought it would. Your mother's death, joining St. Stephen's. Even your wanting to leave caught you by surprise. But everything works out right. As your friend said, you're adaptable. I'm very happy for you."

On the rest of the walk I told her about Jack, how we'd met, what he did, the law classes, the sense of humor.

"Have you met his family?"

"Just once at Christmas."

"I'm sure they loved you."

"We got alone fine."

A car went by and I recognized my next-door neighbor, Midge, at the wheel. We waved to each other. She and her husband had given me a peach tree last summer, and I was crossing my fingers that it would bear fruit this year.

"What a nice place to live," Joseph said.

I thought so myself.

Dinner went without a hitch, although I felt rattled as I cooked. Using Melanie's timetable, I had the apple cobbler baked and still warm when we agreed on tea instead of coffee. That gave me a chance to use the new tea strainer, which added a distinct touch of class to my dinner table.

"You haven't said a word about the murder," Joseph said as I poured the tea. "Does that mean you have it all wrapped up?"

"It means I have endless separate threads that may or may not belong together."

"Well, let's hear it all."

I gave Joseph some paper and a pencil and I took my notes and glanced at them. I started with St. Patrick's Day, the dinner at Petra Muller's apartment, the switching of cars when we left, the Irish coffee at Gillen's Crossroads. I recounted the sound of the bullets, how Jean and I ran in fear to the parking lot to see how our men were. Joseph listened and asked no questions. Then I told her about Scotty's missing birth certificate and what finally developed, his story about a military tour of duty that had never happened. And then the arrest of Ray Hansen.

"He's the one you didn't like."

"It isn't that I don't like him. It's that I can't seem to get through to him. The truth is I think he doesn't really like me. But that's irrelevant. Jack believes Ray is innocent, and he asked me to look into it."

"Because his hands are tied."

"Yes." I told her about the search of Ray's apartment, the discovery of the bullets, the Korean grocery, and Joo's missing gun. Then I told her about the man who telephoned Jean and my eventual disappointment Friday night in Damrosch Park.

"Where does the Dominican nun fit in?" she asked.

"Oh, yes. Harry Donner."

She laughed. "You're right about the threads. I've lost count of how many there are."

"I think I've just forgotten half of them at this point." I talked about Donner and Aunt Benny, my visit to the villa at the convent, my sense that Sister Benedicta knew more than she was saying, but who could tell if any of it was relevant?

Joseph looked down at her notes and asked a few questions about Scotty's birth certificate, Gavin Moore, and Joe Farina. I knew she must be tired. She would have gotten up at five this morning for prayers before leaving for New York.

"Tell me again about the switching of cars."

I recounted how Scotty had tossed his keys to Jack, how Jack had reciprocated, how we had followed in the BMW as Scotty led the way to the bar.

"You think it was Jack the killer was after."

"Yes."

"Let's look at the cars again," Joseph said. "Before you went to"—she looked at her notes—"Petra Muller's apartment, where were you?"

I felt my face redden and knew I would not be able to keep my composure. Jack's car in my driveway overnight was one thing; alluding to my sexual relationship in a conversation with Joseph was another. "We drove from his apartment in Brooklyn Heights," I said carefully. "Jack marched in uniform. He wanted to change out of it before we went to Petra's."

"You drove from Brooklyn Heights in his car," Joseph said, as though I had described a visit to a candy store.

"Yes."

"And before that?"

"There was a huge party given by the Emerald Society at a pier in Manhattan. I met Jack there after the parade and we drove from there to Brooklyn Heights in his car."

"So anyone watching you and Jack leave the pier knew what car he drove."

"Maybe the killer didn't start following until later, when we left Petra's apartment."

"How did he know you were there?"

I couldn't answer that. My beautiful theory was falling apart.

"Tell me again what Jack and Scotty look like," Joseph said.

I described them in quick sketches: Scotty tall, lean, wiry, sandy-haired; Jack shorter by an inch or two, a little heavier, probably broader in the shoulders, curly-haired. "He complained that his uniform had gotten a little tight," I finished, with a smile.

"So you couldn't mistake the two, at least not if you could see them. What about Mrs. McVeigh?"

"She's a torch in the darkness," I said. "A flaming redhead, thin, a little shorter than I."

"But she wasn't with him when he was shot."

"We were both just inside the bar."

"But if someone had been watching Scotty since earlier in the day, it wouldn't have mattered which car he drove in if the redheaded woman was with him."

"Right."

"I wish I could see a motive," she said.

"So do I."

"There doesn't seem to be anything obvious. Tell me again about the Korean man, Mr. Joo."

I went through it once more, the gun allegedly missing the day after St. Patrick's Day and never reported. "Arnold Gold says he'll probably never get a license to carry a handgun again because of this."

"You think he had nothing to do with the killing, don't you?"

"There's no motive," I said. "Scotty helped his family get started."

Joseph smiled. "And you like them. You'll never convict anyone you like. What's interesting about that missing gun is that Mr. Joo said it was stolen after St. Patrick's Day. He must have known that would sound suspicious. After all, he knew Officer McVeigh had died the night before. If he was fabricating the story, it seems to me he would have said the gun was stolen before St. Patrick's Day, not after."

"I agree. That's one of the reasons I believe him."

"Still, it's a disconcerting coincidence. One of those cousins could have 'borrowed' the gun to shoot Scotty and then stolen it afterward so that the case against Mr. Joo couldn't be made conclusively."

"The whole case is very frustrating," I said. "Nothing adds up. Ray is the least forthcoming person I've ever tried to talk to, and all my avenues seem to be dead ends. Not to mention that I'm still worried that it's Jack they're after in spite of your very logical explanation of why it can't be so."

"Mr. Joo's gun can't be a coincidence," Joseph said, as though she hadn't heard me.

"Well, if he's involved, everything he knows will be secret forever. I've gotten him the best defense lawyer in the city. Arnold won't let him answer anything if he's ever arrested. But the police haven't budged on Ray. They're still sure they have their man."

"Is that it then?" Joseph asked. It was getting late for an early riser.

"Not quite." I got up and went to my papers. "I suppose I should show you this." I handed her the letter from Jean to Ray and told her how I had come by it.

She read it and nodded. "I suppose we have everything now: murder; a stolen gun; nuns; an illegitimate birth with a change of identity; and now adultery."

"Do you think the letter changes anything? Obviously, Ray didn't want the police to see it, but that doesn't mean . . ." I let it hang.

"I think it may, Chris. I think Mrs. McVeigh may be the key to this whole thing."

"But how?"

"The motive is still missing," she said thoughtfully. "Perhaps one of those many threads will lead you to it. But I'd keep my eye on Mrs. McVeigh."

"Oh, Joseph! You're becoming a regular sphinx!"

"It only seems that way," she said, with a laugh.

The telephone rang, and I went to the kitchen to answer it. "Chris? It's Jean. Have you heard the news?"

"What news?"

"Another cop has been shot."

"What!"

"Jerry McMahon," she said. "A sergeant in Detectives. Scotty knew him."

My body turned to ice. "He's in Jack's squad. Jack said he didn't come to work yesterday and some of the guys were trying to cover for him."

"Figures. They said he'd been dead for some time. Some-one found his body near Kennedy Airport. I think Ray knew him, too. I met him once at a party. Nice-looking guy, single, real ladies' man."

"Thanks, Jean. I appreciate the call." I hung up and went back to where Joseph was sitting with her notes. "There's been another killing. Someone in Jack's precinct. In the de-tective squad."

Joseph looked at her watch. "I'm going to shower and get ready for bed. There's news at ten, isn't there?"

"Yes."

"I'll come down and watch it with you."

"OK."

She went up, and I tried Jack's number—this was his spring recess—but he wasn't there. I cleared the dessert dishes and got everything washed up, listening to the news on the radio while I worked. They were beginning to put the pieces together—McMahon's unprecedented absence without calling in yesterday, a first in eight years of service.

Joseph came down in a bathrobe as I was putting the last of the dishes in the cabinet. I turned on the television set and switched to a news station. A movie had just ended and the credits were rolling by.

"Your hot water is good and hot," Joseph said.

"It's a good house. Aunt Meg took care of it. Here's the news."

The screen showed a dark field and a figure on the ground covered with something light. Far in the background there were lights, and a plane swooped along a runway and took off to my left. The on-scene reporter was talking about Ser-geant Jerry McMahon, whose body had been found a few hours earlier. The view of the field was replaced with a slightly blurry color shot of McMahon in uniform, probably the picture on his ID.

I turned to Joseph. "I've never seen him before."

The voice started talking about McMahon's work at the Sixty-fifth, and the picture changed again to a snapshot taken during a recent celebration in the squad room, four plain-clothes policemen having a good time. A circle marked Jerry McMahon's head. The man standing beside him needed no introduction. It was Jack.

18

Jack didn't call until the next morning when Joseph and I were finishing the last of our coffee at about eight o'clock.

The first thing he said was, "Don't say it."

I hadn't slept well. "Do they think there's a connection between McMahon and Scotty?"

"I just talked to someone on the phone. Everyone's speculating, but no one knows anything."

"What was he shot with?"

"Looks like a .22. And they're not going to be able to pinpoint the time of death too accurately. He'd been dead several days. Probably killed somewhere else and dumped."

"I'm worried."

"Sure you are. Is Sister Joseph still there?"

"Yes."

"Where she can hear?"

"Yes."

"I'll be good then. Look, Jerry and I got in front of a camera last month. There's nothing more to it. There were two other cops in the picture, you know."

"But only you were in the parking lot the night Scotty was shot."

"Chris, I can tell you McMahon and I had nothing to do with each other, on the job or off. We didn't eat in the same place and we didn't go to the same bar before I met you and you cleaned up my life."

"Maybe McMahon's shooting is unrelated," I said uneasily.

"And someone could have had it in for Scotty, only we don't know why yet."

"But you and McMahon were both in the same precinct and you said yourself you don't like coincidences."

"There are coincidences and coincidences. Suppose all the victims wore black shoes."

"This is different. You know it's different."

"Anyway, I promise I'll look over my shoulder all day. OK?"

"OK." I smiled. "And you'll let me know if anything turns up."

"Have I ever failed you?"

I went back to the table, where Joseph was looking at the paper.

"I hope I'll get to meet him soon," she said.

"We'll drive up some weekend. When he doesn't have too much homework."

Joseph left soon after. On my agenda, but not of immediate necessity, was a call or visit to Carol Hanrahan's thirtysome-year-old address. There were no Hanrahans listed there in the phone book, but someone else might know what had become of her. If she was alive and had given up Scotty at birth, would she know the name of the receiving family? I didn't want to be the messenger of her son's death, even a son she had never known. Also on my agenda, and also low on my list of things I wanted to do, was confronting Jean with the letter she wrote to Ray Hansen. I hadn't been able to do it yesterday, but it would have to be done eventually, and something Joseph had said made me feel it should have my top priority. Third on my list was another trip to see Sister Benedicta. In spare moments I had been trying to think of a way to get her to open up to me. I wanted to know why Harry had almost quit his job and I wanted to know what, if anything, she could remember of Donner's mention of Jack. And if I could get her to recall the last visit Donner had made, perhaps something they had talked about that day would shed some light on his death.

The last thing on my mental list was a call or a visit to Mrs. Moore. The arrest of her husband's killers would surely have revived old feelings of grief, and my motive was no more than to contribute a few words of comfort. A visit, I knew, would be a lot better than a call, but I wasn't particularly anxious to drive down to Brooklyn unless I could kill at least two birds with one stone.

In preparation for a talk with Jean, I called Arnold Gold and got him before he got tied up for the morning.

"I see we have ourselves another body in blue," he said. "Any chance there's a connection to the last homicide?"

"Jack says there's a lot of speculation, but no one knows."

"Or no one's saying and they haven't ruled it out. You taking this one on, too?"

"Absolutely not."

"You still think Hansen isn't the man?"

"I'm still asking questions, Arnold. Later I'll think. I have one for you."

"Make it a good one. My brain is getting fuzzy."

"That'll be the day. I'm in possession of a letter. It was given to me by the addressee, who told me to destroy it."

"But you were too smart to do that."

"Maybe just too curious. I want to confront the writer of the letter with it and try to get an explanation."

"You're being very cagey this morning, Chrissie. I haven't heard a personal pronoun since this conversation started."

"Arnold, it's such a pleasure to talk to a man of letters. Where was I?"

"Talking around the personal pronouns."

"The letter. Is there anything legally or ethically wrong with my taking it back to the writer?"

"You've got everything backward. The person the letter was written to doesn't own it. It's owned by the person who wrote it."

"Really?"

"Cross my heart. If you get a letter from the president, it's not yours to sell unless he gives you his permission. And he may not. He may want it back so he can sell it himself."

"Very interesting. That clears my conscience."

"You sound like you're onto something."

"Arnold, I'm onto nothing, but I have several leads that could explode into something at any point. How is poor Mr. Joo?"

"Very unhappy. He thought the problem with the gun would blow over. I don't think he believed me when I said he'd never get another permit to carry a handgun again, but he's been talking to the extended family and they told him I was right. Now he believes it."

"It's a good thing you don't have an ego," I teased.

"Right. I'm the oldest lawyer in New York without an ego."

I was flipping a mental coin to decide whether to drive up to see Sister Benedicta again or to talk to Jean about the letter when the phone rang.

"Chris?" a young woman's voice said. "It's Angela at St. Stephen's."

"Angela, how good to talk to you. Are you looking for Joseph?"

"No. We expect her back by noon. I'm actually looking for you."

"What can I do for you?"

"Well, I'm on bells this week and I got a call the other day for you, but you weren't home."

"An old student?"

"A policeman from New York, or so he said."

"I see." But I didn't. "What did he want?"

"To talk to you, I guess. I said you weren't here, that you'd left a long time ago, and I didn't know your new address or phone number."

"Thank you, Angela. I appreciate that."

"There's something else. I think he may have called once or twice before. I found a note taped to the switchboard the other day from one of the other nuns who was on bells last week that a man had called asking for you, but he wouldn't leave a name or number. I thought you ought to know."

"Did the one who called this week give a name, Angela?"

"Yes. He called himself Sergeant O'Brien. Try checking that one out in New York."

"Thanks an awful lot, Angela."

We gossiped for a few minutes, and then I got off. Someone was looking for me, someone who had traced me to St. Stephen's, probably through my license plate. Sergeant O'Brien. It was as good a name as any if you were trying to pass as a New York City police officer. It could be the man who hadn't showed up Friday night. In fact, if it wasn't the Friday night informant, I didn't have the faintest idea who it could be.

I called Jean, but she was out. My morning had slipped away in a flurry of telephone calls. I sprayed some water on my seed pots, looking in vain for signs of germination. Brooklyn was out today. I would have to drive up to see Sister Benedicta. But not in jeans. I went upstairs and got a skirt and blouse, a pair of stockings and black shoes, and started to change. The phone rang again when I was more undressed than dressed.

"Chris, I'm glad I got you."

"Jack?"

"I want you to come down here. Can you make it by three?"

"Sure, but why?"

"There's someone I want you to talk to. I think this whole thing is breaking wide open."

"Where shall I meet you?"

"Remember the coffee shop we had lunch in the first time we met?"

"Yes. It's around the corner from the station house. I can find it."

"Why don't you plan to stay over tonight? Then you won't have to drive home in rush hour. I'll bring home a pizza or something."

"OK."

"If it looks like I'll be late, I'll call the coffee shop."

"I'll wait."

"If I'm not there by five, go to my apartment. I'll call you."

I tried Jean again with no success. A call to Sharon Moore ended up with a message on an answering machine. I didn't have the kind of message you could leave, so I hung up without saying anything. That left only Carol Hanrahan. So be it. After lunch, I drove to Brooklyn.

In two of my earlier investigations, either Jack or I had made use of old records in old New York apartment houses, so I was fairly confident that I could successfully do it again.

There are lots of reasons why records of who lived where in the forties and fifties still exist. Most of those buildings are still under rent control or rent stabilization, and from time to time inspectors walk in unannounced to check to see whether landlords have illegally subdivided large single apartments into smaller ones—like Ray Hansen's situation—to increase their rental income. Determining the configuration of the building decades ago is essential when a comparison has to be made with today's floor plan.

The records have other uses, too. It's not unheard of for tenants and landlords to steal electric power from one another. If you can tap into somebody else's line, you can reduce your own bill while raising that of your neighbor's. So utility inspectors also need records dating back a long way when they check out complaints.

According to my map, the Hanrahans' address was near Prospect Park and not far from Kings County Hospital, where Scotty had been born. I found the apartment house, an old red brick building probably dating from before the Second World War, and took the elevator down to the basement, where the super's apartment was. A young black man in work clothes answered my ring. When I told him the name I was looking for, he looked blank. When I said they had lived in the building about thirty years ago, he said, "I wasn't even born then. I've only been here two years myself."

"You must have records," I said.

"Sure I got records. I also got a lotta work to do."

I knew he wanted me to open my wallet and make it worth his while, but I don't do that. I believe people do things for other people if there's a reason. It's up to me to put it in the right terms.

"I'm sure it won't take long," I said. "I represent a member of their family that they haven't seen since they lived here. It's a mother and her son. I've come this far. Please help me find her."

He gave me a bit of a scowl, growled something, and left the room. My time estimate was pretty accurate. He was back in a couple of minutes. "They lived on the second floor, 2D. It's a small building. We got only four on a floor."

"Were any of the tenants on two living here back then?"

He gave me the scowl again. "Mrs. Fisher's always saying she's been here forever. Come on up. I'll introduce you."

Mrs. Fisher was in her sixties or early seventies, a painfully thin woman with steel gray hair that looked as though it had been professionally set several days ago and now had wilted into haphazard curls. Her glasses were large and thick, the frames chosen for use, not style. She wore a full cotton apron over her clothes, and as the door opened, a strong smell of food cooking blew out of the apartment as though looking for a place to go.

I told her who I was and what I wanted.

"The Hanrahans," she said. "I haven't heard anyone talk about them for years."

"Do you know where they are?"

She shook her head. "They had a problem and they moved. A long time ago. It must be twenty-five years."

"Did you ever hear them say where they were going?"

"I don't remember."

"Do you recall their first names? Mr. and Mrs. Hanrahan?"

"Doris," she said. "Doris and . . ." She stood there looking at me as though I could supply the missing name if I just tried hard enough.

"I'm really looking for the daughter, Carol."

Mrs. Fisher smiled as though placating a child. "You won't find her."

"Do you know why?"

"It's a long time ago, dear. Ask Mrs. Kennedy on four. They were friends."

I thanked her, and the super rang for the elevator.

"What she do, this Hanrahan?" he asked.

"I'm not sure."

"Sounds like you got a little mystery."

"A big one," I said.

On four Mrs. Kennedy opened the door when the super called to her. She was small and thin and had short, very thick hair the color of snow and very bright blue eyes.

Something about her made me smile. "I'm looking for the Hanrahans who used to live on two," I said.

"Oh, yes. Doris and Charlie. I knew them."

"They had a daughter, Carol."

"They had a girl, yes."

"Do you know where they are now?"

"Well, they're with God, most of 'em."

My heart fell. "The daughter?"

"She died first. Sad case that was. And Doris next, a few years later." She smiled brightly. "But old Charlie's still around."

"Do you know where he is?"

"Well, I know where he used to be. Haven't seen him for years, but my husband ran into him just a coupla months ago. Said he was livin' in an old folks home around here somewheres."

"Do you remember the name of it?" I knew this was it. If she couldn't help me, I had a lot of work ahead and no certain success.

"It's that big one over the other side of the park. St. Andrew's? I think that's it. St. Andrew's Home for the Aged." She laughed. "That's a funny word now, isn't it? Who wants to be called 'aged' in this day and age?"

"No one as young as you," I said. "Thank you, Mrs. Kennedy."

In the car I looked at my watch. Two-thirty. I couldn't chance missing Jack, so I worked my way over to the Sixty-fifth Precinct and parked at a meter not far from the coffee shop. It was just three when I walked inside.

Most of the tables were empty. I sat at one big enough for three and looked at the menu. When I glanced up, a waitress was standing near the table.

"Get you something?"

"Hot chocolate, please."

"That it?"

"I think so."

I had brought a book to read. Jack doesn't have the kind of job that's predictable. If he was catching cases today, he could be called out and spend hours away from the precinct.

"There you go," the waitress said, setting my chocolate in front of me. "Gave you a little whipped cream."

"Oh, that's nice."

"You're Jack's girlfriend, aren't you?" The plastic bar pin on her uniform pocket said TESSIE.

I felt my cheeks warm. "I'm waiting for him," I said, preferring not to acknowledge our relationship.

"I waited on you the first time you came here. Boy, could I tell he was falling for you."

"I had just met him then," I said.

"But I could tell. He's a real sweetheart, that guy. You take good care of him."

I told her I would. "He may call me here if he's going to be late."

"I'll see you get the message."

But there was no message and there was no Jack. At five to four, I went out and fed the parking meter. I stood for a few minutes looking up and down the street, but there was no sign of him. I went back and ordered a corn muffin and coffee. The muffin came nicely toasted, with butter and raspberry jam, a very New York kind of snack; I ate it slowly.

"You still here?" Tessie was back.

"Still here and still waiting."

"He won't stand you up."

"He's probably out on a case."

"You gonna wait some more?"

"Till five."

"You're a teacher, aren't you?"

"Yes. English."

"You don't look like a teacher. I wouldn't've guessed it if Jack hadn't told me. You don't look tough enough."

"I'm probably not," I said. "Tough enough."

At ten after five I paid up. They had a pay phone, and I called his number at the precinct. The detective who answered said he'd been gone a long time and he didn't know when he'd be back.

I hung up and called Jean McVeigh. There was no answer. I went to my car and drove to Brooklyn Heights.

19

I called Jean again when I got to Jack's place, but again there was no answer. There was no message for me on Jack's answering machine, so I set the table for our pizza and checked the refrigerator. There were a few cans of beer, some milk, some orange juice, and two cans of Coke. We'd do fine.

I didn't like the silence. Jack had said the case was ready to blow wide open and then I hadn't heard from him. I was sure Tessie would have told me if he had called at the coffee shop.

I dialed Petra's number, and she answered quickly.

"Petra, it's Chris. I just wondered if you'd heard anything, if anything had happened."

"Well, the murder of the cop, but you must know that."

"Do they think Ray had something to do with that?"

"They're trying to make a connection. They aren't even sure when this McMahon died, so they're looking for an hour here, an hour there that Ray could have done it. They came to talk to me at work today. Can you imagine that? Two detectives walking into our showroom?"

"It must have been very embarrassing. Did you see Ray over the weekend?"

"The whole weekend, every minute. If he got away long enough to kill someone, it must have been when I was in the shower."

That was a little odd. Ray had said he didn't like to stay overnight; he liked to sleep alone in his own place. Suddenly, on a weekend when a second homicide was committed, he had changed his pattern. Or Petra was covering for him, possibly for the second time.

"You haven't heard from Jean, by any chance, have you?"
I asked. "I've called on and off all day and she doesn't answer her phone."

"Maybe she's at her mother's."

"I think I'll try her there."

Mrs. Costello was home and said Jean wasn't there. "But
you may not get her at home. I think she's unplugged the
phone," her mother said.

"Is something wrong?"

"She said some reporter was after her to answer questions.
She doesn't want to talk to them anymore. She's trying to
put it behind her."

It sounded fishy. Why would a reporter want to talk to her
at this point unless there was something new to talk about?
Something was going on and I had the uncomfortable feeling
that I was the only one who didn't know what it was.

I opened my book and started to read. As I turned a page,
the phone rang. I jumped up and answered it, only to hear a
dial tone. One ring and someone had hung up. I put the
phone back and stood waiting for it to ring again. But there
was nothing.

I couldn't concentrate on the book anymore. I turned on
the radio to see if anything new had developed in the
McMahon murder. The autopsy had been performed today.
The medical examiner said McMahon had died of a bullet
wound in the chest from a gun fired at very close range. His
hands had been tied behind him, making his death appear to
be an execution. He had died over the weekend, probably on
Saturday, almost certainly not where his body had been
found by a bunch of boys riding dirt bikes. If the police had
any leads, they were keeping them to themselves.

Finally, the downstairs bell rang. I jumped up to press the
buzzer, so Jack wouldn't have to find his keys, but I stopped
short. Instead, I called, "Who is it?" on the intercom.

There was no answer. I called again. I thought I could hear
a voice, maybe two voices, but no one was speaking to me.
I went to the door and double-locked it. Even if I hadn't
buzzed him in, someone else might come along and open the
door.

I went to the window in the living room, which overlooked the street. A car was double-parked just to the left of the entrance. Two men appeared on the street, got into the car, and drove off. At that distance in the evening dusk, I could recognize neither, nor could I read the license plate.

They had heard my voice and decided not to come up-stairs. Either they had been looking for Jack, or they had been looking for an empty apartment. Either way, I was scared. If their intentions had been honorable, my voice would not have sent them off.

Jack walked in about five minutes later, carrying a pizza that was still warm. "Sorry about this afternoon, honey." He gave me a kiss as he put the pizza on the counter. "Got a call on a shooting that turned out to be a suicide threat. Took a lot of time to calm him down and disarm him. He's OK," he said, seeing my face. "How're things?"

I told him what had just happened.

"It was probably Tim. Don't worry about it."

"There were two men, Jack. I saw them leaving the build-ing."

"You're sure of that?"

"I heard two voices through the intercom, and then I saw two men leave the building and get into a double-parked car."

I could see he didn't like it. "Let me call Tim."

Tim had already left home to come here. We sat and ate pizza while I told him about my afternoon.

"Tessie let you in on all my personality quirks?"

"I think she likes you. She was very circumspect."

The downstairs bell rang, and a minute later the awaited Tim joined us.

"Chris, Tim O'Brien," Jack said.

"O'Brien," I echoed. "You called St. Stephen's this week."

"Didn't get anything out of them. That's a tight-lipped, protective bunch of nuns."

"Sit down, Tim," Jack said, handing him a beer. "Tell Chris the story."

"I'm Jerry McMahon's partner," he began. "I was," he amended his statement. "We were partners for three years. We knew each other pretty well and we trusted each other. It wasn't like we told each other everything, but damn near.

But some crazy things have happened lately, and last week I knew something was going on that he was keeping to himself. I didn't like to ask. It could be personal. You know."

"I understand."

"Last Friday we were on a four to twelve. Sometime after eleven, Jerry said he had to take a run over to Manhattan and I should leave a line for him. In the log," he explained. "So he could come back and sign out. He would do the same for me." He was a little embarrassed owning up to the deception, something that wasn't all that unusual.

"Yes," I said. "Go on." I wasn't interested in ethics; I wanted to see what he was leading up to.

"I signed out around midnight and went home. I never thought twice about it. When he didn't come in on Monday morning, I just figured he'd had a blast over the weekend. It wasn't the first time. Jerry was a real ladies' man and he did crazy things sometimes. Anyway, at some point, it occurred to me to check the log. He'd never signed out on Friday night. I didn't like that, so I drove over to his apartment. He gave me the key a long time ago. When you're single, you need a backup like that and he wasn't the kind of guy who'd leave a key on the ledge over the door where anyone could find it.

"The apartment looked OK," he said. "The bed was even made, so it didn't look as though he'd just gotten up after spending the night with a"—he paused to find the right word—"a woman," he said, using an uncontroversially correct word. "I made a cursory search of the place and didn't find anything much until I saw a piece of paper sticking out under the phone." He opened his wallet, took out a folded note, and handed it to me.

It opened to about three by five and written on it in ballpoint ink was my license plate number. "He was going to meet me Friday night near Lincoln Center," I said.

"I couldn't say for sure. I checked the plate and got your name and the upstate address. You understand, nuns aren't the kind of women Jerry hung around with. So I called St. Stephen's and asked for you."

"But they didn't tell you anything."

"Nothing. Lots of pleases and thank-yous, but nothing

else. Then last night, after they found Jerry's body, I was having a beer with one of the guys and he said Jack had a girlfriend named Chris who used to be a nun. This morning we put it together."

"He was coming to see me," I said, feeling a shiver. "Did he leave you early enough to get to Lincoln Center by midnight?"

"Plenty of time."

"What's happened to his car?" I asked.

"There's an alarm out for it," Jack said. "They've been cruising his neighborhood since Monday, but it hasn't turned up. Hasn't turned up anywhere else, either."

"Did Jerry know Scotty?" I asked.

O'Brien shrugged. "Maybe."

"Jean said she saw him at a party once. I wonder if he knew Harry Donner or Gavin Moore."

"Sure he knew Donner," Jack said. "We were all at the same place at the same time for almost a year."

Jack had been there, but Scotty hadn't. I turned to O'Brien. "I'm sure you've both been through all this, but you said Jerry had something on his mind."

"I wish I could tell you more. Jerry was a funny guy. He was like two different people. I mean, this guy could pick up a girl and end up in Bermuda for the weekend, but on the job he was cool and tough and reliable. If something was bothering him and he wasn't talking about it, I would figure it wasn't any of my business."

"But this is our business," I said. "He knew something, or heard something, that had to do with Scotty McVeigh's murder and the only way he could talk about it was to an outsider. Do you know where he was a week ago Monday in the morning?"

O'Brien opened a little book he took from a pocket. "That was last week. We were on four to twelves all week. He could've been anywhere during the day."

"You know, someone called Ray to tell him his apartment was about to be searched. Remember?"

"I remember," Jack said. "That's when I left."

"Ray didn't know who it was. It was like someone was calling anonymously. I wonder . . . ?"

"He calls Ray and then drives over," Jack said. "He wouldn't have seen me, but he would have seen you because you stayed for the search."

"So he knew I was a friend of Ray's, and if he followed me, he knew I was also a friend of Jean McVeigh's. He can't follow me home because he's working at four, and besides, he thinks he doesn't have to because he can get my address from my plate."

"And when he can't," Jack picked up, "he calls Jean to get in touch with you."

"Maybe he thought I was Ray's girlfriend. Or if he picked me up outside Jean's house during the week and followed me, he might figure out I was trying to clear Ray. I went to the Korean grocery and Harry Donner's next-door neighbor—in fact, I rang a lot of bells on his block—and I saw Gavin Moore's widow."

"You've been around," O'Brien said.

"But I don't have anything. Jerry McMahon had something."

"Yeah," O'Brien said. "And it looks like it was heavy enough to kill him."

20

After Tim O'Brien left, Jack told me very seriously that he wanted me to drop my investigation. "Whoever this killer is, he's made the connection between you and me."

"Unless it's you they were after all along."

"OK. I admit that's a possibility. But if the guy who came here tonight is the guy who killed McMahon, he may have gotten plenty from McMahon before he killed him. I think all three of us are in danger, you, me, and Tim O'Brien."

"What are you going to do?"

"I'm going to find someone I can trust and dump it on his desk."

"What do you mean, someone you can trust?"

"I mean, whoever this killer is, he knows a lot about cops."

"Or he's a cop himself."

"Right, or he's one of us."

That's the nightmare to end all nightmares. You can't go to the cops because the cops are the enemy. "All right, listen to me. Only you and I know about Harry Donner's aunt. And only you and I—and Ray—know about the letter Jean McVeigh wrote. I don't want Sister Benedicta involved in a police interrogation, and I don't want another soul to know about that letter. I have to pursue those two leads myself."

"Tell Jean to meet you somewhere. Don't go to her house."

I explained that she wasn't answering her phone.

"I'll drive over in the morning and set something up. I won't tell her what it's about."

* * *

143

Jack arranged for Jean to meet me at his apartment as soon as she could get there. She had to drop off her kids at a baby-sitter's first. I kept the door double-locked and looked out the window frequently. When the doorbell rang, I used the intercom before I buzzed Jean in.

"What an adorable apartment," she said when she came in. "How are you?"

"Fine. What's going on outside your house?"

"Some reporter got wind of Scotty's background, that his name wasn't McVeigh. She sticks a microphone in my face every time I go in or out, and she called me so many times, I pulled the cord out of the jack. Mom told me you were trying to get me."

"I think I have some information on Scotty's birth," I said.

She looked at me with a face that expressed more hesitancy than eagerness. "Do I want to know?"

"It's up to you. There's nothing horrible about it, Jean. Lots of people were brought up by families they weren't born into."

"Give it to me," she said.

"According to someone who knew them, both his mother and grandmother are dead. His grandfather is supposed to be living in a home for senior citizens—an old age home is what I was told. I haven't been to see him. I don't know if you want me to. Maybe you'd rather go yourself when you feel up to it."

"I wish I knew what I wanted. I don't want to drop in on him out of the blue, Chris. Maybe he doesn't know Scotty's dead. Maybe he has a grudge against Scotty."

"I'll see if I can find him," I said.

"Is that coffee?" she asked.

"I just made it. Jack's sister sent over some coffee beans she's trying out. She's a caterer, you know, and she's generous with her samples." I poured for both of us, happy to be given a brief reprieve. I wasn't looking forward to the next part of our conversation.

"It's yummy."

"You can really tell the difference, can't you?" Come on, Kix, I said to myself. Get it over with.

"Jean, we think the man who didn't show up last Friday

night to meet me may have been Jerry McMahon," I said, stalling again.

"The one who got killed?"

"Yes. He may have been on his way to see me when it happened."

"What could Jerry McMahon have known?"

"I don't know yet. I've got two loose ends to track down. Maybe one of them will tie him in or at least tell me where to go next." I pulled my bag over and opened it. "I didn't want to ask you about this, but I think I have to know now." I took the letter out and handed it to her.

Her face lost its color. "Where did you get this?"

"I was at Ray's apartment when it was searched. He put it in my coat pocket so it wouldn't be found. When I found it, he asked me to destroy it. I didn't."

"You should have." There was a hard edge to her voice, a set to her lips. The hand holding the envelope was shaking a little. "This letter is none of anyone's business. It has nothing to do with Scotty's murder or Ray being charged."

"I have to decide that for myself."

"This isn't evidence, Chris. This is dirt. It's beneath you. Forget about it."

"I can't."

The phone rang, and I went to answer it. It was Jack.

"She get there all right?"

"Yes."

"You in the middle of something?"

"Yes."

"Talk to you later."

I hung up and looked at Jean. Two tears were making their way down her cheeks.

"It was last November," she said. "The Hansens were going somewhere on a Saturday night and at the last moment their baby-sitter couldn't make it. Betsy called me and asked if I was free. I was. We had a problem with the car, I don't remember what, and Scotty didn't want me driving it. He drove me to their house himself." She breathed in deeply and let it out in a rush. "I know you won't understand this. I've known Ray for years and there's always been a little spark in the air when he was around. Neither one of us ever did anything about it. For a long time I wasn't even sure he felt it. It was just a crazy thing, a spark waiting to ignite, a big ball of fire somewhere that would never happen. Those things don't happen to you, Chris, because you and Jack make your own sparks and your own fire. Scotty and I did, too, but this was different. This was outside my real life."

I had been standing near the table while she spoke, afraid that pulling out a chair might stop the flow. During the pause, I sat. Jean pulled my cup over and filled it. She was looking for something to do to delay the inevitable end of her story. I should have stopped her there to spare her, but unless you're a lawyer questioning a witness in court, when you know the answer before you ask the question, in real life when you ask a question, you never know for sure what the answer will be. There could have been more—or less—than I expected. I took a sip and waited.

"I knew the Hansen kids and they weren't any trouble. After they went to sleep, I watched a movie and fell asleep myself. Betsy and Ray came back about one o'clock, maybe later, I'm not sure. Betsy at least had had a good time. She looked great, all smiles. She thanked me about twenty times while I put my coat on.

"Ray and I went out to the car. He took my arm because there was a little ice on the driveway, and when he touched me I felt . . . You know how I felt. We got in the car and he asked a very crude and very sexy question and I said yes. It wasn't just my mouth that said yes; it was my whole body. I hadn't felt that way for years. He drove to a motel if you can believe it and we just went in and did it." She dropped the letter on the table. "I wrote and told him how I felt. It was crazy for me to write. Not crazy, stupid. I didn't want it to happen again. It was over, it was done. I had a husband that I loved even if Ray was thinking of splitting up with Betsy which I didn't know at the time. I wish it hadn't happened. I wish I hadn't written the letter. I wish he'd burned it when he got it. That's the story, all of it."

"When he left Betsy, did anything happen between you? Did Ray say anything?"

"Nothing, I swear to you."

"At the Emerald Society party on St. Patrick's Day, I saw

you looking at him—at them. There was something about the look . . ."

"I didn't know I was so obvious."

"I don't mean you looked lustful. It seemed to me you were sort of mother hennish."

"That's just what it was," she said. "I like Petra very much. She's good for Ray. I told you this once, didn't I? I was happy for them. I wanted everything to work out, and I wanted Ray to know I felt that way. That's why—"

The phone rang again, and I got up to answer. There was a pause, then a mechanical voice came on. I didn't wait for the pitch. "Computers," I said.

Jean forced a smile. "They're taking over."

"Jean, the night Ray was charged—"

"I went over to see him. I wanted him to know I didn't believe he'd had anything to do with Scotty's murder. That's all it was, just a friendly visit. Chris, I loved my husband."

"I believe you." But Internal Affairs had gotten hold of this somehow. If Ray was innocent and someone had planted those two bullets in his apartment, maybe his apartment had been entered before and someone had read the letter. Maybe someone had seen them at the motel. Maybe he'd left the letter on his desk at the station house before taking it home and someone had picked it up while he was out on a case.

"What are you going to do with the letter?" Jean asked. She sounded scared.

"Legally it belongs to you," I said. "If I were you, I'd get rid of it."

"Thanks, Chris." She scooped it off the table and put it in her bag.

21

After Jean left, I went down to my car and started driving out of the city and upstate. Something had begun working in my head, but it was so amorphous, I couldn't hold on to it, much less define it.

The other thing that kept me thinking was my newly reinforced sense that people are unpredictable. Chacun à son goût was about as right-on as you could be. This man that I could not even manage to feel faintly positive about generated sparks of sexual desire in Jean McVeigh. What on earth had she seen in him? She had a husband who was warm and kind and open, much like Jack, but with a different personality, and she was attracted to a man who lived in a shell, who spoke in monosyllables, who rationed smiles as though they cost him. It was a burden for me to be around him, and Jean had ached to get into bed with him.

The whole idea of it almost made me laugh. I drove to the convent feeling very happy about my own relationship.

I got there about the time I had arrived on my last visit. On the way I stopped for a quick sandwich. The sister who opened the door recognized me, but she shook her head when I asked to see Sister Benedicta.

"I'm sorry, I don't think you should disturb her today. She's had a tragedy."

"Is she ill?"

"No. It's her work. She's in her room and I think she wants to be alone. You aren't family, are you?"

"No. I came to ask her about her nephew. We talked about him last time I visited."

"Yes, the policeman. I remember when he used to come.

He was such a good person. All right, go on up. But use your judgment."

I went up the stairs and found her name on a door. It was quiet inside and I was afraid I might wake her. I tapped lightly.

"Yes," Sister Benedicta's voice said dully.

"It's Chris Bennett."

"This is a bad day."

"Can I get you anything?"

"No."

I took my notebook out of my bag. "I'll leave you my name and phone number, Sister Benedicta. If you want anything, if you'd like to take a drive, call me."

"Come inside."

I opened the door. The old nun was sitting in her chair, almost lost in the white habit. "They told me something happened," I said.

"I lost my little boy this morning."

"I'm so sorry."

"Seven years old," she said.

I understood it was a child she had read to. "Would you like me to walk you to the church?"

"I've walked to the church for sixty years. I suppose I can get there under my own power for a few more. Sit down. You look as if you don't know if you're coming or going."

I didn't. I pulled out the desk chair and sat. "I'm very sorry," I said.

"No platitudes?"

I shook my head.

"We live in a world of platitudes. I don't believe any of them. I haven't been for a drive for a long time."

"My car is downstairs."

She got out of her chair with some difficulty. "Get me my coat."

I opened her closet and took out a black wool coat and helped her on with it. She picked up a sturdy black leather bag with two worn handles and put it over one arm.

"Thank you for the towels. They're the best I've ever had."

"Enjoy them."

"You want to talk about Harry, don't you?"

"Not today. We'll just go for a drive. If you don't feel like talking, then don't."

"I won't."

I had no idea where I was going, but as I reached the edge of town I found a road and took it. There were houses that looked suburban and farms that looked traditional, a mixing of generations. We passed cows grazing and fields that had recently been plowed for the spring crop. I wondered if any of my seedlings had sprouted yet.

"What do you want to know?" Sister Benedicta asked. We had been driving for ten or fifteen minutes without exchanging a word.

"Why did you take a leave of absence?"

"That's pretty old news."

"I'm interested."

"I learned something that I couldn't live with. It was too painful. I had to get away."

"Something in the convent?"

"In the hospital." She looked out the window. "It was embezzlement. A few people in the hospital figured out how to steal from the hospital's funds. I was a bookkeeper in those days and I knew something was going on. I also knew it couldn't be done without the complicity of one of the nuns."

That hit home. At St. Stephen's, while I didn't love all the nuns equally, I trusted every one of them. "That put you in a terrible position."

"Think of the position it put her in."

I almost smiled. I liked her view of the world. "What did you do?"

"I tried to find out as much as I could. I never learned whether the nun actually benefited from the scheme or whether she simply looked the other way—or why she did it. I think she must have gotten something from it. When I had my proof, I took it to the Mother Superior."

I knew that was what I would have done. "Then why did you leave?"

"The nun committed suicide."

"Oh, no." I felt my body convulse as ice went through me.

"A Catholic," she said. "A nun. I still ask myself how she could have done it."

"She would have been forgiven," I said, as though the poor nun were there to hear me.

"She couldn't forgive herself."

"You told Harry about it," I said.

"He was such a nice youngster. He was so patient. He cared. That's what it amounted to; he cared. We talked, and eventually I went back."

She made it sound simple, but I knew it had to have been agonizing. She had told me on my last visit that she had remained away from the convent for ten months. I could imagine that she had spent the time thinking about what had happened, her part in it, the poor nun, and asking herself all the obvious questions and rejecting all the obvious answers. "Was this your convent?" I asked.

"This was it. I've spent my life here and I'm still asking questions and still hoping for answers."

"They'll come," I said, hoping she wouldn't consider my words a platitude. It was something I still believed.

"Some have come already," she said. "Some will never come."

I thought of the little boy who had died this morning. "Will you tell me about Harry?"

"He was always my favorite. I think he liked to talk to me as much as I liked to talk to him. Even when he married Dottie, we never lost track of each other. He'd been on the force—'the job' he used to call it—over twenty years when he had his own crisis. It was so much like mine that I took it as a sign. But it wasn't some poor little nun this time; it was tough, hard cops who were corrupt. He knew it and he saw it and he told me he didn't want to work around it."

"What was going on?" I asked.

"False reports. Petty thievery. Shaking down small businessmen. It was a whole little group inside the precinct. He said he was angry and ashamed and he didn't want to be part of an institution that was supposed to be a moral example and instead was corrupt."

It certainly was very similar to her own problem of years before. "How did he work it out?"

"The way I did. He took what he knew to someone he trusted. The men were tried and convicted and Harry stayed on the force."

"Was there much publicity about him? I mean as a whistle-blower?"

"They kept it quiet, but he said there were rumors. People looked at him as if they knew. They kept away from him. He was transferred to another precinct."

"Sister Benedicta, before Harry died did he ever tell you about anything going on that could have led to someone killing him?"

"You think someone killed him because he knew something?"

"I don't know. If Harry was a man who wasn't afraid to expose corruption, he may have found it again."

"It's possible," the old nun sitting beside me said. "I didn't think of it at the time, but now it seems possible."

"A policeman I knew was shot to death in a parking lot—"

"A parking lot," she interrupted.

"Yes."

"Harry was killed in a parking lot."

"I know. This was about three weeks ago. I can't find any reason why he should have been killed. A friend of his has been charged with the murder, but there's no reason why he should have done it. When I was here last time, I asked you if you recognized the name of the victim, Scotty McVeigh, and you didn't."

"No. I never heard it."

"He was in a parking lot with a friend when it happened. The friend's name was Jack Brooks." I waited.

"You asked me that one, too. Harry told me about— I think Harry mentioned the name."

"Do you remember anything else?"

"It had nothing to do with the corruption," she said. "He was talking about a young fellow in the precinct. That's all. He used to talk about the people he worked with and I talked about my patients and the nuns. We were a couple of old gossips."

I smiled. "But he did more than gossip. He told you things that bothered him."

"Yes. He always told me those things."

"That's why you think he found something going on before he was killed."

"Something was going on, I'm sure of it. Someone came to him for advice, someone he'd known a long time ago."

I had reached a crossroad and I made a wide U and started back. "What kind of advice?"

"It was about drugs. They were selling drugs."

"Who?" I asked.

"The police. The defenders of society. They had become the criminals."

"But Harry only heard about it. He hadn't seen it for himself."

"No. This fellow told him. He wanted to know what to do."

"What did Harry tell him?"

"To do what he did. To go to someone he trusted. Harry said he'd back him up."

"When did this happen, Sister Benedicta? Was it just before he was killed?"

"No. It was before that, weeks before, months before. That's why I didn't think about it as a cause. It was just someone who talked to Harry."

I glanced at her. She had turned toward me and her face was anxious. "Did he mention it only once?" I asked.

"Maybe more than once. Maybe he said something a second time." She sounded more eager now, her interest aroused, her mind challenged.

"Do you remember the name of the man?" I asked it softly, hoping.

"Irish," she said. "A very Irish name."

"McMahon," I said. "Jerry McMahon."

"Oh, no. Nothing like Jerry. It was just very Irish, the first name, I mean."

The first name. Scotty, Ray, Jack, Jerry. What kind of first name was Irish? When it came to me, I knew it had to be the right one. "Gavin," I said, almost triumphantly. "Gavin Moore."

"Gavin. That's it," Sister Benedicta said. "The young man's name was Gavin."

22

"Just tell him to call Chris," I said to the very polite man who had answered Jack's phone. I hung up and watered the brown squares of earth in which my intended seedlings were still hiding. Then I took a piece of paper and sat down at the dining room table, where I had left my notes and doodlings.

Jack had looked through the histories of all three police-men who had died in unsolved homicides and hadn't found any place where their lives overlapped or where they crossed Scotty's. But Sister Benedicta had said Harry had known Gavin Moore from a long time ago. Somewhere their paths had crossed, they had gotten to know each other, and Moore had developed a respect for Donner so great that he turned to Donner when he learned something he couldn't deal with. Somehow we had to find that point of crossing.

Jack didn't call till after six. "Hi," he said. "Just got your message."

"I saw Sister Benedicta this afternoon. Harry Donner knew Gavin Moore."

"You're sure?"

"Absolutely. Moore talked to Donner a few weeks or months before Donner was killed. Something was bothering him. It was about cops selling drugs."

"Jesus."

I didn't even wince. "We have to find out how they knew each other. Maybe somehow Scotty was part of it." I filled him in on what Sister Benedicta had told me.

"The problem is I can't get hold of Donner's or Moore's personnel files. Those are like top secret documents, and un-less you've got a friend at Personnel—and I don't—you just don't have access to them. Their superiors do, but I don't

154

know them. It's not something I can punch up on a computer."

"I'll try Sharon Moore," I said. "Maybe somehow she'll be able to dredge something up out of her memory. If we can figure out where Donner and Moore met, maybe we can get Scotty into the picture."

"I hate to put a damper on your theory, Chris, but one of those guys they arrested last Friday really seems to be part of the gang that killed Moore. He's named names and come up with details that only the killers could have known."

"You're telling me everything's a dead end."

"No, I'm not. I'm intrigued by the Moore-Donner connection. I think it may mean something. I wish I could figure out what. I'll do the best I can to find out where they could have met. Did she say when this happened?"

"I don't think she knew exactly. Donner told her it was a long time ago."

"This is a crazy one. I have to admit, I didn't think that nun was going to yield anything."

"Nuns always yield something," I said.

"You got it."

I went back to the dining room table and looked at the scribblings I'd made before he'd called. Coincidences, things that happened without explanation, without good reason. Two of the dead cops had been killed in parking lots. Moore told Donner about some cops involved in drug selling a few months or weeks before Donner was killed. It had occurred to me at about this point that I wasn't sure when each of those men had died. In my early notes I had written "three years ago" for both of them, but nothing more. I didn't have a specific date for either one. The night Jerry McMahon had intended to see me near Lincoln Center, the killer of Gavin Moore was suddenly arrested. That was a most intriguing coincidence. So was the disappearance of Mr. Joo's handgun the day after St. Patrick's Day.

Suppose all the victims wore black shoes, Jack had said. Maybe the .44-caliber guns were the black shoes. Maybe all the coincidences were just that. Many times in my life I have looked around and seen someone for the first time in many years and not attributed any sinister meaning to the meeting.

But I was dealing with a homicide here, with several homicides. No coincidence was a happy event and nothing could be considered chance. Maybe Sharon Moore would remember a meeting between her husband and Harry Donner. Tomorrow.

Sharon Moore opened the door seconds after my ring. She invited me in but excused the appearance of her house. The vacuum cleaner was in the middle of the living room floor and the furniture had all been moved away from the walls so that the room looked as if she was half moved in or out.

"It's what I do best when I'm depressed," she said. "When they called last Friday to say they'd arrested the guy that killed Gavin, I pulled out the Lysol and Brillo and got to it."

"I'm sorry. I wanted to come earlier in the week, but I couldn't get here. I kind of thought it would rake up all those old memories."

"And then some. Sit down. I'm ready for a break and the kitchen's as clean as it'll ever be."

She was right about that. The windows looked like panes of crystal and the sun shining in on the sink made the faucets look like sterling silver.

"I hear this guy Hansen had a thing for McVeigh's wife," Sharon Moore said.

"Where did you hear that?"

"The wives talk." She sponged the table. "I baked. Can you eat a piece of apple pie?"

"Sure."

"If the kids left any. Oh, there's enough. I'll make some coffee." She filled a percolator and tossed some coffee into the basket with the careless expertise of someone who did it all the time. In a minute the pot started making bubbling noises. "You didn't really come to say nice things, did you?"

"Mrs. Moore—"

"Sharon."

"I'm Chris."

"I remember."

"I thought you might be feeling—the way you feel. But something happened yesterday. I found something out. I have to talk to you about it," I finished uncertainly.

"I don't know what there is anymore. I told you how I thought Gavin died. Now it looks like I was right."

"Sharon, some time before Gavin died, he talked to Harry Donner."

"The other cop who was killed?"

"That's the one."

She moved her shoulders. "He never told me about it. He never even told me they knew each other."

"Do you remember which of them was killed first?"

"Sure. It was Donner. He died in the spring. Gavin was killed in September. The kids had just gone back to school."

That made sense to me. If Gavin Moore had needed encouragement from a mentor, there was a good chance he wouldn't do anything on his own if Donner was murdered. Also, he might not have thought there was a connection. But from what I had learned about Donner, I felt strongly that if Moore had been killed first, Donner would have gone public with what he knew from his conversation with Moore.

"You look as if you're thinking very hard," Sharon said.

"I didn't know it showed."

"Was that so important? Who was killed first?"

"I'm not sure."

She poured two mugfuls of coffee and cut two slices of her pie. "Gavin was killed by a bunch of rotten punks who had nothing better to do that night. How can there be any connection between that and Donner's killing?"

"I don't know. I'm just trying to put things together." I took a sip of coffee. "When Donner was killed, did your husband say anything? I mean, did he mention he'd known him or heard of him?"

"I told you. He never said a word. If he knew Donner, that was his secret."

"I know this isn't easy, but can you think back to that summer before Gavin died? Did he change at all? Was he nervous, worried, a looking-over-his-shoulder kind of thing?"

She said, "Yeah," so quickly that she surprised me. "I thought it was just the pressure of the job. He had a lot of vacation coming and he said, 'Let's get the hell out of New York. Let's really get away.' We drove out West, all of us. It was expensive, but he really wanted to do it. And since you

brought it up, it wasn't like him to do that. He was pretty
careful what we spent. You think he was afraid of something
after Donner was killed?"

"I think it's possible," I said carefully.

"How do you know Gavin talked to Donner?"

"Donner told someone."

She looked at me hard. "You're telling me you found
someone a police investigation missed?"

"I think I did. But remember, after Harry Donner was
killed, no one was looking for a connection between him and
Gavin."

"Right. I see that."

"The pie is great."

"I cooked a lot for Gavin." She put her fork down and
looked away from me. "Gavin Moore was the sweetest man
that ever walked the face of this earth. All he lived for was
his family and his job. I knew what kind of work he was
doing, but he didn't talk to me about it much because he
didn't want me to worry. You can imagine I worried anyway,
but he kept most of it to himself. That's the way he wanted
it. I stayed home with the kids, I kept a nice house, I worked
for the church. He came home and the kids jumped all over
him and he just ate it up. I don't know how a guy like that
ever became a cop. He should have been a kindergarten
teacher." Tears were rolling down her cheeks now. "He was
such an innocent. He trusted everybody." She wiped her face.

"He must have been tough, Sharon," I said. "The kind of
work he was doing . . ."

"He carried a gun. That's where the toughness was. He
never believed anything could happen to him. I'll tell you,
I'd give everything I have to have him back, but I never
want another one like him for the rest of my life."

23

Jack met me for lunch, an infrequent pleasure in our lives. He had one of his famous folded sheets of paper in his jacket pocket, and when we had ordered, he took it out, did some refolding, and smoothed it out in front of him.

"I can't put Donner and Moore together anywhere, Chris. I've made phone calls and talked to people who knew one or the other of them and I'm pretty sure they never worked together. It's almost impossible to find out if they were ever in a hall in a courthouse on the same day and had a conversation. It's possible, but it's hard for me to believe that something like that could have led Moore to seek out Donner for advice or help if there was the kind of problem your Sister Benedicta talked about."

"She wasn't dreaming, Jack."

"I know. I came up with something and I think this could be it."

"You really found something?" I felt my spirits lifting.

"Guys like Donner, real pros with a specialty, often get tapped for the CIC, Criminal Investigation Courses. They give these courses to new detectives, and I found someone who's sure Donner did it every year for a long time. His specialty was drug investigations and Gavin Moore was on a special drug task force."

"How does it work?" I asked.

"It's a couple of hours four nights a week down at the Academy. The way it works, the detective gets a note in the mail one day telling him this is the week to do it."

"And it wouldn't be unheard of for a member of the class to go out for a beer with the instructor when the class was over."

"Having a beer after anything has never been unheard of in this job."

"OK. I really like that," I said. "What I'm thinking about now is Scotty. Would Scotty have been likely to take the same course?"

"Couldn't have happened, Chris. Scotty was never out of uniform and those courses are just for detectives. And while guys like Donner sometimes also teach rookies, I can tell you Scotty didn't know him. We went through the Academy together and we talked all the time when we were rookies."

"Then I guess we still can't tie Scotty to the other police homicides."

"Chris, Gavin Moore was killed by a group of guys in a park. There is absolutely nothing to indicate his death was part of anything else."

"Jack, who arrested those guys last Friday night?"

"I don't know. Why?"

"Can you find out?"

"Sure." He made a note. "Something cooking that you haven't told me about?"

"I'm just thinking of the coincidence angle."

"Fine." He wrote something else down on the folded sheet.

"I talked to Joseph about the case when she stayed over and she said something before she left that I haven't really followed up on. She said to keep my eye on Jean. Jean left us the afternoon of St. Patrick's Day to take her kids to her mother's. I think I should ask her what happened during that time."

"You haven't told me about your talk with her about the letter."

I hadn't told him because I hadn't wanted to. I had wanted to forget the whole thing. "She said it happened once. That's it. She went into more detail than Ray did."

"While he was still with Betsy?"

"Yes."

"Shit."

"Yes."

"How the hell did the IAD get onto it? You think Betsy knew?"

"She could have put two and two together." I told him how it happened. "It must have added at least half an hour to his trip that night."

"Half an hour," he echoed. "What a dumb thing to do."

"You know what? I think I should talk to her. She's the only person in the whole group we haven't considered."

Betsy Hansen lived in the house in Brooklyn she had shared with her husband until a little after Christmas. The ornate *H* on the front door had been painted by Betsy, and there were other touches of her talented hand on and around the house. It was several months since we had last met, but she recognized me and invited me in. She seemed to know that I was looking into Scotty's murder and sounded a little surprised that I had not been to see her earlier.

"I guess when you're separated you're out of the loop," she said.

"It isn't about who lives with whom. I just want to talk to people who may know something that will help me."

"You're trying to clear Ray?" She was a pretty, young woman with soft hair that was naturally blond and bright blue eyes that today lacked their usual luster.

"I just want to know who killed Scotty. And why. I'm not convinced Ray did it, and I don't know why he would."

"I feel a lot of hurt," she said. "Anger. What-have-I-done-to-deserve-this kind of thing. But I don't think Ray killed one of his best friends."

"I don't, either."

"What's she like? The girl he's living with. I hear he picked her up in a bar."

It wasn't the kind of conversation I wanted to get involved in, but there wasn't any easy way out. "I don't think they live together." It wasn't the answer she was looking for.

"Have you met her?"

"Yes." I knew I had to do better. "She's single, from Germany. She works for some decorator."

"Husky voice and very sexy, I suppose."

It was pretty accurate. "She's nice-looking," I said. "I think she's a nice person. I was very sorry when you two split up, Betsy. I thought you were a good couple."

"So did I." She fiddled around with the beads she was wearing. "Ray had a roving eye." She pushed her hair back. "And some cooperation."

"From whom?"

Her lips pursed and relaxed. Her eyes had filled. The wound was still very new and very painful. "Jean McVeigh, for one."

"I see."

"Not that I think there's any connection. I just can't forgive Jean. She had a husband of her own, a really nice guy. What did she need mine for?"

"Did something happen?"

"They used to look at each other as if they wanted to rip each other's clothes off. So eventually they did." She swallowed and her mouth trembled. "It wasn't anything; it was just sex. They had the opportunity and the means, they really didn't need a motive."

"I'm sorry, Betsy."

"It happened at a party last summer. Labor Day," she corrected herself.

"What?"

"A party. One of the older guys was retiring. His wife gave him a big party at their house on Long Island."

I didn't want to cause her any more pain, but I couldn't just drop it. "How do you know something happened?"

"I went looking for him. It was getting late and it was time to go. I couldn't find him outside near the barbecue, so I went inside. I remember it was very cool. The whole house was air-conditioned. There were a couple of people in the kitchen and a couple in the living room, but Ray wasn't there. I thought maybe he'd gone upstairs to the bathroom. I went halfway up and called him. All the doors were closed up there except the bathroom door, but I heard a woman's voice, you know, just a sound, and then Ray said he was coming right down. Then a door opened and some man I didn't know came out of one of the bedrooms and down the stairs. I went back down and Ray came down a minute later."

"With Jean?"

"By himself. When we got outside, we ran into Scotty. He

asked us if we'd seen Jean, and Ray said she was in the bathroom."

But of course she hadn't been, at least not the one upstairs. "Was Jerry McMahon at that party?" I asked.

"The one whose body they just found?"

"Yes."

"He may have been. There were a lot of people from different precincts, people the man who was retiring had known at one time or another."

"Betsy, is that the only time Ray and Jean may have gotten together?"

She shook her head. "It was the first that I saw myself. There was another time that I'm pretty sure of."

"When was that?"

"Last November." She drew in a deep breath. "Our babysitter pulled out at the last minute and we had tickets to go somewhere. I couldn't get anyone so I called Jean. I thought it was safe. She'd drive over and drive back and that would be it. But she got Scotty to drive her, so Ray had to drive her home. I can tell you how long it took him if you really want to know."

I didn't. She was hurting so much I wished I had a painkiller to give her. "I'm really sorry," I said.

"You think Ray killed Scotty over Jean?" She smiled. "Do men still do that?"

"I don't think so, but I'm sorry it all happened."

"It's awful for the kids. Their friends in school know he's been arrested. I wish I could take them away till it's all over." She reached over to the coffee table in front of her and picked up a folded newspaper. When she unfolded it, there was a familiar picture of Ray Hansen, in uniform, shadowed and unsmiling, the kind of ID photo that makes you look old and weary. "I have to throw the paper out before they come home." She folded it again, so the picture of her children's father was hidden.

"Betsy, did you ever talk to Ray about what happened with Jean?"

She shook her head. "I didn't really see anything. I heard a voice behind a closed door. I heard Ray lie about Jean being in the bathroom. I clocked how long it took him to take

her home that night she baby-sat. Maybe I should have said
something, but I couldn't. I thought it would work out. I
thought if I was just patient, he'd come back to me and we'd
be the way we were before. Instead, he got more distant.
And after Christmas he walked out." Her voice choked on
the last sentence.

I didn't stay much longer. I asked her if Ray talked much
about his work and she said he didn't. Before I left she
showed me the St. Patrick's Day decorations the kids had
made in school. I knew she'd rather be showing them to Ray,
but I didn't mind being a substitute. She asked about Jack
and me, and I said we were happy together, and she said she
thought we made a good couple. Then she said she was going to work full-time soon, and I told her I thought that was
a good idea. At the door, she gave me a hug. I wished I had
stopped by sooner.

The street where Jean McVeigh lived was clear of all but
a few cars that probably belonged to the houses they were
parked in front of. Maybe the reporters had given up when
they found out they couldn't bully Jean or wear her down
into talking to them.

I pulled into the empty driveway and got out of the car. A
little boy walked over from the front lawn of the next-door
house.

"Who ya lookin' for?" he asked, licking a candy bar.

"Mrs. McVeigh."

"That's where she lives."

I smiled. "Thank you." I went to the front door and rang
the bell. There was no answer. I hadn't called in advance because I assumed she wasn't answering her phone. I rang the
bell again, but the house was perfectly quiet. I walked around
to the back, the little boy following me.

"You from the TV?" he asked.

"No. I'm Mrs. McVeigh's friend."

"Oh." He seemed disappointed. Who could be interested
in a friend when there was the possibility of getting your
chocolaty face on the six o'clock news?

The back door was locked and two attempts on the bell
brought nothing but silence.

"She went out," my little friend said. I wasn't sure whether his statement was the result of logic or if he had seen Jean leave.

"Did you see her go?"

He shrugged.

I went back to the car and sat behind the wheel. The boy stood in the driveway watching me as though there were something interesting about the way I sat. Once or twice he came right up to the car and pressed his face against the window, leaving chocolaty marks on the glass.

Suddenly there was a sharp rap on the opposite window, frightening me. I turned to see an old man with a cane peering in at me angrily.

"What are you doing here?" he said.

"I'm waiting for Mrs. McVeigh."

"She doesn't want to see you and *we* don't want to see you. So how about leaving us alone?"

Enough, I thought. For all I knew she was gone for the weekend. I started the motor and backed out of the driveway, watched on each side. When I got to the curb, the little boy waved, but the old man stood holding his cane aloft like a weapon. The neighborhood had had its fill of unwelcome visitors.

24

As I left Jean's house, I remembered Carol Hanrahan's father. Pulling over to the curb, I checked my map of Brooklyn, then worked my way to the area where old Mrs. Kennedy had said St. Andrew's Home for the Aged was located. A drugstore with a phone book gave me the exact address, and the pharmacist assured me the home was close enough to walk to, so I left the car and took off. When I reached it, I didn't need to check the number or the street. It was easily recognizable as Catholic and institutional, a very old building made of large, square rust-colored stones, a patch of concrete in front which may once have been grass that was too much trouble to maintain, and a hideous chain-link fence around the perimeter, whether to keep outsiders out or insiders in I did not want to consider.

The front door was locked. After I had rung the bell twice, it was opened by a young woman who was probably a nurse's aide. I told her I was looking for Charles Hanrahan.

"He's probably in the community room," she said, locking the door behind me. "Are you a relative?"

"A friend."

She started to direct me, but I asked her to show me the way. "It's been a long time," I said. "I'm not sure I'll recognize him."

She gave me a skeptical look but started walking. The community room was in the back of the building and was filled with old men and women, many in wheelchairs, others with canes and walkers at arm's reach. There were a few card games going on, some knitting, some rocking, some talking, some television watching. The aide walked to a man holding cards and said something in his ear. He looked over at me and shook his head. They conferred again and he put his cards down and got up from the table. He was fairly tall and very thin, and he hadn't shaved for several days, which made him look dirty, although he wasn't. He was wearing a jacket over a tieless sportshirt and his clothes looked very clean.

"Do I know you?" he asked as he reached me.

"No, you don't. My name is Christine Bennett. May we speak privately?"

"Did I win the lottery?" he said, with a grin.

"It's not about money. It's about family."

The aide was still standing there. "Everything OK, Charlie?" she asked.

"Everything's fine. We'll just sit in the foyer if you don't mind."

She smiled and waved and left the room. We walked back to the entrance area and sat in a corner, each of our chairs on a different wall. Although it was a large area, we were completely alone.

"What family are you here about?" he said.

"Your daughter Carol and her son Scott."

He said, "Ah," and looked down at his hands. "That was a long time ago. A whole lifetime ago."

"I know."

"Carol's been gone over thirty years and the boy just died a few weeks ago."

"I know. I knew him."

"You his wife?"

"No. My fiancé is on the police force. He was one of Scotty's best friends." It was a milestone in my life. I had referred to Jack as my fiancé.

"So what are you here for?"

"Scotty never told his wife that your daughter was his natural mother. I'm sure he meant to, but he didn't. She wants to know about his family—for the sake of her children."

"It's a good family," he said. "My wife was a good woman. Carol was just unlucky. It happens."

"She had a baby before she married."

"He wouldn't marry her. He had big plans for himself and my Carol didn't fit in. He gave her a little money." He said it as though it had been a very meager contribution to her welfare.

"Do you know who he was?"

"Oh, I know. Carol made me swear—made us both swear—we'd never tell and I can't break my promise. He got what he wanted, a big career. Married another girl a few years later."

"What does he do?" I asked.

"He's a big man in the military, lots of gold braid on the uniform, lots of medals. He would have been proud of the boy, but he never kept up with him. Nothing."

"And your daughter?"

"Suicide," he said curtly, and my heart jumped.

"I'm so sorry."

"She just couldn't take it, I guess, his leaving her like that with a little baby. Doris already had cancer and we knew the end was coming for her. I couldn't raise a little fella like that and hang on to a job. We put him up for adoption."

"Did you know the McVeighs?"

"I saw them now and then. They let me see the boy. They were nice enough people." His offhandedness was probably more of an indication of what a wonderful parent his daughter would have been rather than any fault on the McVeighs' part.

"So you got to see him. That's nice. Did you know he was married?"

"Oh, sure. He used to drop in here once in a while. Good-looking fella in his uniform."

"Did you tell him who his father was?" I asked.

He stalled, looking pained. "I told him," he said finally.

"What about the McVeighs?"

"Oh, they've passed on. They were an older couple when they adopted the boy. Been waiting a long time for one of their own."

"Mr. Hanrahan, do you know why Scotty never told his wife about you?"

He shook his head slowly and rubbed a hand over the stubble on his face. "That's how he wanted it," he said. "I think it shamed him, his father leaving like that, his mother a suicide. My Carol, she was a beautiful girl, a good girl. There was nothing to be ashamed of."

I wondered if he had been as accepting three decades ago, if his daughter's suicide had been at least partly the result of a tough father's disapproval. It was all moot now and none of my business. "Would you want to meet Scotty's wife? There are two little children, your great-grandchildren."

"I know what they are to me," he said, letting me know he had all his faculties. "I would see them. Why not?"

I took his lack of enthusiasm as a sign of the wall he had built up over all the years when he was privy to his grandson's life only at the pleasure of other people.

I smiled at him. "I'll call before we come," I promised.

"Thanks for coming," he called as I walked across the stone floor to the big door.

25

On the way to Jack's apartment I heard a news report that Jerry McMahon's car had been found in the water not far from where his body had been dumped. It had been hauled out this morning and identified positively as belonging to him. Besides bloodstains on the front seat, there was a bullet hole in the back of the seat, the one bullet that had missed its mark. The bullet that had been dug out was a .22, the same size that had killed McMahon.

Jack was home at six-thirty, and I had dinner ready to go when he walked in. He was carrying a bottle of wine, which he put on the table before we hugged.

"Hear about McMahon's car?"

"On the way here. How'd they find it?"

"It must have been pushed into the water and gotten stuck on something. Someone saw it and called 911. It's been pretty dry lately and the water level was down. Just plain luck that it turned up."

"It sounds like he was shot in the car."

"Looks that way. A .22 doesn't make much noise. I'd guess they followed him, got into his car, and held the gun against his chest. Just sounds like a couple of pops inside a closed car."

It wasn't a conversation I wanted to pursue. I had rice cooking and all the makings of the stir-fry I had cooked for Joseph on Tuesday. I got it started as he put his gun and holster away and started to change into more casual clothes. "I think I'm getting somewhere, Jack. I talked to Betsy this afternoon."

"I'm listening."

As I followed Melanie's directions, I told him about the

retirement party the Hansens and McVeighs had attended on Labor Day. Jack hadn't been there, but he knew the man who had retired, a lieutenant named Connelly who was probably as old as Donner. I told him Betsy's story right down to the man who came out of a bedroom while she was standing on the stairs waiting for Ray.

"Everyone was there, Jack: Scotty; Ray; and Jerry McMahon. I have a feeling something happened that day, somebody said something or did something that got Scotty killed."

"Six months later?"

"Maybe St. Patrick's Day was the first opportunity. Maybe what happened at that party was just a beginning. I know I sound vague, but that's because I can't put my finger on it yet. Can we find this Lieutenant Connelly? I'd like to get hold of their guest list."

"They sold their house and moved to Ireland. The pension goes further there. Even if I could find him, I doubt whether his wife took along a list of people she invited to a party. What are you cooking?"

"Melanie Gross's fail-safe stir-fry."

"Beef," he said. "What a woman."

I added the last two ingredients and poured some light soy sauce into the pan, then some dry sherry. "We're almost there." I peeked into the pot of rice, then fluffed it up. I could smell success.

"Smells terrific," Jack said, reading my mind.

"What would I do without Mel?"

"Probably start with chicken like the rest of us."

He told me it was great so many times that my ego was soaring. We were dishing out seconds when I remembered what I'd asked him at lunch.

"The arrest last Friday night," I said. "Did you have a chance—?"

"It's in the works. I asked someone I know in Manhattan to check it out. He's working nights. We ought to hear from him soon." He poured some more wine, a Beaujolais his sister had recommended. "Like it?"

"It's nice. You know I have underdeveloped taste buds. It'll take time before I can really make a judgment. I'm glad your sister has taste."

"Does she get to cater our wedding?"

"I hadn't even . . ." A catered wedding. In my imagination, I saw us kneeling at the altar at St. Stephen's. There was nothing before or after, just a lot of black and white and two gold rings. We were totally disengaged from anything else. Were there people behind us in the pews? Was there a meal waiting to be served in another building on the convent's grounds? Were there children with rice and rose petals waiting breathlessly for us to leave the church so we could be showered? I had no idea. I had no sense of the down-to-earth realism of getting married.

"Something wrong? If you don't want her—"

I put my hand over his. "I think I ought to talk to Melanie's mother. Something tells me she knows a lot of things that I don't."

"You know enough for me," he said. "It's a great stir-fry."

On that sweet note, the phone rang. From the half of the conversation I could hear, I could tell it was Jack's friend from Manhattan, reporting on my question. Whatever the answer was, it surprised Jack. He said, "Interesting," twice and "You sure about that?" once. When he hung up, he just stood by the phone, looking as though he were trying to puzzle something out.

"It wasn't someone from that precinct, was it?" I said.

"I'm starting to feel a cold chill go through me. The arrest was made by a Brooklyn cop who just happened to be in the city that night and just happened to see a suspect in Gavin Moore's murder commit a felony."

"On the night Jerry McMahon may have been murdered."

"How did you know, Chris?"

"I didn't. I just didn't like where everything was leading me. I was really hoping you'd tell me something else, that the arresting officer was on duty in his own precinct."

"I have to make a call." He picked up the phone and dialed, asked for someone, then asked for someone else. Then he asked for some phone numbers and wrote them down, hung up, and started again. "Al, Jack Brooks. Got a quick question. The name Tom Macklin mean anything to you?" He listened and made agreeing sounds. Then he said, "What about before that?"

When he got off the phone there was no remnant of the warm, cozy man I had been sharing dinner with. "It's not good, Chris. This guy Macklin who made the arrest is part of an undercover group that works on busting drug gangs, intensive surveillance, linking, heavy investigation, interagency cooperation, the works. He's been at it for a couple of years. Before that he was part of the team that Gavin Moore was on."

"Sounds like he was following that guy last Friday, waiting for him to do something that could get him arrested."

"And take the attention away from Jerry McMahon's disappearance. I really hate this. I really, really hate this."

"I have to talk to Jean," I said. "Maybe she remembers something about that retirement party that Betsy didn't tell me. And maybe something happened the morning of St. Patrick's Day. There has to be a missing piece somewhere."

"I'll give her a call. I don't want you going over there yourself."

While he telephoned, I cleared the table, leaving the two glasses of wine behind. I sipped mine and let it go down slowly. I certainly liked wine a lot better than hard liquor.

"She's home, let's go," Jack said, hanging up. "Leave the dishes. We'll do them in the morning."

"You can't be there when I question her. It's pretty sensitive stuff."

"I'll drop you off and wait outside. Maybe I'll take a ride. I'll figure something out." He went to the closet and got his ankle holster, the one he wore when he didn't have a jacket on, and smoothed the Velcro flaps around the leather and padding. He also put a pouch of extra bullets on his belt, quickly, efficiently. "Let's go," he said, fitting his off-duty gun into the holster. I could see he was in no mood to wait.

The lights were on in the McVeigh house and the streets were empty of little children and old men with canes. Jean opened the door on the first ring.

"Where's Jack?"

"He'll come back later. I just want to talk."

"Talk." She sat on the sofa in front of a stack of sealed envelopes that lay on the coffee table. She had been writing notes to thank people for their comfort in her time of bereavement. It couldn't have been a very uplifting task.

"You said you saw Jerry McMahon at a party. Could that have been on Labor Day?"

There's a certain look people give you when they realize you've been checking up on what they've told you. That's the way Jean looked at me at that moment, as though she knew she had to watch herself, that there were other sources of information that could confirm or cast doubt on what she said. "It was Labor Day," she said.

There was giggling upstairs. The kids were playing before going to bed.

"Is that where you saw him?"

"Him and a lot of other people. It was a big party."

"Did you and Ray end up in a bedroom together there?"

"No," she said vehemently. "No, we didn't. Is that what Betsy told you? She's hallucinating."

"Did anything happen that day with Ray?"

"We talked. We gave each other looks. We never touched each other, Chris. We were never alone together anywhere."

Maybe Betsy *was* hallucinating. Someone was mistaken or lying and both women struck me as utterly sincere.

"Then the motel was the only time," I said.

"I told you that already." She looked at the stacks of notes she had written to people who had cared about her husband. "And since you're obviously getting bits and pieces of information from unreliable sources, let me tell you the rest, so you'll have the story. You know this much and you're not stupid and I'd rather have you hear it from me and not guess at things that may or may not have happened. There was nothing wrong with our car that night. I asked Scotty to drive me to the Hansens' because I said I didn't feel secure on icy streets. I knew Ray would take me home. I wanted to be alone with him in the car for the ride home. OK?"

"Could anyone have seen you that night?"

"I can't imagine how."

"What about at the party? Could someone have seen you and Ray together and made something of it?"

"I don't think so, Chris. I was just walking around, talking to people. I went inside once to look at the house. It was a gorgeous place. I went upstairs and used the bathroom. It was all marble inside, really beautiful. I didn't see any of the bedrooms, though, because all the doors were closed. There were people in one of them. Men. I could hear their voices. You know cops. They can't talk about anything else besides the job, even when they're at a party."

"You said you saw Jerry McMahon at that party. Do you remember where or who he was with?"

"He was just sort of around. He was there with a gorgeous blonde with a lot more up here than I have." She patted her chest. "But I saw him just walking around, talking to people. Oh, yeah." She sounded as though she had just remembered something. "When I left the bathroom, he walked into the bedroom where I heard the voices."

"Did you see anyone else in the room?" My heart was beating faster now.

"No one. He just went in and shut the door."

I got up and went to a credenza against the wall. There was a group of family pictures at one end—the children, Jean and Scotty, the whole family in the backyard, and one of three grinning rookie police officers in uniform: Scotty; Jack; and Ray. I held it in my hand for a long time before going back to where Jean was sitting and watching me.

"They were so young and happy there," she said.

"Tell me about St. Patrick's Day," I said, sitting down.

"Again."

"I'm afraid so. Start with the morning."

"We had breakfast together. Scotty put his uniform on and took the car. He was going to park it at the pier and then find his unit to march with. The kids and I left later. We went by train. We had a long block to walk in Manhattan to meet you and Petra. That's it."

"After Scotty marched by, you left."

"I took my kids to my mother's in Brooklyn. You know that."

"And then you came back to the pier for the party."

"I took the subway." She flashed a smile. "I was the only sober one on the whole train."

"I can imagine. Anything happen on that trip? Could you have been followed?"

"If I was, I didn't know it."

"Did you walk from the subway to the pier? The pier was all the way over on the river."

"I took a cab. It was only a few blocks, but I knew I'd be on my feet at the party."

"We all left the party on the pier together. Where did you go?"

"We went to Petra's. We all went upstairs for a little while. Then Scotty and I left. My mother's house is so close, we just left the car and walked over. He had some clothes there he changed into."

"And you walked back later in time for dinner," I said, knowing I shouldn't be putting words in her mouth.

"Yes. What is it you're looking for?"

"I wish I knew." Someone had to have followed them when they left Manhattan, someone who saw them go into Petra's apartment house. Had he then waited for hours for the McVeighs and us to leave and then followed us to the bar? "You only stayed in Petra's place for a little while? After the parade, I mean."

"Ten minutes. They were giving each other looks like they couldn't wait to get into a bedroom. And I was really happy for them. I wanted something good to happen with them. There was nothing between Ray and me, there never had been. It had been a crazy flirtation and I was sorry for it. I really was," she said, looking at me earnestly. "And I had just told Ray that."

"When? At the party on the pier?" I had seen her look at him, but I hadn't seen her talk to him alone. Besides, having a private conversation in that mayhem was an absolute impossibility.

"On the way home."

"What?"

"Scotty gave the keys to the BMW to Ray, so he could drive it to Brooklyn. You know Scotty. He has a new toy, he wants everyone to try it out."

"Ray Hansen drove the BMW to Brooklyn when you left the party?"

"And I went with him. It was just perfect. I would get a

chance to talk to him and Petra knew how to get to her place, so she could show Scotty the way."

"Jean." I got up and went to the credenza where the pictures were. "Look at this picture." I handed her the one of the three friends. "If you were describing Scotty, what would you say?"

"Six-one, a hundred seventy or so, lean, fair, sandy hair, blue-gray eyes."

"What about Ray?"

"He's about the same height, maybe a few pounds less than Scotty, dirty-blond hair ... What are you telling me?"

"That in the dark, one man of that height and weight with a redheaded woman at his side could be mistaken for the other one."

Her face paled. "They were after Ray?"

"Someone was watching Ray leave the pier on St. Patrick's Day. He went to a BMW with a redheaded woman and drove to Brooklyn. Maybe the killer saw you and Scotty leave ten minutes later, maybe he didn't. But when the four of us left about eleven that night, Scotty was with the redhead."

"But we switched cars."

"I know, but there was no mistaking Jack for Ray Hansen. Or me for you. Maybe the killer realized at that point that we'd switched cars. When we went into the bar, he pulled into the lot and waited. Sure enough, when the redhead's companion walked up to the BMW, he knew it was the same man he'd seen leaving the pier that morning."

"I think it's crazy," Jean said, but her voice was low and unsteady. She looked at the photograph and ran her finger over the faces. "You think if I'd driven to Brooklyn with Scotty, he'd still be alive."

"Don't think about it, Jean." I patted her back and got up. "I saw Charles Hanrahan this afternoon. Scotty's grandfather."

She stared at me. "You found him? You talked to him?"

"Yes. He knows all about you and the children. Scotty used to drop by and see him."

"Poor Scotty," she said. "How could he have thought it would make a difference to me?"

"He'd like to meet you. We can talk about it when things have settled down." As I put my coat on, the doorbell rang.

Jack was standing on the doorstep. "I was getting cold," he said. "Hiya, Jean, honey. How're you doing?" He hugged her, and she wrapped her arms around him.

"I'm kind of worn out," she said. "But that's nothing to the way you're going to feel when Chris gets finished tonight. I think you've got some running around to do."

It was no exaggeration.

26

"You want to go where?" Jack said, backing out of the driveway.

"To the Korean grocery on Scotty's beat, the Happy Times. My map's in my car, but I think I know how to go."

"I know where it is. What've you got?"

I didn't have to tell him much for him to see what I was driving at. It did take a minute of reflection to see that Scotty could have been mistaken for Ray.

"You've known them so long," I said. "You saw them as individuals. If a killer only had an ID photo to go by, if he spotted Ray at the party and watched him get into a BMW with a redhead, then saw that redhead late at night with a man the same size and shape as Ray, it's an easy mistake to make."

"So what are we going grocery shopping for?"

"Because of Joo's gun. I just don't like the disappearance of that gun twenty-four hours after Scotty was killed."

"Well, let's find out."

The lights were all on in the Happy Times Grocery. As Jack pulled into a space across the street, I wondered when those poor people slept and where they got the energy to work such long hours.

Jack stayed in the car, and I crossed the street. Two customers were looking over the fruits in the bins along the sidewalk and two more were inside. I nodded to the young woman at the cash register and went to the back where Mr. Ma had been on my previous visits. He was there, helping Joo to open some crates.

"Excuse me," I said, and they turned around. I reminded them who I was, but I didn't have to.

"I know you," Ma said. "You came with Mrs. McVeigh."

"That's right." I hoped he wouldn't associate me with Joo's arrest for not reporting the stolen gun.

"And you got a good lawyer for my cousin."

"He's a very good lawyer," I said. "I hope everything is all right."

"Not all right, but a little better. Can I help you?"

"After Officer McVeigh was killed, did the police come to ask you questions?"

"Many questions."

"Do you remember when they came?"

Joo turned to me and said in English, "They came about lunchtime on the first day after Officer McVeigh died."

"Monday?"

"Yes."

"I thought you went to school on Monday."

"I go Monday afternoon, Monday evening."

"Did they ask you about your gun?"

"No."

"They ask me," his older cousin said. "I have no gun. I tell the truth."

Jack had said that the Koreans had claimed to understand no English during the canvassing. "Did you speak in English to them?"

"We say little. We not understand. It is better with the police."

"So nobody knew about the gun till after it was stolen?"

"No, no," Ma said. "They come back at night."

"Who came back? The ones who questioned you at noon?"

"Other police. Very mean. They ask for my cousin. I tell them he is in school. They go away."

"Did they come back again after that?"

"No."

"Thank you very much," I said.

"You know who killed Officer McVeigh?" the older cousin asked.

"No," I said. "I'm sorry about your gun, Mr. Joo."

Jack was watching as I crossed the street. Not many other businesses were open, but the Happy Times looked as if it was ready to go all night. "Here's what I think," I said as I got into the car. "The detectives assigned to Scotty's homicide came to ask the Koreans questions about noon on March eighteenth. They asked Mr. Ma if he had a gun and he said no, which was true. The Koreans volunteered nothing and they pretended to speak very little English. Joo was there. He left for his classes later. At night other cops came and asked about Joo, but he was at class. I think they were the ones who killed Scotty and they'd discovered their mistake. During the day, they probably checked everyone who works on Scotty's beat, not just the storeowners, and found Joo had a .44."

"OK," Jack said. "So now they've got a fall guy, someone Scotty had a relationship with. They've made a mistake and they're frantic. If nothing else pans out, they can point the finger at Joo. All he has to support his alibi that he was working on St. Patrick's Day is his family and nobody'll believe them because that's what you expect a family to say."

"But what they really want is to build a case against Ray, a case that will hold up under investigation, that will convince a D.A. to take it to the grand jury, one that will stick in court."

"Right. When they found they'd killed the wrong man, they decided to nail their target as the killer. They must have scrambled all that week to build a case and leak what they had to the team investigating the homicide."

"And the case had to be that Ray was in love with Scotty's wife." I could just feel things fall into place. Besides the detectives assigned to the case, the killers were also out canvassing. Who would know if they were questioned by the real team or the shadow team?

And poor Joo. If they hadn't found the gun in his apartment while he was at class, they probably would have waited for him to come home and gotten it from him then. How could he have imagined he was being set up to stand in for a killer?

"So we're pretty sure it's a brother officer we're looking for," Jack said.

"It's the same people who killed Donner and Moore."

"Honey, Moore was killed—"

"I know. And I can't really figure out what's wrong there, but something is. That Tom Macklin who arrested the kid last Friday has to be part of it. And he was connected with Moore."

"OK. I can guess where you want to go next."

"I don't look forward to it, but we have to talk to Ray."

"Let me find out where he is."

There was a pay phone on the corner and I waited in the car while he called. I didn't want to do this in front of Petra—I didn't want to do this at all, but I had to.

"He's at Petra's," Jack said, getting into the car. "We'll meet him at his place. I have a strong sense that we've ruined his evening, both their evenings."

"I'm not apologizing."

"I'm not asking you to." He patted my thigh.

I wanted to be back at his apartment with him as much as Ray wanted to be with Petra. But there wasn't time for anything else right now. Whoever they were, they might be only a few steps behind me. Someone had rung Jack's bell the other night, probably to break in if he wasn't home. If they were selling drugs that they picked up on raids, there was big money involved and a long prison sentence if they were found out. There was very little risk at this point in adding another body to their collection.

Ray was just walking up the driveway when we pulled into it. He unlocked his door, and we followed him inside.

"Look," he said when we had dropped our coats on a chair, "I have a very competent lawyer who knows what he's doing and the best thing you can both do is stay out of the case."

"Chris has learned a lot in the last couple of weeks," Jack said.

"I don't want to talk to Chris," Ray said irritably. "I don't want to talk to you, either, buddy. Look, you're a nice girl, Chris, and I know your heart is in the right place, but I wish you'd leave this to the professionals."

I really hate being patronized. I started to say something when Jack stepped in. "It was Chris that figured out that you were the target, not Scotty, and that when the killers found out they'd gotten the wrong guy, they decided to set you up for the killing. You take the collar, they take a walk."

He didn't look at us. He got up off the sofa he'd been sitting on and walked nervously away, then back again. I kept trying to see him as Scotty, the long, lean body, the hair that might once have been gold. The only difference was the facial details and the lack of a smile. Scotty had always seemed to be on the verge of smiling.

"I knew something was going on," he said, stopping and shoving his hands in his pockets. "I'd gotten a couple of warnings on the phone, nothing specific, just somebody saying, 'Mind your own business.' "

"Any idea who it was?" Jack asked.

"Yeah," Ray said, with a little laugh. "I thought it was McMahon till they found him dead."

"Why McMahon?"

"Because I saw him in what you might call a compromising situation and I don't mean sex."

"At the party on Labor Day?" I said.

He said, "Yeah," and I could tell he was impressed that I knew.

"Who else was there?" Jack asked.

"I didn't know the others. I hardly got a look at them. I'd seen McMahon, I knew who he was, and he knew I'd heard what was going on in that room."

"What did you hear?" Jack and I asked almost together.

"There was going to be a raid. They didn't mention a place or a time, but it was obviously something that was ready to go down. And this was going to be a big one, big enough that they could do their scam. They didn't say anything specific, but it was pretty damn clear they were going to hold back a sizable chunk of the haul and merchandise it themselves, somebody said a key." He looked at me. "A kilo. It was also clear they'd done it before, but I got the feeling they didn't do it every time, just selectively, when they thought they could get away with it. Understand I didn't hear much, but I didn't have to. I knew what the hell they were doing. And then the door opened, and I was looking right into McMahon's face."

"You get on it?" Jack asked.

"Sure I got on it. I talked to McMahon's partner and got nowhere. I even asked you about McMahon because I knew he was at the Six-Five."

"I remember."

"You didn't tell me a damn thing I could work with."

"You didn't tell me what you were looking for."

"I wanted to keep the trouble in my own house."

"Well, you sure did that."

"Ray," I said, "I think it may have been McMahon who called you the day after you were charged and told you they were coming with a warrant to search your apartment."

"Why?" he asked, suddenly interested in what I had to say.

"Because I think McMahon was trying to help you without blowing his cover. He may have known about the .44-caliber bullets. It was probably McMahon who arranged to meet with me a week ago tonight near Lincoln Center, but he never came."

"They must have gotten to him first."

"I bet you were warned to keep quiet about what you heard on Labor Day or they'd expose your relationship with Jean McVeigh."

"It wasn't a relationship," he said in a low voice.

"Were you?" Jack asked. "Threatened? Blackmailed?"

"I told you, it was a couple of calls. One said, 'Keep quiet or we'll talk about your girlfriend, the redheaded Irish one.' I didn't want to get Jean in that kind of trouble. It would have killed Scotty."

I didn't mention that it already had. "How many were in that room?" I asked.

"Maybe four besides McMahon. Maybe only three. I only saw inside for a second." He turned away from us and rubbed his forehead. "You know, besides the threats, someone did call to warn me before St. Patrick's Day. Just a quick call, something like, 'Watch your back, Ray.' If you're right, that could have been McMahon."

"Ray, could anyone have seen you and Jean together the night you went to the motel?"

"I'd say that's pretty near impossible. I didn't know it was going to happen until it happened."

"Did the threats mentioning your Irish girlfriend start after that night?"

He didn't stop to think about it. "No. That came later, after I'd moved out of the house."

"Then how the hell did they know?" Jack asked.

"Beats me. After they found those .44 bullets in my drawer, I figured if someone broke in here to leave them to incriminate me, someone must have broken in earlier and found the letter."

"But the letter is signed 'Jean,' " I said. "There's no return address. Even if someone read it, it's not an obvious connection."

"Well, someone sure as hell made it," he said, with anger. "I never talked about it, and I'm sure Jean didn't, either."

I felt a small sick sensation. "Did you give Petra a key to this apartment?" I asked.

"Leave Petra out of this," he said, his voice rising.

"Did you?" Jack asked.

"This is crazy. Petra has nothing to do with any of this."

"Answer me, Ray," Jack said.

"I didn't give her a key till St. Patrick's Day. That afternoon, when we got home from the parade. OK?"

I didn't want to pursue it further. I liked Petra. I trusted her. I was absolutely convinced she was crazy about Ray. But I couldn't overlook the obvious. "Did you ever leave her alone in the apartment?"

He stopped pacing. His back was to us. "Once or twice," he said dully. "After we met. I went out to buy some cake or something. She stayed here to make the coffee." He turned around. "OK, it's possible, but I don't think it happened that way."

"Did she know who Jean and Scotty were?" I asked.

"Sure she knew. I talked about them. I talked about you guys. I think she met them." He stopped. "Not long after we started going out."

He looked grim now, worried. He was a professional who asked questions for a living, put two and two together and saw them add up when others told him it couldn't be, it wasn't possible, it was all a mistake. His face showed what he was going through, the metamorphosis from witness to investigator, lover to accuser. He was starting to look at this as a case and himself as the detective in charge. I felt deeply sorry for him, sorrier still that I had a hand in generating all these suspicions.

"OK, we have a possibility," Jack said. "Let me get something straight. Did you indicate to the guy who called that you'd cooperate and keep quiet?"

"At first, yes. I wanted time to see where it was going, to find out who was involved. And I wanted to keep Jean out of it."

"But you changed your mind."

"I never changed my mind, damn it! I was just waiting for the right time to get those bastards. What I said to them and what I was doing were two different things."

"When was the last time you heard from them?"

"Before St. Patrick's Day. A few days, maybe a week."

"And you lost your cool," Jack said.

"Right. I told them to go to hell."

And that had signed Scotty's death sentence.

Jack turned to me. "Anything else?"

There *was* something else. Betsy had said Ray was in a bedroom with a woman during the Labor Day party. Jean had sworn it hadn't happened. The time had come to clean up loose ends. "You were in a bedroom with a woman at the party on Labor Day."

Ray's lips loosened to a half smile. "Right."

"Would you mind telling us who it was?"

"You're not going to believe it, but here goes. The woman was Sharon Moore."

27

He was right that I couldn't believe it. I couldn't even find my voice to say something.

"Lay it out," Jack said.

"I saw her outside the house. I'd never met her before. She was sitting alone, looking depressed. I sat and talked to her. It was almost two years since her husband had been killed and she was feeling it."

"What was she doing there?" Jack asked.

"Lieutenant Connelly had run that little group Moore was part of."

The big house, the marble bathrooms, the lush green acreage. Pretty nice for a lieutenant just earning his salary. "Ray," I began.

"You don't have to ask. She started to cry and I took her into the house. It wasn't a bedroom, it was a study on the second floor. We just sat and talked. I went out to use the bathroom and that's when I heard the conversation in the bedroom and McMahon opened the door. I went back to Sharon and we talked till Betsy called and I went downstairs. Sharon stayed in the study. I never saw her again."

"Did she know your name?" She hadn't said anything about having met him when I talked to her.

He shrugged. "Maybe. I don't know. It wasn't a very big deal. She was more wrapped up in her grief than about who I was."

I said, "Thank you," and Ray nodded.

"We done?" he asked.

"Not yet," Jack said. "The name Tom Macklin mean anything to you?"

"Yeah. It does." Ray sat down across from us. "Sharon

Moore mentioned him that day. He was part of Moore's team. She said he came to the house to bring her the news the night Moore was shot even before the chaplain came. That's not procedural."

I looked at Jack but didn't say anything. Sharon Moore had said her husband was killed in an out-of-the-way place on his way to a bust. A week ago the boys who had presumably shot him had been arrested. How did Macklin happen to be the person who carried the bad news to Moore's widow? It didn't seem right; it seemed like an amazing coincidence.

"He's the guy who picked up one of Moore's killers last Friday night," Jack said.

"Sounds like he's always first man on the scene. Why don't you two tell me what you know? I've been answering a lot of questions tonight. You owe me a little information."

"Chris found a connection between Moore and Harry Donner."

"Interesting."

I told him about it, adding what Sharon Moore had told me that morning, that her husband had become very nervous after Donner's death, taking his family out of the city and far away during that summer.

"You think after Donner got it, Moore thought he'd be next?"

"It looks that way," I said. "But I don't think his wife had any inkling." As I spoke, something occurred to me.

"What's wrong?" Jack said.

"Sister Benedicta. Ray, may I use your phone?"

He pointed to it, and I called information for the number of the convent. I must admit that after I wrote down the number, I stopped and reconsidered. Nuns go to sleep early because they're up at five for morning prayers. Old nuns go to sleep even earlier. It was now after eleven and the entire convent would be asleep, but I knew I had to do it. I dialed and bit my lip.

"Yes," a woman's voice said shortly.

"Excuse me, Sister. My name is Christine Bennett and I am concerned about Sister Benedicta who lives in the villa. I visited her—"

"She isn't here."

"Can you tell me where she is?"

"No, I cannot. She had some business in New York and she took a train there several hours ago. I don't know what all this interest is in Sister Benedicta, but—"

"Has someone else called?" I asked, interrupting.

"They have called, they have visited, they have upset my convent."

"I'm very sorry," I said. "Did Sister Benedicta leave an address with you where she can be reached?"

"Yes, she did, and I am not giving it to you or anyone else. And now, if you don't mind, we have come to the end of this conversation."

I hung up and turned back toward the large room that was Ray's entire apartment. "She's gone."

"Gone where?" Jack got up.

"She wouldn't tell me. There have been calls and visits. She said Sister Benedicta had business in New York. I'm worried, Jack. I've left a long trail in the last two weeks and Moore's old group may have questioned some of the people I've talked to. It wouldn't take much for someone to find Sister Benedicta just the way I did."

"Who would she see in New York?"

"I don't know. Maybe Macklin or another member of Moore's group lured her into the city. But I can't believe they'd talk to her in a station house. An old nun in a long white habit is very visible."

"They could have met her at the train and taken her somewhere."

I started to feel panicky. "Let's go. I have to think." But what I was thinking was scaring me to death.

28

"We won't get anything out of Macklin," Jack said as we got into the car. "We have to build a case against him."

"I know. What I'm worried about now is Sister Benedicta. With Donner and his wife gone, there can't be anyone she'd go to unless someone convinced her somehow that he was working to find Harry's killer."

"How savvy is she?"

"She's no innocent, Jack. She once found some people in the hospital embezzling. She worked it out herself. And Harry told her Moore had come to talk to him. Maybe she just left the convent to protect herself."

"You want to get some sleep?"

"Desperately." I laughed. "But I think we should talk to Petra first. Before Ray does."

"Let's do it."

We had to ring several times before Petra answered on the intercom. People trying to get into an apartment house often ring several bells, hoping someone will buzz them in, so if you hear a ring in the middle of the night, your instinct is to ignore it.

"Who is it?" she called finally.

"It's Chris Bennett. Can I come up?"

"Chris? Now?"

"Please, Petra. It's very important."

The buzzer rang, and Jack pushed the door open. The elevator was on the ground floor, and we rode up, saying nothing. I leaned sleepily against Jack until the elevator lurched to a stop.

Petra had the door open a crack, and we went in without saying much. She had put a robe on over a white nightgown, yards of which swirled around her ankles. She looked only half-awake.

"I was sleeping," she said.

"I'm sorry." I sat down in my coat, feeling cold and tired myself. It was a gamble, and if she was clever—or innocent—it wouldn't work. Jack and I had agreed to let me make the first try. He stood away from us, admiring Petra's pretty things, but I knew he was listening to every word. "You found the letter in Ray's apartment when you were there alone a couple of months ago."

Her eyes opened. "What letter?"

"And you told Tom Macklin about it." It was the only name I knew.

Her body flinched, then stiffened. "I don't know what you mean," she said, but it was clear that she did.

"How could you do that to Ray?"

"Do what? I love Ray. You know that. We love each other. I believe in him. He's innocent. I'm his witness."

"Petra, Ray left you alone in his apartment a couple of months ago while he went out to buy something."

"It's possible," she said. "I don't remember everything that ever happened. Do you?"

"But you remember that because someone asked you to dig up something ugly about Ray. You read the letter and you left it there, so he wouldn't know you had seen it. You set him up, Petra." I had a hard time saying it. I still only half believed it, and if she kept denying it, I was lost.

"I thought you were my friend." Her voice shook and her mouth trembled.

"I was your friend. But you betrayed Ray."

"Get out of here," she said in a voice nearly out of control. "Both of you. Now. Don't ever come back."

"Come on, Chris," Jack said.

I got up. "I'm sorry, Petra, but we know the truth. You gave someone your key to Ray's apartment, so they could get in while Ray was being arrested. They left incriminating evidence there, false evidence, evidence that might convict him."

"How dare you! I never did that. I never gave anyone the key. Never." She was awake now, enraged. When I had accused her of finding the letter, she had been surprised but relatively calm. She wasn't calm now, she was furious. I had a sense that I was beginning to understand the truth.

Jack had the door open and when he closed it, we heard the bolt snap and the chain shoved angrily into place. "Let's go," he said, and immediately put a finger to his lips.

The elevator was still there. He pressed the button, and, when the door opened noisily, he reached in, pushed a button, and stepped out. The door closed, again noisily, and the elevator went down. Quietly we walked back to Petra's door and listened. We could hear her voice, although what she was saying was pretty much unintelligible, except when she said "No!" loudly. The building was solid and the only reason we heard anything was the absolute silence of everything else on the floor.

The conversation ended abruptly. Then we heard Petra's voice again, this time at a lower volume. It was a short call, and I wasn't entirely sure when it ended. Jack signaled me away from the door. We went down one flight of stairs, where the elevator was waiting, and rode the rest of the way to the lobby.

"Let's give it some time," he said as we walked to the car. "She may be going somewhere."

"I didn't do very well."

"You did fine. She knows we're onto her."

"You know, Jack, I had the feeling she definitely read that letter from Jean and passed the contents along, but she was so enraged about the key, maybe she didn't give it to anyone. Maybe she changed her mind between January and March."

"Could be. Look down the street."

A private cab was coming slowly toward us, stopping to check house numbers. Petra was on the move. As though I had awakened from a restful sleep, I felt myself suddenly get a second wind. I was alert again. The taxi stopped right at the entrance to her apartment house. Two minutes later a woman, wrapped in a warm coat, came out and slid into the backseat. It wasn't all that easy to identify her in the darkness, but I was sure it was Petra. Jack turned the key, waited for the cab to pass, made a U, and started to follow. He was halfway down the block before he put his lights on.

We kept well behind as the taxi led us through Brooklyn streets. It was too dark to read the street names, and I felt thoroughly lost until we turned into a wide street.

"You know where we're going?" Jack asked.

"I have an idea."

A car turned in from a side street, putting a little distance between us and the cab, but it wasn't hard to keep an eye on our prey. In fact, it made me feel a little easier in case the cabbie glanced in his rearview mirror once in a while. When he made the next turn, I tensed.

"I don't believe it," I said.

"Neither do I."

A few blocks more and we were in a familiar, quiet residential area. The cab's brake lights went on and Jack stopped abruptly and turned his lights off, letting the cab pull well ahead of us. We were too far away to identify the house, but I had no doubt whatsoever. Petra was already on her way to Jean McVeigh's door.

The cab remained in front of Jean's house. After a minute, the door opened, and Petra went inside. The cab's lights went off. Inside the McVeigh house, one upstairs light was lit and a couple downstairs.

"I can't believe Jean is involved in this," I said.

"Did you mention her name to Petra?"

"No. I was very careful. I only mentioned Tom Macklin."

Jack left his ignition key turned just enough so that the digital clock was on. Petra stayed inside about twelve minutes. When she came out, she went directly to the cab. The rear lights went on just as the first-floor lights in the house went off.

"Let's see where she goes next."

I hoped it would be to Macklin. I needed a concrete connection and everything I had was supposition. Jack followed with his lights off for several blocks. When a series of left turns took us back to the street that led to Brooklyn, Jack turned his lights on, and I resigned myself to driving back to where Petra lived, which is what happened. Jack didn't bother turning into her street. He stopped at the corner, where we could watch the cab. It let Petra off, and she hurried into her building. The cab pulled away. She had finished her traveling for the night.

"Let's get some sleep," Jack said.

I relaxed and closed my eyes. What I needed to figure out now was where Sister Benedicta was. I had to assume the men on Moore's team were at least as capable as I at tracking down a witness. If they had interviewed Harry Donner's next-door neighbor, it wouldn't have taken much to find his aunt Benny. I drifted into sleep, awakening when Jack put his hand on mine.

"We're home," he said. "Can you walk a couple of blocks or should I drop you off at the apartment?"

"I can walk," I said groggily.

"Sure?"

"Mm-hmm."

We got out, and he put an arm around me. I wasn't sure what street we were on. Brooklyn Heights is full of streets with narrow buildings that were once single-family homes and are now split up into apartments. One street looks very much like another, especially at night. We walked around a corner and there was an air of familiarity. Half a block more and we would be home.

We were almost at the front door when someone literally stepped out of the shadows.

"Brooks?"

Jack tensed and I froze. I could sense Jack's right hand move toward his gun as he stepped in front of me.

"Who's there?" he said.

"Relax. It's Tim O'Brien."

Neither of us relaxed. Jack said, "Stay here," to me and he moved forward alone as I thought how crazy our lives had become. Two days ago Tim O'Brien was someone we trusted. Tonight everyone had become a suspect.

The men spoke quietly for only a minute. Then Jack turned. "It's OK, Chris. We're going up."

"You guys are really uptight," O'Brien said as we went up the stairs.

"These days you can't tell a friend from an enemy." Jack unlocked the door, and we went in. The answering machine was blinking.

"That's me," O'Brien said. "I called a couple of times and finally decided to come over and see if you were in. They found something in Jerry's car, in the trunk. They called me over to see if I could identify it. It's a bunch of old clothes that still reek of alcohol and a bag full of rags. The coat hasn't dried out completely yet. They found something in the pocket that looks like it could be a false beard or something like that. It's pretty much falling apart now."

"What do you make of it?" Jack asked.

"It's crazy. It's like the stuff actors wear and some of the guys when they work in decoy units. Jerry never worked in a decoy unit. I've seen him five days a week for over two years."

"The homeless man," I said.

"I really blew that one, didn't I?"

"There's something else," O'Brien said. "They found a gold ring in the clothes. It's hard to tell if it came out of the pocket, but the guys who took the stuff out of the trunk think it did. It's a high school ring from Forest Hills High and it has the initials *G.J.B.* in it."

"Any ideas?" Jack asked.

"I checked with the PBA. They've got a George Barker, middle name John. Jerry talked about him once. Said he'd met him somewhere on the job. I asked a few questions. A couple of years ago Barker worked with Gavin Moore."

"You know who the rest of the team are?"

"I found out tonight. There's a Ricardo Ramirez, a Paul Dorgan, and a Tom Macklin. At one time or another, I heard Jerry mention all of them."

"Figures."

"Our homeless man must have dropped his ring in his coat pocket last Friday night," I said, "so you wouldn't see the gold."

"You know who this guy is?"

We explained.

Then I added what I had finally decided really happened over two and a half years ago. "After Gavin Moore talked to Harry Donner about what was going on in his buy-and-bust team, Donner started asking questions. Someone in that group killed him and Moore knew why. He was nervous that summer and took his family out of New York. But when they got back, he was sure they were going to kill him. I think he even guessed the night it would happen. Maybe he decided not to show up that night, maybe he couldn't make up his mind. He drove to a park that wasn't on the way to the place where they were meeting, but someone was following him. I think it must have been Tom Macklin. He saw his chance to kill Moore right there, but a bunch of kids got to him first. Macklin knew who those kids were and he's probably kept an eye on them since the killing. He picked up that one last Friday night because that was the night they planned to kill Jerry McMahon."

"Because they were tailing him and they figured out he was trying to help Ray Hansen," Tim said.

"Right. And solving the Moore killing when McMahon disappeared would prevent anyone from connecting McMahon to the Moore team."

"Not bad," Jack said.

"I want to see the kid who was arrested last week, the one who named names. I want to ask him if Macklin was in the park that night two and a half years ago. And in case it wasn't Macklin, we'll need photos of the other members of the team."

"That's tough," Jack said. "Especially on a Saturday."

O'Brien was rubbing his forehead. "I've got a friend in Personnel, someone I worked for. He's a very straight arrow. He'll do it for me."

"On Saturday?"

"He'll have to. I'll meet him at headquarters, get the pictures, and make up some photo layouts. I'll meet you at Rikers."

I shivered at the prospect, but we agreed on a time and place. I had the sense that we were getting somewhere, that the end was close. But I was too tired to think about it. For me, the long Friday night was finally over.

29

It was a busy Saturday. Jack made arrangements to interview the prisoner whose name was Johnny Waldo. When he finally hung up from making all his calls, the phone rang. It was Jean McVeigh. Jack did more listening than talking.

Afterward he said, "Petra told her you and I knew about the letter and wanted to make it public to smear Jean's name. At least that's what Jean got out of that unannounced visit. Petra said she was doing her best to protect Jean, that she'd been questioned this week about whether she knew of a relationship between Ray and Jean and that she'd denied having any knowledge of it. Jean's feeling a little confused. I told her Petra was just covering herself, looking for support. I promised we wouldn't say anything to anyone. By the way, she said she called last night and left a message. I guess I should have listened to that tape." He pressed the Play button.

The first message caught me by surprise. It was a solemn female voice, speaking slowly and carefully. "This is Melanie Gross. I am trying to reach Sergeant Jack Brooks of the New York Police Department. I must speak to Chris immediately. If I have reached the right number, please call me right away."

I said, "Uh-oh," and went to the telephone. The next message was from Jean. The last three were from Tim O'Brien. "I'd better call."

"Make it quick. We have to meet O'Brien."

Mel was overjoyed to hear from me. "You won't believe this, but you have a guest."

"A what?"

"A nun named Sister Benedicta."

197

"She came to visit *me*?"

"I found her on your doorstep around dinnertime. You know, you've never given me Jack's address or phone number, but I was pretty sure it was Brooklyn. You wouldn't believe how many messages I left last night."

"You're an angel, Mel. Is she all right?"

"She's terrific. I'm thinking of opening a home for friends of Chris Bennett. They're all so nice. She's reading to the kids now and they're teaching her to play some of their games. Is it all right if she gambles?"

I laughed. "She knows exactly what's right for her. Mel, I can't get home till tonight. Do you have a pencil?"

"In my hand."

"I'm going to give you four names. Ask her to think about them, whether she recognizes them or not." I dictated the names, and Mel read them back to me.

"Dare I ask if you're making progress?"

"Tremendous progress. We just don't quite have it all in place. I'll see you tonight and I thank you more than I can say."

"You don't have to. I think my prestige in the community just went up several notches."

When I hung up, we dashed out of the apartment. The weather had suddenly decided it was spring, something the calendar had decreed a couple of weeks earlier. It would have been a wonderful day to walk in the park or sit with the sun on your back and read a good book. Instead we drove to Rikers Island.

Rikers Island is actually part of the Bronx, but you approach it through the Steinway section of Queens, Steinway as in pianos. The old piano factory is located there. A causeway formally known as the Rikers Island Bridge crosses Rikers Island Channel and Bowery Bay and you can see LaGuardia Airport from it. Jack gave me the Cook's tour as we approached the island, a place I could have happily lived a complete life without ever visiting.

He had arranged our meeting while I was still asleep. An irritable young lawyer with thinning hair and a newish-looking attaché case reluctantly joined us. On this day, he would surely have preferred to be doing what I wanted to do, but I was grateful he had given up his leisure and I told him so.

What you never forget about Rikers is the smell and the noise. The odor of unwashed bodies competes with the equally unpleasant smell of the disinfectant used to cleanse the effects of the other. The two together made me long for the fresh air we had only minutes before left behind. The other assault on your senses is the buzz. There doesn't seem to be a moment of stillness in that place. Some voices rise above the constant murmur, announcements are made over a public-address system, there are angry shouts and bursts of laughter.

For Jack there was the unsettling moment when he relinquished his gun. No one is armed at Rikers, including the corrections officers. Nor, it turned out, was the prisoner we were visiting handcuffed.

We met Johnny Waldo in a room with a couple of small, high windows, a table bolted to the floor, and benches bolted down as well. This was a place where no one in a fit of anger could pick up and throw furniture. Waldo had a face marked with adolescent acne, a nose that may have been broken once or twice, and a sullen look that didn't make me feel confident we would get anything out of him. Tim O'Brien remained outside the conference room, and by agreement, I did the talking.

"You remember the night two and a half years ago that Detective Moore was killed?" I began.

"Yeah," Waldo said, looking at me with curiosity.

"We have some pictures for you to look at. I'd like to know if anyone in any of these pictures was in the park that night."

Jack handed me the first layout, and I placed it in front of Waldo. Each layout contained eight snapshots, each about an inch and a half square, of police officers. Tim O'Brien, who had put them together for us this morning, had cropped the pictures so that very little uniform showed. For the most part, they looked like men staring into a camera, a hint of shirt collar and tie, and little else. The way the layouts were arranged, one of the members of Moore's old team was on each one; the other pictures were selected because they showed some similarity to the person we were interested in. The layout with Ricardo Ramirez contained only Hispanic officers. The one with George Barker, who sported a thick mustache, contained seven other mustachioed faces. I put the one with Barker on the table first. Waldo looked at the faces carefully.

"None of these," he said.

I tried the Hispanics next and got the same response. Paul Dorgan, a typical son of Ireland, nestled among the faces from the Emerald Society. Waldo pushed it away after looking at it. Finally I showed him the layout with Macklin.

"This is the guy that busted me last week," Waldo said, pointing.

"Did you see him in the park two and a half years ago?"

"I never seen him before last Friday night."

"You sure of that?" Jack asked.

"Yeah, I'm sure," Waldo said, as if he were picking a fight.

"Thank you, Johnny," I said. I picked up the last layout and handed it to Jack.

"That's it?" the lawyer asked, with disgust. He had put on a clean shirt for five minutes of work and he wasn't happy about it.

"There was a guy in the park that night," Waldo said as I got up.

"There was?"

"Yeah. But it wasn't any of them guys. It was someone else."

"Would you recognize him?"

"Yeah. You show him to me, I'll recognize him. What's it gonna get me? I didn't kill nobody. You know it and I know it."

"We'll talk about that," Jack said.

"You're damn right we will," the lawyer said. "My client's been very cooperative."

We walked out of the room, and Johnny Waldo was led away into the unceasing smell and din. Watching him go, I felt an unreasonable welling of sympathy for him.

"I forgot about Lieutenant Connelly," I said to Jack.

"You think a lieutenant was playing hit man that night?" O'Brien said, with disbelief.

"Well, someone was. We'll just have to leave it for another day." I felt discouraged. I had been so sure Waldo would identify Macklin as the man.

The lawyer reminded Jack again that his client had been very helpful. Then he ran ahead of us to get out of the place. Jack retrieved his gun, along with O'Brien, and we went out to the parking lot together. I didn't say anything till we were in the car. We drove onto the causeway to Queens and then back toward Brooklyn.

"Petra knows," I said.

"If we can break her."

I hated the sound of it. Somehow her involvement in this was all wrong, but I was convinced she was part of it.

When we got back to the apartment, I called Melanie Gross. Sister Benedicta came to the phone.

"You have very nice friends, Christine," she said.

"Thank you."

"With smart children. I like smart children."

"I hope you're all right."

"I feel very safe here. I got a phone call yesterday that worried me. It was a man who said he was a police detective working on Harry's murder and he wanted to meet me and talk to me. It didn't sound right. I told him I'd be at the convent and then I decided to visit you, even though I called and you weren't home."

"You did the right thing. Did Melanie give you that list of names?"

"They mean nothing to me. But there was a name Harry mentioned. I've been racking my brain to get at it. It's right there, but I can't get it out."

"Could it have been Connelly?" I asked hopefully.

"No, no," she said impatiently.

"Maybe it'll come back to you. I'll be home later and we'll go out to dinner and relax."

"It was a name like— Oh, I don't know. It was something like—" She sighed into the phone. "Cereal," she said. "You know what I mean?"

"Searle?" I said. "Sorrel?"

"No, no," she said again. "That stuff we used to eat when we were children." She'd been a child about fifty years before I had and I had eaten Rice Krispies and cornflakes until I switched to English muffins in my teens. "Didn't your mother ever cook you cereal?" she said.

"Farina?" I asked as it hit me.

"That's it, that's it. I couldn't think of it. Harry said a man named Farina was the middleman, the one who sold the drugs. Do you know him?"

"I certainly do. God bless you, Sister."

"And the same to you. I'll see you when you get home."

There was music playing inside Petra's apartment. She hadn't answered the downstairs bell, so we had waited for someone to open the door for us. I pushed the doorbell and heard her approach.

"Who is it?"

"Chris."

"Go away."

"Petra, I have to talk to you about Joe."

The music stopped. The bolt was turned and the chain released. The door opened, and a somber Petra let us in. The shelves were empty and there were cartons on the floor. She was packing to leave.

"You're ruining my life, do you know that?" she said. She looked a wreck. She was wearing old jeans and a faded floppy top; her hair hung limp and out of control. Although she never looked made up, this afternoon her face was pale and washed out. She walked on bare feet to a chair and sat down. "I didn't do anything, but everyone wants something from me. Well, they all got it and there's nothing left. I'm going back to Germany, where they can't get me anymore."

"When did you meet Joe Farina?" I asked.

"Last year sometime. In the fall maybe."

"You went out with him?"

"A few times."

"Did he introduce you to Ray?"

"He took me to a bar where Ray went sometimes. He said Ray was a dirty cop and they needed information on him."

"Why did you do it, Petra?"

She looked desolate. "I had problems with immigration. My visa. Joe said . . . He threatened me if I wouldn't do it."

"Tell us what you did."

She took a deep breath. "We talked a lot. I asked him questions. But I didn't get anywhere. Finally, one day I told Ray to go buy something while I stayed in his place and made coffee. I went through his closet and his desk and found some notes and things. Then I looked in the drawers in his dresser and there was the letter from Jean. I knew right away who it was and I guessed what happened."

"You told Joe?"

She nodded. "I told him and I said that was it. I said Ray and I were finished; we broke up and it was over. I couldn't get any more information for Joe."

But of course, that had been enough. *Unsubstantiated information on an overheard.*

"You mentioned Tom Macklin," Petra said.

"Did you know him, too?"

"Maybe I met him once, I don't remember. But Joe used to talk about him a lot. He said Tom had worked for the Auto Crime Division for a year and he could get into any car in ten seconds—except a Mercedes." She pronounced it in German and spoke with pride. "That took longer. They're very secure cars."

So they had someone who could steal a car easily.

"What else, Petra?"

"Nothing," she said vehemently. "I was crazy about Ray. I couldn't believe what Joe said about him. After that, I never went to Ray's apartment with him again."

"What about the day Ray was arrested? You had the key."

She covered her face with her hands for a moment. "When he called me and told me, I went to his apartment to get the letter. I didn't know what I would tell him, but I wanted to get it out of there. It was the first time I ever used the key. I went in and someone was there, a man with a big mustache. I said, 'Who are you?' and he pushed me out of the way and ran out. I was shaking, I was so scared. I wanted to call the police, but I was afraid. I didn't know what to do. I locked the door and looked for the letter. It wasn't where I found it the last time. When I saw some kids playing in the driveway, I left. If he came back, they would see him."

The mustache could have been Barker, but we didn't have the layouts with us.

"Did you ever see Joe again?"

"Never. He moved in with some woman he was seeing. He was seeing her before he met me and he went back to her after." She clasped her hands and looked at me. "You talked to Ray, didn't you? He knows, doesn't he?"

"We talked to him last night before we saw you. He didn't believe you had done anything."

Her eyes filled. "He won't talk to me. I called and called. Is it my fault Scotty got killed?"

"It's not your fault," Jack said. "Don't go away, Petra. Nobody's going to immigration about you."

"Did Joe do it?" she asked in a small voice.

"We don't know. Chris, I think we have one more stop to make."

30

We drove to a nearby Laundromat, and Jack called Sharon Moore's number. Joe Farina was working. I directed Jack to the Moore house. Farina's car wasn't around, but Sharon's was in the open garage. I was starting to feel distinctly ill. Petra's situation was bad enough; this one was much worse.

Sharon answered the door. She was wearing a bright red shirt with jeans and she looked better than she had yesterday morning. The furniture was all back in place, her catharsis over. I introduced her to Jack, and we went into the living room and sat down. I could hear kids inside and out. It was Saturday afternoon and they were having fun. I wasn't.

"Hi," she said, shaking hands with Jack.

"We'd like to ask you some questions," Jack said. "There's nothing official and you don't have to answer them if you don't want to."

Some of the color left her face. "Is this about Gavin?"

"It's about a lot of things," I said. "It's about Joe."

"Joe?" Her face tightened. "What about Joe?"

"Do you remember where he was on St. Patrick's Day?"

"He was home."

"All day?"

"He was on call. He said they'd call him if they needed him."

"Did they?"

"Yes. They did."

"When?" I asked.

"Late. I was getting ready for bed when the phone rang. He took it downstairs. He came up and said there was trouble somewhere, rowdy kids or something. He had to go." She looked frightened. "Why are you asking me this?"

"Mrs. Moore," Jack said, "do you remember when he came home?"

"I was sleeping. I really don't know. That was the night of the shooting, wasn't it?"

"Officer Scott McVeigh. He was my friend."

"Why do you think Joe would know anything about it?"

"How long have you known him?"

"A long time. He knew Gavin. He knew the whole team. We used to run into him at, you know, get-togethers. He was always very nice to me. He still is."

"Mrs. Moore, I don't have a warrant and you can ask us to leave if you want, but I'd like to look at Joe's gear, if he keeps any in the house."

She stood and looked at each of us. "I think I'm going to be sick," she said.

I started over to help her, but she put her hand up. "It's OK. It's OK. This is because he knew about Scott McVeigh's wife and Ray Hansen, isn't it?"

I wondered if she had heard about that from "the wives," as she had told me. "It's about a lot of things."

She looked directly at me. "Tell me he didn't kill Gavin."

"He didn't." But I didn't add that someone had saved him the trouble.

"You can look all you want. It's my house. You have my permission."

She led the way upstairs. There were three bedrooms, one with the door closed. She opened it, and we went in. From the closet she pulled out a nylon bag, the kind people carry sporting equipment in, and put it on the bed. Jack opened it and looked inside without touching anything.

"Anything there?" I asked.

"A couple of guns. One of them looks like a .44."

Sharon gasped. "I know he has an off-duty gun. But it's small."

"We'll have to check the serial numbers. If you wouldn't mind, I'd like to take the whole bag with me."

"Go ahead."

"And I'd like you and the children to come to the station house with us. I don't think you should be home when Joe gets here."

She stared at him hard. Then she said, "Anything you say."

Jack pulled a ballpoint pen out of his jacket pocket. Leaving it unopened, he poked around in the bag as Sharon and I watched. "Take a look at this," he said, and I took a step over to the bed and looked inside. There were three guns in there, but that wasn't what he was pointing to. The pen was holding something in place, faceup. It was a police ID photo of Ray Hansen.

Jack took us to the nearest precinct, which is what the *Patrol Guide* says he should do. It wasn't Farina's precinct and it wasn't Jack's, but the detectives we spoke to took our story as seriously as if the crime had occurred in their backyard. Jack made sure that Sharon Moore signed a statement that she had given permission for us to make a search and to take the gym bag from her home. While we were in the station house, they ran a check on the guns in the bag. One of them was legally owned by Joseph Farina. One was a .38 that did not belong to him. It was the kind of gun that had killed Harry Donner, but tests would have to be run to determine whether it had, in fact, been the murder weapon. The third gun, the .44 caliber, also did not belong to Joe Farina. Nor was it likely to be the murder weapon in the McVeigh homicide. It was registered to Sang Joo of the Happy Times Grocery.

It was later than I had anticipated when I got back to Oakwood. Joe Farina had already been taken into custody, along with the members of Gavin Moore's team. There was still a lot of work to do, a lot of evidence to gather, but now they knew what they were looking for, and I was confident it would all fall into place.

Sister Benedicta had already had dinner with the Grosses when I got back, so I took everyone out for ice-cream treats at a favorite spot in the Oakwood shopping center. Then I took her to my house, fixed up the room Sister Joseph had slept in, and we went to bed. On Sunday morning we went to early mass, and later in the day I drove her back to the convent. She was a changed person. She had lived to learn the truth about her nephew's death, and she had helped to uncover that truth. We had a long conversation as we drove back, her recollections of the convent forty, fifty, and sixty years ago absolutely mesmerizing me. When I left her, I felt as though I had known her for years and I promised to visit.

At home, the first of my seeds were just sprouting and my window was filling with that brilliant new green that is never duplicated after spring. From morning till night I could see changes in the little seedlings, a leaf opening, a little plant bending toward the sun. I was absolutely enthralled.

Jack called in the evening with an update. Johnny Waldo had picked Joe Farina's picture out of a layout and identified him as the man in the park the night Gavin Moore was killed. It looked like my theory was right, that Joe Farina was following Moore that night, perhaps to kill him, when the group in the park did the job for him. Probably he had then alerted the team, and Tom Macklin had taken the news of Moore's death to Sharon Moore.

"I saw my folks this afternoon," Jack said when he finished the story. "We have to talk. And I really didn't see much of you over the weekend."

"If I come in tomorrow, I'll have to leave very early Tuesday morning. I'm teaching, remember."

"My sister gave me some goodies. We can have a late dinner together. I don't mind getting up early."

The story was in all the papers Monday morning, full of errors, but essentially correct. Jack was mentioned, and, happily, I wasn't. I had asked specifically if they would keep my name out of the news. While I was getting my house back together and laundry done, the phone rang. It was Ray Hansen with a thank-you and what I took to be an apology. The charges had been formally withdrawn and he had had his badge and weapon returned. He was feeling like a cop again.

A little while later the doorbell rang, and a florist handed me a box, which turned out to have a dozen roses in it from Ray. It was a strange feeling for me. Having spent all those years in the convent, these were the first flowers of my life. Like the nun I used to be, I started thinking whom I could give a few, to share the pleasure. Then I decided this was one gift I didn't want to share. I put them in a vase on the coffee table in the living room, and every time I walked through the room, I smiled when I saw them.

Jean was the next call. "Something crazy just happened, Chris," she said. "You know that Armenian jeweler on Scotty's beat?"

"I remember seeing it, yes."

"The owner just drove over. He gave me a gold chain Scotty ordered for my birthday. It's just beautiful."

"The things in their window were lovely. Is today your birthday?"

"Yes. Scotty was probably going to pick it up. It makes me feel weird."

"It should make you feel good, Jean."

"That must have been part of the three thousand. I wish he'd gotten something for himself."

"He got the car."

"Oh. I forgot the car. We'll get together soon, Chris. I'll make lunch and I'll wear the chain. I want you to see it."

I promised we'd do it. Then I went out and did some food shopping.

In the evening I drove down to Brooklyn. A radio news report announced that one of the guns in Farina's gym bag had been confirmed by ballistics experts at the police lab as the gun that killed Harry Donner almost three years ago. Farina wasn't talking; his lawyer said everything was circumstantial and the guns had been planted in the Moore house. So, I guessed, had the prints on them.

I found our dinner in a familiar foil container and warmed it up while I waited for Jack. It smelled of curry. Jack's sister was getting daring. I put some rice on and set the table.

When he came in, I could see something was up. "Stay here," he said, and went into the bedroom. When he came out, he said, "Close your eyes."

I did. He took my hand and folded it around something. "Look."

I looked. It was a diamond ring. "Jack." I swallowed, hardly able to speak. "It's beautiful." It was a square stone that sparkled as I turned it, releasing flashes of color. "I don't know what to say."

"Just say you'll wear it."

"I will."

"It's my mother's. She scrubbed it up and gave it to me yesterday. She said she wanted to keep it in the family."

I could feel my eyes tearing. "I will. What a wonderful surprise."

Late the next afternoon I called Arnold Gold. The comfortable sound of Mozart was in the background, and he was glad to hear from me.

"So you put another notch in your belt," he said. "How come I don't see you getting any credit in the papers?"

"I don't need it and I don't want it. There's lots of stuff I can tell you that won't be printed. Next time I come to work, let's get together for lunch."

"You can come tomorrow; we've got the work for you."

"Arnold, I have to ask you something." I waited so long to continue that he prompted me. "I'd like you to give me away. Jack and I are getting married."

Now it was his turn to pause. "You don't want me, Chrissie. I'm a Jew, remember? How can I fit in in a Catholic ceremony?"

"You're part of my life, Arnold. We'll make you fit in."

"Well. I'd be honored. I'd be absolutely honored."

I was brushing tears away at that point. "Thank you," I said.

"Oh, no. I'm the one to give the thanks."

31

A couple of weeks later Jean called and said she'd like to meet Scotty's grandfather. I called St. Andrews and made an appointment for us to visit. I met the McVeighs near the home, and we walked over. The children were all dressed up and Jean was wearing the exquisite chain Scotty had sent her for her birthday. Charlie Hanrahan was waiting in the large foyer, as dressed up as his great-grandchildren. We sat in the same corner where he and I had talked. Jean told him about her husband and the children, and he laughed as he watched them. When they had settled in, I got up and walked away, finally finding an old woman sitting alone in the community room who was anxious to talk and didn't care very much who she talked to. Half an hour later, when I went back, they were still there, still talking.

"You know what," old Charlie said, bouncing Andrea on his knee, "I got a surprise from Scotty not so long ago. I didn't tell you, miss," he said, looking at me, "because it was a family matter. Got a check from him for my birthday. A thousand bucks. Can you believe it? Came in the mail with a little note the day after he died. He musta mailed it that morning."

"On his way to the parade," Jean said.

"A thousand bucks." He beamed. "That's how come I have on such a nice new suit today. It's a present from your daddy, kids. What a nice boy he was."

They never found the gun that killed Scotty, but Farina and the members of the team will go to prison for a long time. They found at least some of the buyers Farina sold drugs to, and they're still working on that.

211

The way we figured it all out, Macklin stole the car the morning of St. Patrick's Day and followed Ray and his red-headed companion in the BMW back to Brooklyn. He must have sat a long time waiting for them to leave, and when he finally got to Gillen's, he phoned Farina to take over. Macklin was working from an ID photo and didn't know either Ray or Petra, or Scotty for that matter. When Farina took over the watch, he was looking for Ray, a redheaded woman, and a BMW. He saw what looked like Ray going to the BMW and decided that was his man. After the killing, he probably ditched the gun he used.

Ray split up with Petra and after a while went back to Betsy, but I'm not sure it'll last. One thing that happened, he's a lot easier to talk to now.

Of all the deaths, it was Jerry McMahon's that left me with the most painful feelings. George Barker, who had posed as the homeless man, eventually turned state's evidence against the others. He and Ricardo Ramirez had followed McMahon when he left the station house that Friday night. Members of Gavin Moore's old team had been suspicious of McMahon for some time and had kept close watch on him after Ray was charged. They were pretty sure something was going down that Friday night when McMahon left the station house early and headed for Manhattan. By the time Barker was sitting on the sidewalk on Amsterdam Avenue, McMahon was probably already dead or dying. We couldn't have known it, of course, but it hurts me to think that we were only blocks away from him while he was still alive.

And then there's the three thousand dollars. A thousand for Jean's gold chain, a thousand for Charlie Hanrahan, and what else? Did the used-car dealer pocket it in spite of all his protestations? I suppose so. But maybe not. Maybe Scotty has a surprise put away, something for the children, perhaps, that will pop up just at the right time to give them some happiness.

I wouldn't put it past him.

The novels of
Lee Harris
are available in bookstores everywhere.

THE GOOD FRIDAY MURDER

Christine Bennett has just left the cloistered world of the nuns when she is enlisted to solve a forty-year-old murder. Pursuing this mission with her old religious zeal, she'll move heaven and earth to exonerate a pair of retarded savant twins, now senior citizens, of their mother's murder on Good Friday in 1950.

THE YOM KIPPUR MURDER

When ex-nun Chris Bennett can't get into Mr. Herskovitz's apartment to accompany him to Yom Kippur services, she discovers that her friend has been murdered. The police arrest someone almost immediately, but Chris is not convinced, and she is determined to uncover the sacrilegious truth.

THE CHRISTENING DAY MURDER

Studsburg was evacuated by the government and flooded to create a reservoir thirty years ago. Now drought has uncovered the town's forgotten church, and Christine Bennett stumbles upon a skeleton in the church's basement. Christine must put together a sordid puzzle from the past to find a killer.